PENGUIN BOOKS
MALAYAN SPY

Kam Raslan is a Malaysian writer and broadcaster. Originally a filmmaker working in London, Los Angeles, Malaysia, and Indonesia, he has written for many publications including the *Economist, Mekong Review,* and he had a long-running column in the *The Edge Malaysia.* He hosts two shows on BFM Radio: *A Bit of Culture* and *Just For Kicks.* Kam Raslan is the author of *Confessions of an Old Boy,* a collection of short stories, the various adventures of Dato' Hamid from the 1940s to the 2000s. The book was first published in 2008 and has been re-printed in 2024.

Malayan Spy

Kam Raslan

PENGUIN BOOKS

An imprint of Penguin Random House

PENGUIN BOOKS

Penguin Books is an imprint of the Penguin Random House group of companies whose addresses can be found at global.penguinrandomhouse.com

Published by Penguin Random House SEA Pte Ltd
40 Penjuru Lane, #03-12, Block 2
Singapore 609216

First published in Penguin Books by Penguin Random House SEA 2025

Copyright © Kam Raslan 2025

ISBN 9789815233858

Typeset in Century Schoolbook by MAP Systems, Bengaluru, India

www.penguin.sg

To The Wife (and The Cat)

Prologue

Kuala Lumpur,
Malaysia
2012

Is it late, or is it early? Tonight, I don't know.

I have never read Marcel Proust, but I know he used to go to bed early. Not me. There is so much to do in those late or early hours while the rest of the world, and The Wife, are asleep. In Kuala Lumpur, when the heat of the day has passed, there is nothing finer than to enjoy the cool of a tropical evening. I leaf through old books, gaze at my Poussin, listen to my Chopin, or sense the rustlings in the forest just behind my house.

I live deep in the city but have the remains of a forest at the end of my garden. At night, I can look out from the veranda into the darkness and see only the blinking eyes of an unknown animal looking back at me. Perhaps, by day it lives up a tree or down a deep hole.

Perhaps, it is the rare and elusive goat-like serow, which I have never seen except as a head mounted on a wall—a hunting trophy of my father's that he had bagged with his trusty Purdey shotgun. In the silence of the night I imagine that thoughts pass between us and that we share the understanding that we are the only ones awake.

A jungle, a real jungle, is never silent at night. I know this from my childhood. A real jungle is alive and loud at night. In the treetops above, scampering over your feet below, and in the distance, beyond the nearest trees and the flickering light of the campfire, there is unknowable movement. A meaningless small stream might suddenly roar into a terrifying torrent and then just as suddenly die down again to return to its tranquil way; except that huge and seemingly immovable rocks have been rearranged. And nobody in the whole world apart from my father and I (and half a dozen unhappy but faithful family retainers) would ever know that it had happened.

But this hacked-off limb of a forest behind my house is silent at night. It is the shipwrecked remains of a once mighty vessel now washed up on an isolated hill and surrounded by the sea of a sprawling, noisy city—a city that will not be satisfied until this tiny remnant has been engulfed. The local residents have decided this will not happen, and we have held meetings, formed committees, and written petitions, but the city never listens, and we will eventually lose the fight. Soon, the life and darkness behind my house will be snuffed out, and my mysterious nocturnal friend will die alone and unnoticed.

I don't want to go to bed early. I don't want to sleep at all. I want to stay awake forever, enjoying whatever vestiges of my world remain to me. I want to lie on my chaise longue, under the whirring ceiling fan, surrounded by my lovely things, with my wife slumbering in the room above, knowing that I am alive and that I have lived a life worth living. Now that I am older (never old!), I want to remember, and occasionally forget, the things I have done in my lifetime.

My memories, many of which I cannot even share with The Wife, are my happiest possessions, and I like to enjoy them at night, safe in the knowledge that I am where I want to be, even if I am—like the forest behind me and my nocturnal friend—an endangered species, threatened with extinction by my own country. My entire working life, for at least every other day or so, I had loyally served a nation. A nation that had not even been imagined when I was young, but I had served and understood. And then, it became something else, something that did not need me any more.

Sometimes, The Wife will find me in the morning, asleep on the chaise longue. She will replace the photo of our son, The Ayatollah, which I usually hide away because it spoils the mood, and she will ask me what I have been doing all night. 'Nothing, darling,' I will always say.

It was not always the case that I would have been happy being where I am now. If you had asked me five decades ago where I wanted to be, I would have said anywhere but Malaysia. I wanted to be far away from this tiny new country and its jungle. But I have been on a journey since then, and along the way I have experienced things that make me what I am today— an older man comfortable in his own skin. Along the way I have experienced love, loyalty, divided loyalty, misunderstood loyalty, beauty (oh, such ravishing beauty), trust, and above all, betrayal—or was that real loyalty?

There is one thing I share with Marcel Proust, which is that a seemingly insignificant scent can trigger a flood of memory. For Proust, the smell of a cake unleashed 3000 pages of remembrances of things past. For me, it happened yesterday.

I was walking through one of those infernal Kuala Lumpur shopping malls that are all noise and crowds— 'Buy Now!' and '20% Discount!'—when a simple, dark scent suddenly gave me back my youth and took me on a journey though haze, smog, and mist to a time of love and fear, of Empire, of being chased by tanks and of moving towards my true goal: The Wife. It has been a journey from which I am only now, this morning, beginning to groggily emerge, thankful to be alive but left wondering what it is that I have learned.

I loathe having to be anywhere with so many exclamation marks, because an exclamation mark is like a loud bang and therefore a shock to the system. I want my world to be quiet, safe, predictable, and filled with nice things. Numb, but in a nice way. But I had to be in a shopping mall because I was desperate to escape from the horrors of The Haze—that dreadful pall of dense smoke that drifts across the Malacca Straits from the burning forests and peat swamps of Sumatra. I can remember when Malaysia's air was sharply clear, but now, The Haze is a regular affair, and I needed to escape into a shopping mall's cocoon of air-conditioning. Only inside the limited horizons of a shopping mall is it possible to ignore, even if it's just for a moment, the fact that one can barely see 100 yards through the sickening smoke and escape from the stench of a burnt jungle and its charred, homeless animals. I also had to go to the shopping mall because The Wife's birthday was fast approaching, and I needed to buy her something.

Despite the fact that we have been married for so very long, I still find myself utterly unable to think of anything for her birthday. It was perhaps at least thirty years ago that I realized she no longer wanted cravats, tweed jackets, or even umbrellas from James Smith & Sons of New Oxford Street, and ever since then, I have truly struggled. What does one get for the woman who has everything? Surely, I always suggest, I should be the best possible present. But apparently not. Her birthdays had become a chore and an annual event almost as unwelcome as the godforsaken Haze.

So, there I was, disconsolate and wandering aimlessly through a department store, gazing at mysterious lady's apparel, when a young Malay person popped out of nowhere and squirted something in my eye, immediately inducing a searing pain.

'What the bloody hell are you doing?' I demanded.

'Rapture for men?' she chirped.

'I think you've blinded me!'

'The new fragrance from Calvin Klein.'

'Unless Calvin Klein is an ophthalmologist, I'm bloody well not interested.'

'It has a cinnamon bouquet with lighter, fresher notes for today's metrosexual.'

'How dare you! I have never been so insulted in all my life.'

With my one good eye, I managed to see that her nametag said Eena, and that she appeared to be concerned at having upset me.

'But it's Rapture for men,' Eena repeated quietly, a little confused, as if it was a spell that had inexplicably failed to work.

'That may be true for some but it's agony for me.'

'For today's metrosexual,' Eena continued with her incantation, nonetheless.

'I am an innocent shopper and now I'm having my sexuality impugned. What is happening?'

'No, sir . . .'

'. . . Dato'.'

'No, Dato',' soothed Eena, realizing her mistake. 'Metrosexual. Like David Beckham.'

'I have absolutely no idea what you're talking about.'

Eena considered her next words carefully and took a different tack, one that instantly captured my attention.

'Like Prince Charles.'

'Really? But he seems so normal.'

'Perhaps Dato' would like a more mature fragrance? . . . for old people?'

'You're wasting your time,' I interjected. 'I only use Caron's Pour Homme. It's good for all occasions and it's what a real man smells like.'

Eena gently turned my wrist and sprayed on some perfume.

'Try this Dato', I think you might like it.'

I breathed in a heady aroma of pine and citrus and was immediately transported back to Africa in the 1960s. Vast low skies, an open Veldt, and frightened Portuguese settlers trying to escape down a desperately slow river that had always been their friend but now was not. And two dark-eyed Bulgarian sirens.

'It's delicious,' I lamented. 'I haven't smelled this for years. What is it called again?'

'Pino Sylvestre,' said Eena, her spark returning at the possibility that her spell might be working after all.

'How could I have forgotten? I used to wear this all the time.' It had been my scent until that upstart Zain stole it from me.

'Try this, Dato'.' Eena grabbed my other wrist and sprayed.

Lavender, coumarin, and ginger, Tunku and my father in a cloud of cigarette smoke discussing my future but unable to come up with any ideas. A classic English fragrance from the dying days of the Empire, but I couldn't remember its name.

'Penhaligon's English Fern,' said Eena eagerly.

'Of course. How could I have forgotten?'

I was beginning to swoon in a perfumed cloud of long forgotten memories. Meanwhile, Eena could smell the blood of a big sale, and she started peppering me with perfumes from every angle: Vetiver, Monsieur Balmain, Blenheim Bouquet, and the unmistakable Tabarome from Creed, which used to be my scent. Why did I ever stop wearing it? What happened to me?

I knew them all, and yet I had forgotten them all, but now each one brought back times, places, youth, longings, regrets, and even some triumphs. Eena was grinning at her strategic onslaught, and I was powerless to resist the magic.

So, I reached for my only weapon and pulled out my credit card.

'I'll take the lot,' I pleaded.

'Would Dato' like them gift-wrapped?'

'No, just give them to me and let me go,' I continued to plead.

'Would you like something for a lady?'

'Who?' I didn't know what she was talking about.

'Your wife?'

'My wife? Yes, of course, my wife. I need a birthday present. Could you choose something? I don't know her scent.'

'Is she a younger lady? Or old like you?' Eena asked indelicately.

'She is older. A mature lady, the same age as myself, and therefore not old!'

'A lot of the Datuk and Tan Sri have their third or fourth wife when they're old like you. And they get younger and younger,' Eena lamented.

'She is my first and only wife.' I said proudly. I am not like my son, The Ayatollah.

'Perhaps your wife would like this, it's called Paris.'

'I don't think so. Paris is a beautiful city, but it smells like a latrine. Besides, it looks mass produced. I think my wife would want something a little more singular.'

'We have this. It's very special. Fleur de Thé Rose Bulgare from Creed.'

Her pronunciation was dreadful, but the perfume was divine.

'It has rose and green tea mixed with fiery Sicilian mandarin, Italian lemon, and Spanish bergamot,' Eena incanted blankly. 'Like a dewy pink rose straight from the garden.'

'No, it's not,' I ventured excitedly. 'It's like Ava Gardner in a bottle. Sumptuous. I'll take it.'

Once again, Eena could sense that my defences were weakening, and she reached for a bottle. It was on its own shelf, as if exiled by the other more gregarious perfumes. It was a small, dark bottle, like something a genie might inhabit.

'This is very special, Dato'.' Eena told me. 'It's an old fragrance that has just been reintroduced. Now it's called Everlasting.' She sprayed some onto a card and wafted it under my nose. 'But it used to be called—'

The scent stunned me.

'—I know what it's called. It's Betrayal.'

I do not have a clear recollection of what happened next. Presumably, I paid for the perfumes and staggered away. Perhaps I thanked Eena, perhaps I did not. I was lost to the present world of sales staff, bargain hunters, and tourists.

Thin wisps of long-lost memory were swirling in around me and steadily thickening into a deep fog as I, no doubt, stumbled through the department store looking like a crazy old man. The scent of Betrayal had seeped into my pores, clouding my thoughts, and it was taking me back.

Part I

London

1952

Chapter 1

I was inching my way through a fog so thick I was unable to see my hand in front of my face.

I clutched onto a railing, pulling myself along tentatively. I became aware that my fog of memory had a smell, and it did not smell like the burnt wood of The Haze. This fog had the acrid, acidic stench of sulphur, it was cold and heavy, and my eyes were burning.

It was nighttime in my fog, streetlamps and car headlights were glowing uncertainly, and sounds were beginning to infiltrate. Somewhere in the distance, a car crashed into what sounded like something solid. Glass crunched, and a woman screamed. I was clutching a book as if it were a dark sin and I was wearing a rough wool suit that offered no warmth. Despite the cold, I was sweating with nerves, frightened that I might step into the path of a car I could not see. What was this hellish place? It certainly wasn't Malaysia. And then, a jolt of fear. A hand grabbed my shoulder, and a voice, the voice of an Englishman.

'Is that you, Hamid?'

'Who are you?'

Deep through the fog of my past, I could see a man stepping towards me. He was an outrageously handsome man in his early thirties, square jawed, with a look of deep concern that morphed into a look of happiness, one that's bred by familiarity. He had short blond hair and a long-healed scar along his cheek. It was an imperial face that no longer exists.

'It's me, Thomas. Tom Pelham, old boy.'

I was in London, and it was the winter of 1952. It was the year of the Great Smog. I was young again, at an age when I had neither known who I was nor become numb to that knowledge when it had been gained. He was Tom Pelham, the man who would change my life.

'Tom, how are you?' I remember demanding excitedly, shaking his hand. We were outside Saint Martin in the Fields, but the normally delightful church could not be seen through the smog and instead could only be felt as a foreboding spirit.

'I haven't seen you since before the war. How is your father? And your mother? And your sister?'

'I'm fine, they're all fine. They would love to see you. How the devil are you? What are you doing in this infernal place?'

'I'm studying. None too successfully, I must admit.'

'We have a lot of catching up to do. Do you have some time? Let's get out of this wretched smog. I would take you to my club, but I don't know if I can bloody well find it. There's a Lyons Cornerhouse nearby. Come. Hold onto my coat, we don't want to lose you.'

I grabbed a handful of his gabardine and stepped forth warily, following Tom with youthful trust as he strode easily through the dense smog, guided by some innate sense of direction.

The disgusting Great Smog of 1952 went far beyond the pea-souper fogs that enveloped the London of Sherlock Holmes. This smog was the combined effort of smoke belching from eight million coal fires and a particularly cold and breezeless winter. Who knows how many had died that winter, asphyxiated by the smoke, frozen by the cold, or hit by cars driving blindly through the gloom. Dozens, perhaps hundreds? Somebody told me it was 12,000. The smog was a far cry from the clean, bright, clear air and heat of my home in Malaya.

I hated gasping for every breath, but otherwise I was having a whale of a time in London. In between the lectures I was not attending, there was plenty of time for fun. Besides, I was confident that I could find some Indian fellow to sit my exams (surely all Hamids would look the same to them).

Without the benefit of having seen any alternative horizons, I was resigned to a predictably tedious future as a civil servant in Malaya married to Irma. But I did silently dream of delaying the inevitable for as long as possible. So, for now, I was enjoying my youth by living it up in the bosom of London—with as many bosoms as I could get my hands on, which wasn't many.

But bumping into Tom Pelham in the deep smog, what were the chances of that?

Trailing behind Tom, I caught a hint of the scent of his perfume—Vetiver—that helped only slightly to mask the stench of the smog. I studied his back as he weaved us through the streets around Trafalgar Square, looking at his watch and occasionally telling me to mind my step or avoid a car. He was taller than from back when I had known him nearly fifteen years ago. His shoulders were broader, and his gait had changed. He walked quickly with a supreme sense of confidence and alertness. He seemed to be able to see through the smog and anticipate obstacles long before they appeared. I was happy to entrust my safety to my boyhood hero, but the way he was constantly checking his watch reminded me of the White Rabbit from *Alice in Wonderland*.

Eventually, we came to the Lyons teashop opposite Charing Cross station and as we opened the door, the outside smog swirled in and intermingled with the plumes of cigarette smoke being generated inside. Tom indicated for me to sit while he went to the counter and bought the customary tea and teacakes. What else could one have at a Joe Lyons? I have to say that I would much rather have gone to his club because my student life in London was an endless drudgery of cheap restaurants and disgusting English food, enlivened only occasionally when Salim cooked a curry. I could see that the pretty Welsh waitress was obviously struck by Tom's manly good looks, but he appeared to pay her no heed.

'Isn't this smog disgusting?' said Tom, returning to our table with the tea. 'It is inescapable. I was feeling quite miserable and then I saw you and memories of Malaya came flooding back.'

'How did you see me in the smog? I can't see more than two feet ahead.'

'I saw you in a bookshop on Charing Cross Road. I lost you in the smog, but I managed to hunt you down in the streets.'

I was somewhat embarrassed to have been seen at the bookshop. 'I was buying a book for my studies,' I managed to splutter.

Tom uncurled my fingers from around the book I was clutching.

'*Lady Chatterley's Lover*. Hamid, what are you studying? This book is banned.'

'Good heavens! The man told me it was about conveyancing law.'

'Are you studying law?'

'No.'

'Hamid, there's more to you than meets the eye.' Tom laughed away my shame.

'There is?' Nobody had ever said that of me before and the compliment, if it was one, made me glow. Especially because it came from Tom Pelham.

'I should think so, but don't worry, Hamid, your secret is safe with me. I've already read it, in Italian, and it's not particularly smutty. How is Malaya?'

'Hot and sticky,' I said dismissively.

'And how is your father?'

'Hot and sticky,' I said regretfully.

Now that we were inside, I could finally see his face. This Tom Pelham was different from the one I had known before the war. That Tom had been capable of displays of serene charm when the occasion called for it, but it was only a temporary mask for a latent anger. An anger with the old men and their ways, an anger with his father's world of white solar topees and colonial governance, and most of all, an anger with the provincialism of England—despite the fact that they ruled half the world.

This Tom Pelham was all charm and no rage, but he was also older. Much, much older. I imagined that the scar on his face that I had never seen before might hold a clue to his change.

'How did you get that scar, Tom?'

'This? Just a stupid accident during the war.'

'How was your war? What did you do?' I yearned to know.

'Nothing extraordinary. I had a quiet war. Back-room staff. How was yours?'

'Not as bad as we thought it would be. Hungry years, but my family fared better than most. Your father got out just in time.'

'Yes, retirement saved him. I don't think he would have survived Changi. Did you know that the Japanese didn't serve soda with the whiskey? Barbarians.'

Tom's flippancy did not make me forget the intense shock I had felt when I saw the British being forced to bow to the Japanese in my hometown in January of 1942. On display in the middle of the main road, Carter-Ruddock, the manager of Harrisons & Crosfield, Bamforth of the railways, Scott the judge and a dozen boy soldiers from the slums of Glasgow wide-eyed with terror. The only person missing was The Resident, Tom's father, who had retired a month before. The protection the British had always promised had evaporated in a month, swept aside by Asians like myself, but also so very different from me. All of us Malayans had to understand that shock and negotiate new loyalties in our own way.

Me? I had kept my silence.

'I used to imagine,' I dared to break the silence, 'that they would send you back to Malaya with Force 136.'

I was giving too much away. I had always been in awe of Tom Pelham. Throughout the war, I used to dream that Tom would come back and liberate us from the Japanese, deposited alone by a submarine on a secluded beach, striding into our town, tommy gun in hand, the Japanese who made us bow instead bowing to him as he restored the old order. But, of course, he never did. I think Tom sensed my adolescent disappointment.

'They never asked me, Hamid. And I never offered. I didn't really know Malaya. I only visited my father during the long vacations, and that did not make me an expert. There were others, like that Chapman. Do you know him?'

'I've met him.'

'A brave man.'

'Probably. A planter.'

'Trade?' Tom laughed at me. 'You're such a snob, Hamid.'

'You always were,' I whispered it, 'a socialist.'

'Our beliefs can change,' he grimaced. I was young enough then to imagine that beliefs never changed. Tom changed the subject. 'Why didn't you tell us you're in London?'

'I don't know, I thought about it, I didn't think you'd remember me. It was all so long ago.'

'I know, everything before the war feels like a dream. But of course, we remember you. I know my sister does.'

'How is Clare?'

Clare, that lanky tomboy, nine years old, pushing up her spectacles, big teeth and blonde hair in a ponytail, the Malayan sun bringing out her freckles. I hadn't thought of Clare for years, but now my stomach flipped as I remembered her. Somehow, in my memories of Clare, it never rained, it was always sunny, and yet, never hot.

My mother had disapproved of me spending any time with the white girl, but Clare would come to our house each morning and talk in Malay, the only language my mother spoke, charm my mother, and then whisk me away for a day of childhood adventure. We would climb trees and be bitten by ants, throw rocks into the river trying to hit the catfish, emerge into a kampong even I had never visited before, and chat with an old man about the big flood in '27.

It had been scandalous behaviour for us to be running around together like a pair of feral animals, but where we were separated by race and gender, we were united by class. She was the daughter of The Resident and I was the son of the most important Malay in the state, after The Sultan himself.

Once, we had bumped into Irma who was sitting by the river, singing a sad song, and brushing her hair.

'Who is she?' Irma demanded to be told while putting a hibiscus flower in her hair.

'Irma, this is Clare.'

'I like your flower,' said Clare.

'Hhmph,' Irma declared. 'Help me with my homework tonight, Hamid. You're always so clever.'

'Er, I'll try.'

'You'll do it!' And then Irma walked away, singing a happy song.

'Who is she?' asked Clare.

'That's Irma. She says we're going to get married.'

'Yuck. I'll never get married.'

'Why not?'

'I hate boys.'

'I'm a boy.'

'You're different. Let's go further up the river. I heard there's an old white crocodile up there.' And she dragged me away.

It was the first time I had been caught between two girls, and I had quite liked it.

A thousand years later in the smoke and gloom of London, stirring my watery tea, I asked Tom tentatively, 'Is Clare, married?'

'No,' Tom stated, as if the very concept were ridiculous. 'She's studying as well. She's become quite bookish. Is that the time? I'm afraid I have to go now, Hamid, but please come and stay with us if ever you want to visit England.'

'But this is England.'

'This is London. England is another country, and I don't suppose you've ever been there. Will you be able to find your way back to Bryanston Square?'

'Yes, I think so. How did you know I'm living at Bryanston Square?'

'All Malayans live at Malaya Hall. Goodbye, Hamid, it's been wonderful seeing you again, and please keep in touch,' he said, writing down the Pelham's telephone number. 'It will give us a chance to really catch up, and to talk about your future.' Tom gave me a bone-crunching handshake and strode out of Lyons.

For some reason, my future was a subject of endless interest for almost everyone who knew me, as if it were a conundrum as mysterious as the inside workings of the Kremlin. Obviously, my future path had already been mapped out for me by my father, and by Irma. When the time was right, I would become a civil servant. For now, I was heartily enjoying my present, but I did find it curious that Tom should have any concern for my future when this was only a chance meeting.

Tom had appeared out of the smog as an apparition from my past and I did not know it then, but he was making plans for my future. Within two paces, he had disappeared into his future, inside the sickly yellowish smog where nothing could be seen but from which emanated the car horns, screams, and swearing of unknown chaos.

Chapter 2

As I stumbled back to Malaya Hall among the other frightened people of a broken London, I realized that I had just had my first real conversation with Tom Pelham. Before that, before the war, our 'conversations' had been a series of lectures delivered with passionate fury by a younger Tom in the clear air of my hometown in Malaya. Tom would stride back and forth on the veranda of the magnificent official home of his father, Sir Alfred Pelham KCMG.

In 1940, Tom's father was the British Empire's chief potentate in my home state, his title was The Resident and his home was unsurprisingly called The Residence. Sir Alfred Pelham, like many Residents (but by no means all), was widely respected having worked in Malaya for most of his life. I grew up always understanding the power of The Resident. The title seemed so benign and unthreatening, as if he were a rarely seen houseguest who inhabited a spare room, but nothing happened in the Malay states without the say-so of the British Residents. Whenever I went past The Residence, I could feel the hum of global power, as if there was an orchestra buried beneath it, playing Elgar. And nobody personified the Empire's impressive power, tact, and subtlety better than Sir Alfred.

The Sultans had absolute authority over religion. They represented the hopes of their peoples. But it was the Residents who made sure that the flow of tin and rubber continued unimpeded. In return for this convivial relationship, the Sultans were feted and handsomely rewarded. They could speak of the British King Emperor as a royal equal and stayed at Windsor Castle when occasion required. His Highness tried not to, because the place was apparently too cold and draughty. Most of all, the Sultans were promised protection: protection for their lineage and for their state.

My father? He was The Sultan's right hand man, just as his father had been before him. My father worked closely with The Sultan and The Resident on the day-to-day running of a state that required prosaic things like taxes, roads, and water works. If The Resident wanted something done, he would say to my father, 'Perhaps His Highness might wish to . . .' Or, if the mood were darker, 'His Highness would be strongly advised not to . . .' My father happily complied, and he sent his son to a school that was the Eton of the East—Malay College Kuala Kangsar (MCKK)—where I learnt how to play cricket and quote Shakespeare.

In the royal towns of most Malay states, the Residence was situated high on a hill, higher even than the Sultan's palace. The ostensible reason was to be above the possibility of being flooded by the unpredictable river, but really it was a symbolic gesture to make sure that the reality of the true order of things was not lost on anybody.

But in our state, the Sultans had long ago taken the highest point, and The Residence had to settle for being slightly lower down the hill on a man-made promontory overlooking the road to the palace, so that The Resident could see everyone who came and went.

I grew up with the architecture of the British Empire, and I was not alone in finding it impressive. Only with age and with travel did I begin to understand the inspirations for the peculiar mishmash of styles. But even as a child, I knew it always spoke of somewhere else, somewhere that the British owned. Where the Dutch in Jakarta wanted to merely recreate Old Amsterdam or the French in Indochina to rebuild Paris, the British would build an even grander version of Whitehall next to a railway station that was a dream of distant and vast India and a printing press that was a fable of Arabian nights—all built with Glasgow wrought iron.

My home was lovely, but it was made of wood. Although it was very cool inside, having been built from hundreds of years of accumulated wisdom, I felt a trifle ashamed of it when I saw the iron, stone, and brick of the British Empire that promised to stand for a thousand years. My mother loved our old home, but my father knocked it down as soon as he had the money to pay CB Hong & Sons to build a peculiar house in a style that can only be described as Chinaman Hacienda. My father was very proud of it, but I hated it. For me, the finest house in our hometown, one that spoke of power, permanence, and whimsy, one that would have been presumptuous to copy, was The Residence.

When I arrived in London, it came as a surprise to discover that for the British, the British Empire was something that happened to other people. I grew up assuming that buildings in Britain must have looked just as they did in its Empire, but then, I discovered, that they did not. I was shocked that nobody in Britain had ever heard of Sir Alfred Pelham, when, to me, he was surely one of the most important people in the whole world.

The British Empire was virtually unknown to the British. Their Empire was merely a map on the wall where a third of the world was painted pink. It was a point of pride, but these places had no real meaning because very few of them ever ventured into these faraway lands.

The very first moment I arrived in London, an Englishman had begged me for some money. He begged me, a subject of his Empire. It was suddenly obvious to me that the vast majority of the British were simply too poor to be able to visit their Empire as tourists. In time, I realized that the whole vast Empire was peopled by only a tiny handful of Britishers left alone to their own devices. They had the complete freedom to perfect an England of their dreams.

Our Residence was one such English dream. It had been built just before the First World War, long after the Empire's first flush in the 18th century when it built itself as a dream of an enlightened New Athens of justice and rational governance and when the new port cities were invariably called Georgetown. I have visited three Georgetowns, and a pair of Wellingtons. In those long-ago times, before the Empire had properly arrived into my great grandfather's life, every courthouse looked like a temple to Athena and every Britisher succumbed to malaria, beriberi, shipwreck, or alcohol before their thirtieth birthday.

The Empire fully arrived in my grandfather's life in the Victorian 19th century, at which time, the dream had changed from Athens to Sparta. The pleasures of the flesh were forsaken for the dour, dark-stoned Gothic of Victorian clean-limbed, sports mad, muscular Christianity where Britishers could persuade themselves that drinking copious amounts of gin and tonic was healthy because the tonic water contained quinine for the malaria.

As a rule, Malayans do not stand around under the sun, and I paid the price for Sparta by having to sweat on MCKK's cricket pitch for endless hours. I was, I had been told, learning about teamwork when I was far more interested in learning about a gin and tonic.

Although my father could never have imagined it at the time, I had been born at the end of the Empire's life in the 1930s—when it had decided to join the machine age. In my childhood, everything was being built with the sleekness of Art Deco so that every building looked like it was a Ford motorcar factory. And then, when I was around ten years old, in 1942, the Japanese Imperial Army came, and it all ended. Coincidentally, the British surrendered to General Yamashita in a Ford motorcar factory.

But before that, and just before the British became shell-shocked by the First World War, there came a dainty intermezzo when the Empire briefly decided that it could be about fun. Sparta was exchanged for Italy, not a New Rome but an everlasting Imperial Tuscan holiday of costume parties, tennis parties, and cocktail hours, dotted with exotic Princes and Sultans, a Somerset Maugham and the occasional Noël Coward. Mercifully, my family never attended these parties. However, most of my hometown was built during this time and it looked as if it were a wonderful dream of Empire.

It was a place where Michelangelo journeyed through the Raj with a caravanserai for a thousand and one nights and where a Medici played chess with a Mughal Emperor in the Alhambra. Our huge new mosque had more than a hint of the Taj Mahal, as did the new palace, and The Residence was a large, beautiful, and ornate Italianate affair with curling Moorish flourishes for windows and awnings. It had acres of polished teak floors, ten bedrooms, and was surrounded by a terraced garden where, somehow, roses were coaxed into blooming under the tropical sun. Gleaming white, it rose above the point where two rivers met (one crystal-clear from the jungle, the other tea-coloured and heavy with mud from the tin mines), and it commanded a view across the royal town, arresting the eye wherever one stood. But over there, at the bottom of the hill and in the town, the streets were ordered, and the buildings were sensible.

My town hummed with the constant sound of metal being bashed. The stink of rubber being processed would mix with the heady smell of food being cooked. Malays, Chinese, Indians, and Europeans would busy themselves with the everyday practicalities of life.

The town spoke of what the Empire had really always been about—industry and trade. Fortunately, I did not come from that world.

The town itself, like all royal towns in Malaya, sat beside a river. But in our case, we were not near the sea, but in the interior of the peninsula. Our town was an island in the deep green sea of the jungle that stretched all around, up the sides of the mountains in the distance, cresting over the ridgeline with a spray of perpetual cloud that splashed down into our neighbouring state, or was it vice versa? Apart from a tiny handful of Temuan tribespeople, there was nobody in the jungle because civilized people only lived along the river or by the sea.

I once saw the town from the jungle on one of my father's hunting trips, from the top of a waterfall that was a two-day trek away from the town. A river is the only place in a jungle where one can see more than ten yards ahead, and where a river bursts out of the jungle and cascades down a waterfall, one can see very far indeed. From the top of the waterfall, I could see the town in the distance. There was the large golden dome of the mosque, the smaller domes of the palace, the tiled roofs of the huddled town below, the rubber estates lining the roads, and the gleaming white beacon of The Residence. The jungle was a chaos of trees and animals, but the town was an order that I understood, the only kind that my father had ever known. It was an order that I was being raised to serve.

In the far distance, mostly obscured by the trees in the jungle, was the scar of the flat flood plain and the red earth of the countless tin mining pools that paid for everything. It all looked so small in the vastness of the jungle, but it was civilization. It was comforting, strong, and permanent. I have, however, since learned that permanence is an illusion. I couldn't linger for long on the waterfall because our Temuan guide had sensed that there had been rainfall further upstream and that a flash flood might be coming. So, I took one last look and then hurried away, clutching my father's Purdey shotgun—his most treasured possession that I was only ever allowed to carry but never fire.

I was young then, and I thought I would catch that view again, but I never did. The jungle is mostly still there, but it is now criss-crossed with logging trails. All the big ancient neem and ironwood trees have been cut down and the animals have gone. The tin mines are also all gone and although my hometown still stands, it is no longer of much importance.

Over time, most of the Residences have been allowed to decay, converted into cheap hotels where civil servants gather to eat fried rice at lunchtime or where, at night, young lovers park their cars in its isolation to grab whatever privacy they can. Fortunately, the Residence in my hometown is still well maintained, but it now stands empty because nobody knows what to do with it. The memory of The Residence has become something of an embarrassment and the orchestra that once played beneath it has gone somewhere else to play a different tune.

Before the war, in 1939, when it seemed assured that the Empire would last for a thousand years and Britain had not yet suffered its finest hour, The Residence had been magnificent and on its veranda strode Thomas Pelham, the handsome son of The Resident, declaiming on the correctness of the Republican cause in the Spanish Civil War, the evils of fascism, the injustice of class divides and the sheer, damn wrongness of an Empire that I thought was at its zenith, but, which he told me had already declined and would soon fall.

I had never been invited to The Residence before, but I had been befriended by Tom's sister Clare, who was then squatting on the floor terrorizing a beetle she had caught and not listening to a word Tom said. I was utterly enthralled by Tom. I had never in my young life imagined such outlandish concepts, and I was shocked that the son of the chief imperial potentate could express views that contradicted everything his own father represented.

I would never have even dreamed of questioning my father, and I would have received several painful strokes of the cane if I had. I had always believed the Empire was one enormous happy family with the King Emperor sitting benevolently at the head of the table. I understood that there were people like Gandhi demanding independence for India, but wasn't he just a crackpot in a loincloth? Although I did think of Nehru as a very handsome fellow with an excellent sense of style.

'And that is why the British Empire's subject peoples must be given their independence!' Tom declared at the end of his long tirade.

'Don't be so tiresome, Tom,' Clare said, while examining the beetle in its death throes. 'Papa says that the natives wouldn't even know what to do with independence and that they would all be at each other's throats if ever we left. Papa says that they want our guidance and that we have given them the railways, Shakespeare, and cricket.'

'My father says the same,' I added excitedly, waiting anxiously to see how Tom would contradict my father.

'All men crave and deserve dignity above all else. Where is the dignity in having all of life's decisions made for you?'

I struggled to find an answer. Clare gently touched my arm. 'He's being rhetorical, Hamid. You don't need to answer.'

Tom continued, sweeping back his hair and jabbing the air with his finger, 'Mistakes will be made and societies must be cleansed, but the subject peoples are demanding their independence and who the hell are we to deny them?'

'We're British,' Clare concluded simply while dropping the dead beetle onto an ant trail.

Tom's frustration was palpable. It made him look magnificent as he continuously circled around us, inadvertently treading on the ants, which caused a commotion in their miniature world.

'There is nothing exceptional about Britain and we have no god-given right to be telling anybody else what to do. Assuming there is a god, which there isn't.'

'Mama says it's a demi-paradise,' said Clare, helping the ants digest the beetle with more ease by ripping off a few of its legs.

'It's a sceptred isle,' I added knowingly, despite never having been to England.

'Britain is nothing but an island off the coast of Europe.'

Clare was unimpressed by Tom's argument. 'Stop being so unpatriotic, Tom. Papa fought for our country in the Great War and Uncle Jack died in Gallipoli doing his duty. Mama says we must show them our respect and keep them in our hearts and in our prayers.'

'I have decided that I would never fight for king and country,' Tom declared. 'My loyalty is to a greater cause—to free humanity from the enslavement of capitalism and imperialism. And I'm not just talking about the Empire. We must free the working men and women of Britain because they were the first subject people of the British Empire.'

'Really?' said Clare. 'Papa says it was the Welsh.'

Tom ignored Clare's flippancy and was now in a fine fury. He shook me by the shoulders. 'Independence will come to your country, Hamid. I'm going to give it to you. Are you ready for it? Independence will come to the whole Empire, even Africa.'

'Even Africa?' Clare was shocked at the thought. 'Now you're being preposterous, Tom.'

Clare pulled me by my arm. 'Come, Hamid. Let's follow the ants.'

Tom was holding me by the shoulders and Clare was pulling me by my arm. I wasn't sure which way to go. Tom was practically panting, so caught up was he in his passion. His pale blue eyes bore straight through me. He didn't seem to see me at all, for he was staring at some future horizon. I wanted to stay in his orbit, absorbing the energy that was radiating from his body, from his fingertips through my shirt and into my skin. I felt like I needed to stay under his tutelage, learn from him, join him on his mission. But something told me it would be more fun to follow the girl, so I allowed myself to be pulled away by Clare.

Tom slumped into a chair and called for the servant to get him some lemonade, while Clare and myself followed the dead beetle being borne aloft along the ant trail off the veranda and into the garden. Finally, the body of the unknown beetle disappeared into the Westminster Abbey of the ant's nest. But I wasn't very interested. I was feeling troubled by some of the things Tom had said. Clare and I were both nine years old, but she was six months older, and she had travelled the world, so I saw her as an older woman who better understood life's mysteries.

'Clare,' I asked, 'God exists, doesn't He?'

Clare took a break from tormenting the ant's nest with a stick, and she looked me in the eye.

'Hamid, everything Tom says is simply tosh and nonsense. He's my brother and I know when he's just showing off.'

'That's all right then. Clare, what does rhetorical mean?'

'Actually, I'm not really sure. I think it's when you don't really mean what you're saying.'

'That's all right then.'

Something deep inside me was really enjoying gazing into Clare's eyes. There were strange little explosions going off inside my body, which confused and delighted me. Although I couldn't be sure of it, I sensed that Clare was enjoying gazing into my eyes as well. Either way, neither of us noticed that the ants had had enough of our presence and had swarmed out of their home and were all around us. I felt a painful ant bite first and Clare felt one immediately after. Within seconds, our legs were covered with rampaging ants, and we ran screaming from the garden.

Instinctively, as any Malayan child would, we ran into the kitchen and into the comforting arms of Mak Mina. She brushed off the ants, splashed our legs with water and, on my insistence, applied some Tiger Balm to the bites. Despite the pain, Clare seemed to be enjoying herself. I, however, had tears flowing from my eyes. Mak Mina sang me a soothing Malay song from her native Kelantan, to which Clare listened intently, committing it to memory. It was a happy moment.

Childhood is all too brief.

Chapter 3

A thousand years later, and in the smog and darkness of London in December 1952, I collapsed onto my bed in Malaya Hall, Bryanston Square, and I watched Salim, with whom I shared a room, prepare himself for the evening. He lacquered his hair with Yardley hair cream, plumped up his cravat, and sang smugly about going where fashion sits and putting on the Ritz.

As the years have gone by, Salim's complexion has become progressively darker—and he was really quite dark-skinned to begin with. He had the sharp narrow face of a matinee idol and had always fancied himself to be an oriental Ramon Novarro, the star of *Ben Hur*, which is why we called him Bin Hur.

'What are you getting dressed up for, Bin Hur?' I asked.

'I'm going to the Café de Paris tonight. Johnny Dankworth is playing,' Salim whistled. 'My father has finally left London and gone back to Malaya so now I can enjoy myself again.'

Salim's father had recently been in London with a group of senior Malayan civil servants to initiate initial talks about starting preliminary discussions for first-round conferences about greater self-governance, and even possible independence for Malaya. They had been tasked with ushering into existence a wholly new concept—a nation, one that did not yet have a name.

My father shared Salim's father's scepticism about the viability of the whole thing, but my father was not involved in the negotiations. Despite being a loyal and capable senior civil servant, my father did not have the wherewithal, ruthlessness, and imagination for politics, and few people relish the ruthlessness of politics as much as the Malays. Ultimately my father and Salim's father were merely loyal and capable senior civil servants who were to be swept aside when independence finally came.

My views were always close to my father's. And yet, our relationship was cold and distant—as was once the Malay tradition between a father and his son. Although we shared much in common, I was never more lonely than when in the company of my father. Now, ironically, I am never more alone than when in the company of my own son, The Ayatollah. When I was young, I had been very close to my mother, but then I went into the world and ate the forbidden fruit of French cheese. After that, there was no going back.

Salim had been putting on a good show of being the dutiful son and had accompanied his father throughout the London negotiations, but Salim's views, and more importantly his ambitions, were very different from his father's. Now that his austere and remarkably humourless father had gone, Salim wanted to have some fun again.

'I'm taking Inge,' continued Salim.

'Is she the fat one?'

'No, that's Susan. And don't be so dismissive of the fat ones. I'm probably going to marry Susan.'

'You're going to marry an English girl?' The very notion seemed impossible.

'She's from Lancashire. Is that in England?' Salim asked.

'I think so. You're going to take an English girl back to Malaya?' I was still stunned.

'Why not? The English have been in Malaya for centuries. They don't melt in the sun.'

'But it's not the done thing. She's white and you're practically black.'

'I'm tall, dark, and handsome, Hamid. I am swarthy, if you must. Any mother would be happy to have me as a son-in-law.'

'Is her mother happy?'

'No. But their family has been giving birth and dying on factory floors for hundreds of years, and my father is practically a maharaja.'

'No, he's not. We don't have maharajas, and our families are not royalty.'

'They don't know that, and you're not going to tell them. We're aristocrats, Hamid. Granted we're aristocrats in Malaya but class is class, and we are members of that class, wherever we may be. She'll be marrying up.'

I had to agree that we were aristocrats, but I still couldn't see how he could bridge the race divide. 'But if you take her back to Malaya then she can go to The Club and you cannot.'

'Who would want to join The Club? It's full of upstart, middle-class nobodies eating their cucumber sandwiches and pretending to be the Duke and Duchess of Devonshire. They're just plantation managers and civil servants from Solihull. Is Solihull in England?'

'I have absolutely no idea. Do you really think you can do it? It seems so daring. I can't even imagine it.'

'I know I can, and I will.'

'But what about your father, and your mother? They'll be shocked.'

'I know. It will be delicious. It'll shake them. Turn their world upside down. It'll show that we are the equals of the English, perhaps even their superiors. This English girl will be my wife. Independence is coming, Hamid, and I want to be ready. You could say I'm doing it for my people.'

'Sounds very grand, Salim, but marrying a hefty English girl hardly makes you a freedom fighter. So, if you're going to marry Susan, who is Inge?'

'My Danish pen pal, and she is gorgeous.'

'She has lovely handwriting?'

'No, legs. I persuaded her early in our correspondence to send me a photo of her in her bathing suit. Spectacular. I sent her this.'

Salim whipped out a photo from a drawer and tossed it to me. It showed him looking dark and handsome on a fishing boat somewhere on the South China Sea, and he wasn't wearing a shirt. It was a flattering image, and I knew that he had over a dozen copies of it in his drawer.

This had been back in the days when we all had pen pals. The ostensible reason was to practise our English, but our English was already perfect, so it was mainly used as an opportunity to fine-tune our flirtation skills. For me, writing letters to faraway places also answered some ancient Malay yearning to be part of the world, to travel, understand, experience, and escape. Sadly, this wanderlust had skipped the generation of The Ayatollah and his little friends.

'You look very dashing,' I ventured. 'But if I remember rightly, you started throwing up the moment this boat hit a wave, and you cried like a baby when you were stung by a jellyfish.'

'She doesn't know that, and you're not going to tell her. Remember whose side you're on,' Salim said, snatching back the photo. 'And do you remember my golden rule?'

'Deny everything.'

'That's right, deny everything. If you never admit to it, then it never happened. Come out with me tonight, Hamid. I think Inge has a friend.'

The prospect was intriguing, but meeting Tom Pelham had put me in a thoughtful mood, which remains something I am not used to.

'I think I'll stay here tonight. I want to think about my future.'

Salim seemed shocked by my statement.

'You want to think about your future? Are you all right? Do you have a fever?'

'I do think about the future, you know,' I lied.

'Suit yourself, but Café de Paris will be swinging. You might meet some girl there. Maybe you'll hit it off and then you could marry her and take her back to Malaya.'

'I don't think so.' I snorted.

'Don't you ever think about marrying an English girl?'

'You know me, I fall in love with every girl I meet, but I don't seriously think about marrying them.'

'But what if you did think about it seriously? Who would you marry? Isn't there a girl you could imagine taking back?'

'No. It's wrong. It's against the rules.'

'Those are the old rules, the Empire's rules. Divide and conquer. It's pointless playing by the old rules. Now it's our turn to *veni, vidi, vici*. And first, we shall fight them in the bedroom.'

I was thinking about Clare Pelham, but I didn't know what I was thinking. We had both been nine years old, and she was European. But what was she like now? All I knew was that Tom had called her 'bookish', but what did that mean?

'There's nobody,' I told Salim.

'If you say so. But think about it. We can do it now. We can do anything we want. Anyway, I've got to go. Don't want to be late, you understand. I found a pineapple in the Berwick Street market, so I made a pineapple curry. It's in the kitchen but you'll have to eat it with bread, there's no rice. You owe me a bob. What's the time?'

'I don't know. I don't have a watch.'

'I will never understand why on earth you don't have a watch.'

'I don't want to know the time.'

'Well, it's probably time to grow up. Adults wear watches.'

Salim opened the drawer that held his extravagant collection of watches and chose one.

'It's later than I thought. I have to go. Wish me luck.' Salim dashed out of the room.

The smell of his Yardley lingered in the air, even though the stench of the smog had permeated the room. He had planted a dangerous thought in my mind.

Could I really, seriously, actually marry an English girl? Was such a thing honestly possible? What would Irma do if I took an English girl back? She'd probably kill us both, but the thought of ridding myself of Irma merely made the notion more attractive. I went to the kitchen and ate Salim's pineapple curry. It was delicious and it made me think of home, and of Clare. But I didn't know what I was thinking, we had both just been nine years old.

Back then, a thousand years earlier, our endless summer had finally come to an end. Tom and Clare's mother had always been sickly, and the effort of complaining about the heat and humidity of Malaya only made her worse. She thus decided to return to England, and she took Clare with her. It was my father of all people, who told me about the unexpected departure as he sat listening to a sad song about the river on his gramophone. I ran to The Residence through the rain, but they were gone. Tom had still been there, but somehow, he had changed.

Now I was thinking of Clare, but I didn't know what I was thinking because we had both just been nine years old under the shining sun.

Chapter 4

It took some effort, but I eventually found a namesake Hamid who was prepared to sit my exams for me.

He was from Bengal, was immensely bright but was also a raging and very argumentative communist of the Maoist variety. He was, at first, reluctant to take part in my elegant plan but I managed to persuade him by telling him that sitting the exam for me could be a victory for the proletariat everywhere in the on-going class war against the oppressive, imperialist- capitalist running-dogs. In good dialectical-materialist fashion I was, in a sense, doing him a favour, plus I would pay him £10. With my Bengali Hamid on-board, I was able to settle down to the prospect of a very long Christmas holiday, which, according to my own interpretation of my academic responsibilities, had actually begun in the month of May. Sadly, my Bengali Hamid was later killed when Bangladesh split from Pakistan in 1971.

Despite managing to secure plenty of free time for myself, my Christmas holiday prospects were suddenly looking very bleak indeed. Malaya Hall was steadily emptying out because everybody, except me, had somewhere exciting to go. Even Salim had packed his suitcase for a jaunt to Denmark to see Inge. Naturally, his Susan was extremely displeased, but Salim had tried to console her by convincing her that Inge was a monster of a woman, who enjoyed eating live chickens for breakfast. He was going to Denmark, he explained to Susan, not for his own sake, but because he was determined to teach Inge the rudiments of spoken language. I'll never understand how Susan believed this nonsense, but she waved her noble Salim off at Waterloo Station with tears in her eyes. For a brief moment, I contemplated spending a few weeks consoling Susan. I would like to say I chose not to out of a sense of loyalty to Salim, but it was really because I witnessed how she consumed her cheese sandwich.

The corridors of Malaya Hall, which normally echoed with laughter and chatter, went quieter with each passing day as the boys drifted away. I was to be alone with nothing to do, and I never liked being alone. I would start having thoughts, and I never liked having thoughts.

My entire life had been spent in the company of others: family, servants, and school friends. Always being surrounded by people made me yearn for the romance of solitude. But our empty chatter and the simple tasks they gave me helped crowd out an unpleasant question that tended to arise whenever I was abandoned to myself.

Did I exist if I was not in the company of others? Did I serve a purpose in this world if I was not serving somebody else's needs?

This was why the prospect of a marriage to Irma frightened me so. I would be safe with Irma, but I would merely become an extension of her life and ambition.

Could I even hope to find somebody with whom I could be blissfully cocooned together in solitude, with whom I could share, be me, and yet still be told what to do?

Of course not.

I did not have the spirit to fight off Irma, so I decided to blot out the pointlessness of asking questions by searching for nice things on the streets of London and in the company of its teeming millions.

Stepping out of Malaya Hall, I could see that the worst days of the hellish Great Smog had finally passed but the air remained smoke-laden and unpleasant to breathe. The only thing that had improved was the visibility. Though I could see slightly further than before, all that stood to be seen was a soot-covered and grimy London. At least when hidden behind a blanket of smog, I could imagine that London was a gleaming citadel, an imperial metropolis filled with elegant people saying witty things and that as soon as the veil of smog was lifted, a dazzling city would be revealed.

Instead, with the worst of the filthy miasma having cleared, I stumbled upon the unsettling sight of coffins emerging from numerous buildings where the bodies of those who had expired during the Great Smog were finally being removed. It was saddening to see that far too many of the coffins had onlookers but no family. And now, I could see again, the bombed-out sites that were still empty from the Blitz and the crowds of survivors wheezing into and out of the Underground.

Ever since arriving, I had simply assumed that it was in London's nature for its air to be hard to breathe and for its walls to be as black as any coalmine. And then, one day, I saw a workman washing a wall while somehow keeping his cigarette dry. He was scraping and washing off the layers of posters—calling for wartime vigilance against Nazi spies, old advertising for long dead music hall acts, and a call for recruits to fight for Queen Victoria in Crimea—until he finally reached the unblemished bedrock and revealed the building's glowing and almost golden stone, upon which he plastered a sign saying, 'Bill Stickers will be Prosecuted'. I wondered who Bill Stickers might be and what he had done wrong, but I also realized that every grand facade and statue that was black with soot hid underneath an original London, one that none of us had ever seen. If you scraped at the blackness covering any wall you would have found flecks from the fireplaces of Pepys, Dr Johnson, or Dickens, but would this have been a memento of their genius, or simply their unintended detritus?

Like millions around the world, I had grown up believing that London must be the greatest city in the world and that glimpse of a clean wall suggested that it once had been. But even with its dirt, I still loved it, as someone loves a beloved yet obviously dilapidated old car. London was bigger than all of Malaya's towns and cities combined. And although the slouching masses around me may not have had anything witty to say, they were all busy workers serving this great city. Everyone except me.

All cities are very lonely places when one is alone, but in the short, cold December days, perhaps nowhere is lonelier than London.

I was reduced to wandering the West End streets and re-visiting my old haunts—but without my customary enthusiasm. As usual, I found myself in Simpsons of Piccadilly perusing their trousers but the choices, and quality, were not as I would have hoped.

I was in limbo, caught between nowhere to go and nothing to do, and with nothing lovely to buy that could brighten up my day. I managed to shake myself out of my dark thoughts by reminding myself that my mood was simply matching that of Great Britain and its mourning capital city. Black trimmed photographs of the old King reminded everyone that he had recently died and that the new young Queen had not been crowned yet. Any anticipation for rejuvenation, however, was offset by the return of the seventy-eight-year-old Mr Churchill as Prime Minister again.

During my war in Malaya, the Japanese executed anybody found listening to a short-wave radio set, so I did not hear his wartime speeches until after the war. The speeches were stirring, defiant, even exhilarating, but they offered scant consolation to the memory of what we Malayans had been through. The exhortation to 'fight them on the beaches' merely reminded me of the sight of the men who were beheaded on the beach one day. But now Mr Churchill was prime minister again, and although he had lost none of his eloquence, he had clearly aged, and he looked increasingly like a bulldog that was in dire need of a nap.

The big war had been over for seven years and yet, Britain, in those days, was still on a curious war-footing. Unlike the supposed losers, the victorious British still had rationing with each household entitled to so many eggs and so much coal. This always came as a shock to young students newly arrived from a Malaya that had long since returned to times of plenty. Notions of plenty are relative, for most Malayans it simply meant eating rice and not the ghastly wartime staple of tapioca. We Malayans in Britain did not have ration books, and we bought what we wanted if we had the money and if we could find it. But, alas, London in those days was not the shopping cornucopia it had once been, so there wasn't too much to tickle my fancy.

Yet, in December 1952, it was possible to imagine that the present mood was not simply one of stagnation or an aspect of decline but of the quiet before, well, something. It was possible to imagine that the Empire might be about to enter a late flowering. Certainly, India had gone in 1947, and British soldiers were at war in Korea and Malaya and there were rumblings in Kenya but the real blows and small wars that would eventually drain Britain of all money and hope had not yet happened. Nobody knew then that the Mau Mau insurrection would make Kenya ungovernable, that Cyprus would explode, that there would be such a fiasco at Suez or that the England football team would be beaten 3–6 by Hungary, and at Wembley stadium at that.

But football was a working-class sport, so it didn't really matter, and instead in December 1952, it was still possible to imagine that Britain was actually an immensely important country. After all, Britain had won the war and it retained an Empire in Africa and the West Indies, and it still had Malaya, the only colony that had ever made a profit. Something mighty could yet happen, a Renaissance, a rising from the ashes.

I wandered back to Malaya Hall, not feeling optimistic about the chances of this happening before tea-time.

Chapter 5

It was dark by the time I arrived back at Malaya Hall. The little sunlight that had managed to penetrate the smog had failed to give London any warmth and now that it was dark, the air itself seemed to freeze around me. My flesh, which had been tenderized in the Malayan sun, was feeling the chill. It was still early, so with nothing better to do, I decided to go to a nearby pub that we boys frequented, except that this time I would be alone, which made it feel strange. Normally ordering a G&T in a London pub gave me a frisson of feeling sophisticated—being in the midst of the ale-drinking locals—but on this occasion, it made me feel like a bit of a whoopsie.

The landlord of The George was a friendly fellow who had lost a leg when he hit the beaches of Sicily in '43 (or did he say he was already legless when he landed?).

'On your own are you tonight, Mr Hamid?' he asked.

'Yes.' I have to admit that I was always a little shy when talking to the locals, especially the salt-of-the-earth types.

'Been abandoned over the Christmas holidays?' he asked.

'Yes.'

I was beginning to regret entering the pub on my own. I looked around for somewhere anonymous to sit and quickly down my drink. I caught the eye of a group of Africans who always gathered at the corner table by the fireplace. They were constantly plotting the downfall of the Empire in their countries, and I had no desire to join them. But as the only other dark-skinned fellow in the place, I think we all felt that perhaps it would be appropriate for me to be with them and not with the Anglo-Saxons. The Africans and I nodded to each other, and I mustered a nervous smile as I gingerly took a step towards them.

Little did I know then that among this group of virtually penniless African exiles, wrapped in layers of oversized clothing, were two future foreign ministers, one minister of culture, and two very nearly prime ministers of three different countries. In later years, I would follow their careers in the papers until they ended, often horribly.

Just as I was stepping towards them and a possible future career nurturing African-Malaysian relations, I heard the landlord speak my name and my life took on a different direction. Africa did eventually come to me, but under different circumstances.

'You should speak to Mr Hamid, he's from there,' said the landlord to a bull of a man leaning against the bar.

I turned back towards the bar for the simple reason that I had heard my name being mentioned. That, and because it would save me from the difficult task of pretending to the Africans that I wanted to foment revolution. The landlord introduced me to his large friend.

'Mr Hamid, could I introduce you to my old friend, Jim Plaistow.'

Jim Plaistow was not fat, he was just very big with big fingers clasping a pint of warm beer. Thinning, greying hair topped a large head with a long-ago broken nose burnished by the residue of a suntan. He must have been in his fifties, but was still powerfully built with a chest bigger than his belly—which was more common then than it is now. He was a physically unattractive man, but not disgustingly so, and he towered over me.

'You're from Malaya, are you?' Jim Plaistow said, as if I had been caught stealing a bicycle. I knew immediately that he was a policeman, but not an English bobby, he was an imperial policeman with an unblinking gaze designed to unnerve brown men in hot locales. I'd met enough of these men to know what they looked like, and I knew I had nothing to fear from them. There are two types of people in this world, those who have something to fear from a policeman and those who do not. With my family background, I had nothing to fear, but I also had nothing to say to a British policeman.

'Yes,' I said, with the appropriate degree of disdain. 'I am from Malaya.'

'Jim is thinking of going there. You might be able to help him,' said the landlord before hopping away to serve a customer and leaving me alone with Jim Plaistow.

'Yes, thinking of trying my luck out there. Not much happening here for the likes of me.' Jim Plaistow laughed to himself. 'I hear you're having some bother in Malaya?'

'Yes, Communists causing trouble. Isn't that what they do?' I said, but this time with a studied air of disinterest. I nonchalantly swirled my G&T.

'I hear it's more police action than the army?'

'Both, but police take the lead. It's urban, rural, and jungle. The politicals and police call the shots, and the army do the donkey work in the jungle.' I wanted to sound very knowledgeable.

'The way it should be. Sounds like it could be just the place for me.'

I could have terminated the conversation then. But being away from my Malayan friends, I felt a sudden and surprising excitement. I did not need to conform. For the first time in my life, I could talk to somebody from outside my world.

'Policeman, are you?' I asked.

'Is it that obvious?' Jim Plaistow laughed again.

'Yes. I could tell the moment I saw you.'

'Not surprising. Military police during the war, Palestine Police Force till '48, and a spot in Tanganyika after that. I press my trousers and polish my shoes every day, and I'm good at banging heads together. Do you think Malaya could benefit from a man like me?'

'Probably.' I found myself warming slightly to Jim Plaistow, possibly because, unlike so many Britishers, he appeared to be at ease talking to a brown man. I decided to relax my air of disdain. If I saw him on the streets of Malaya, I would have ignored him, but here on the neutral ground of London, our class differences seemed not so clear cut. He was not a policeman in Malaya yet, he was still a person, and talking to him made me feel like I might be an adult.

'There are lots of Palestinians in Malaya already.' I told him. A whole slew of British policemen moved to Malaya from Palestine after the mandate shut down in '48, and we called them Palestinians. They had a reputation for a lack of subtlety.

'I know,' he said with regret. 'Some good ones. Do you know a chap called Hancock? Or Kelly?'

'No, I'm sorry.'

'I probably should have gone there straight after Palestine. Got bedded in early. Gained some respect from the locals. They treat us Palestinians like we're a bunch of thugs, like we're the Black and Tans, or worse.'

'How was Tanganyika?' I asked, keeping an eye out for the group of Africans. Sure enough, one of them popped his head up when he heard the name.

'Bloody awful,' Jim Plaistow spluttered. 'The locals have the whole place sewn up.' By locals I knew he meant the British. 'Snouts in the trough everywhere and they don't want outsiders asking any questions. The bastards cooked up a story that I was too fond of the sauce,' he said, indicating to his beer. 'Everyone's tanked up from morning till night, the shits. Beautiful country, though. I swear you've never seen anything like it.'

Jim Plaistow tapped his empty glass in the direction of the landlord who was hopping past. He didn't offer to buy me a drink.

'I don't suppose you know anybody in the police in Malaya?' Jim Plaistow asked.

'No, I'm sorry.' I did, but I wasn't going to admit it. 'I don't think I can be of any help. What about your friends Hancock and Kelly?'

'Those two? I don't think so, not those two. I'm not married, you see. It goes against a man. Makes people think he's unsettled. I should be settled down by now, not wandering the world looking for trouble. It's not right being this rootless, just waiting for something to happen. Still, it's what we have an empire for.' Jim Plaistow seemed to find this amusing and he clicked his replenished beer against my empty glass. 'You're a young man, got your life ahead of you. Marry a good woman.'

'You've never been married?'

'I was. She let me down, with my best friend. Can't forgive that kind of betrayal.'

Jim Plaistow struck me as a man who was completely soaked up with regrets, and he disappeared into his pint of beer.

'So, you want to serve the Empire?' I asked.

'The Empire?' Jim Plaistow seemed a little puzzled by the idea. 'I suppose you could say that, but I don't think of it like that. My loyalty is to the police. We're an international brotherhood, there to keep the riffraff and darkies in line. Sorry, no offence.'

'None taken.' I am certainly not riffraff.

At that moment, Atkins, the doorman for Malaya Hall, entered the pub and dumped his scrawny, nicotine-coloured body onto a bar stool.

'Finally,' exclaimed Atkins, 'The wogs have all left, except for one or two sad buggers with nowhere to go. Oh, sorry, Mr Hamid, I didn't see you there.'

'Would it have made a difference if you had?' Jim Plaistow asked.

'Well, I wouldn't have suggested he was a sad bugger.'

'Your usual, Stan?' the landlord asked.

'Er, no. I'm on duty. I never drink when I'm on duty, you know that.'

'So why are you here, Stanley?' asked Jim Plaistow who clearly did not like Atkins—but nobody did.

'I'm here to, er, to give a telegram to Mr Hamid.'

'How did you know he would be here, Stanley?' asked Jim Plaistow.

'Stop being a policeman, Jim,' the landlord said, placing a pint of beer in front of Atkins.

Atkins took out a crumpled telegram from his pocket, handed it to me, and took a swig of his beer all in one movement. I only ever received telegrams from my father and they either said, 'Work harder', 'No more money', or 'I want you to think about your future', usually all together. So, I was not filled with joy and anticipation.

'It's from Tom Pelham,' Atkins said and the landlord and Jim Plaistow both exclaimed an 'ooh' with an air of respect.

'You know Tom?' I asked.

'Don't know him personally, but I know of him,' said Jim Plaistow. 'He's a legend. Parachuted alone behind enemy lines into Yugoslavia during the war.'

'I don't think so. Tom told me he had a quiet war. It must be a different Tom Pelham.'

'There's only one Tom Pelham. Handsome chap, scar on his face?' asked the landlord.

'Yes, that's Tom.' I said, getting a bit excited. 'I knew him in Malaya before the war.'

'What does he want?' asked Jim Plaistow, as if wanting to know the contents of a Christmas present. 'Is he in the police? Can you put in a word for me?'

'He's not in the police. At least, I don't think he is.'

'What does he want, man?' demanded the landlord. 'They say Hitler himself ordered his best SS battalion to find him. Tom Pelham dodged them for six months.'

'And killed half of them and blew up ten bridges before they caught him,' said Jim Plaistow, passing the baton of praise to Atkins by clinking his glass.

'They tortured him, but they couldn't break him.'

'And then he escaped and did it all again,' laughed the landlord.

'It can't be him, can it?' I was trembling with excitement, discovering that my adolescent hero might really be a hero after all.

'What does he want?' they all demanded.

I tore open the telegram.

Come to Pelhams for Christmas immediately. Train to Atherington from King's Cross. Do not hesitate. Leave today. Tom Pelham.

'What should I do?' I tend to panic whenever the word 'immediately' or the phrase 'do not hesitate' are being used in my direction.

'What should you do?' snorted the landlord. 'If Tom Pelham says leave immediately, then you leave immediately!'

'But he's missed the last train,' Atkins pointed out.

'In that case, you stay with us tonight and tell us all about Tom Pelham,' said the landlord. 'And I'll even give you a drink on the house. Another G&T, Mr Hamid?'

'Don't mind if I do.'

'When you see Tom Pelham be sure to mention my name. Jim Plaistow, ex-military police, ex-Palestine. Best not mention Tanganyika, let's keep that between ourselves, shall we? There's a good chap.'

I stayed the rest of the evening at The George as a vicarious and tenuous connection to the astonishing tales of Tom Pelham's wartime derring-do. I discovered much, and I made up quite a lot too. It was most enjoyable, and I was relieved that 'leave today' could actually mean 'leave tomorrow'. As you can imagine, I said some extremely emotional farewells when the landlord rang the closing time bell, but before I staggered back to Malaya Hall, which fortunately wasn't far, Jim Plaistow took me to one side.

'Make sure you behave yourself at the Pelhams.'

'Of course I will. I'm a very polite young man,' I slurred.

'I know you're polite, but something tells me you don't know how to behave yourself. You remind me of my wife.'

Little did I know then that I would one day meet Jim Plaistow again, but that would be in the jungles of Malaya. He would lose none of his regrets and I would discover his dangerous fatalism, and that he was very handy with a Bren gun in a sticky situation. But by the time I collapsed onto my bed, I had already forgotten all about Jim Plaistow and his advice. My thoughts were occupied by Tom Pelham, Christmas with the Pelhams, and would Clare be there? My limbo was over, I had something to do, somewhere to go, something great was going to happen. I was excited, nervous, and then, I was asleep.

Chapter 6

A sense of excitement woke me early in the morning. Early by my standards, that is.

The winter sun was low in the sky, there was sunlight slanting into my bedroom. The smog that still hung in the air diffused the light, making the very air in my room turn an eerie orange.

It was not beautiful because my every breath was a reminder of the poisonous vapour I was inhaling. The sun offered no relief from the cold and while it was not particularly cold, it was cold enough to make me wince at the thought of having to get out of bed and sit on an icy toilet seat. Normally, I would stay in my warm bed, relish the coziness, and decide that I would not attend lectures today—maybe tomorrow. But today, I leapt out of bed, enveloped myself in my chilled silk dressing gown, and hurried about my morning ablutions.

Today, I was in high spirits. Today, I was going to see Tom and, hopefully, Clare. What should I pack? How long would I be staying? The telegram did say until Christmas at the very least, but after that, what then? These questions needed answers for me to make the best possible wardrobe choices. Being invited to the Pelhams was, I felt, something of an honour because Sir Alfred Pelham had once been the esteemed

Resident and, therefore, the King's representative in my state. So in my world, this was akin to being invited to Windsor Castle.

Having been raised by my father with standards of etiquette that were strictly formal and deferential, I felt that I had to cram my dinner jacket into my suitcase. I also borrowed Salim's most debonair trilby hat, and a few of his other nicer things. The pickings were slim because he had taken the best stuff with him to Denmark. My only regret was that, unlike Salim, I did not have a photograph of myself looking rugged and shirtless to leave for Clare in case she was not there. That one regret aside, I checked each of my wardrobe choices in the mirror, satisfied that I was looking very dapper. For the journey, I chose tweeds and my finest Crombie overcoat, which was actually an uncomfortably warm combination, but sometimes, one must suffer for style. Finally, I grabbed some clean collars and put on my old MCKK school tie, and then I was off to King's Cross station, practically skipping past the weary and the lame of London.

It is a fact oft cited by those of us who can remember those times, such that it has become a tired cliché—it was when you travelled on a steam locomotive that you really knew you were travelling somewhere. The engine itself was alive, hot to the touch, and constantly being fed by men shovelling in coal and checking its temperature—much like the Siamese elephant mahouts I knew from Malaya. Its moving parts would pump and turn on the outside for all to see. It spewed out smoke, steam, and sparks, and when it struggled up a hill, you wished it well.

The wheels of my locomotive first spun helplessly on the tracks, then managed to find a grip, and then made some deep, slow, effortful chugs. My train began to move, and I was suddenly gripped by an exciting understanding. I was making a journey away from the London that I knew well, and into a place about which I knew nothing. A place that was essentially a blank space on my map, one that said, 'Here be cream teas,' a place that even the many Scotsmen in Malaya grudgingly imbued with a mysticism. I was travelling to England.

At first, there was not much to see from my train except the dreary urban sprawl of north London caught in a sudden drizzle. One was privy to a glimpse into the backs of people's houses, and I caught a glimpse of some of them visiting the outdoor privy. It was just damp streets, damp, tired people, grey slate roofs, and the smoking chimneys of houses and factories everywhere adding to the sickly yellow miasma of smog.

My locomotive was also adding a healthy portion of smoke. In its swaying and chugging, it was having a private conversation with me, commenting on sights of interest, pointing out the two women talking over a fence while one bashed clothes on a washing board, the man walking his dog, the coffin leaving the house, the rag-and-bone man patting his horse. This was surely the landscape of Jim Plaistow and Stanley Atkins. No, not of Jim Plaistow, he was a cut above, but certainly of Stanley Atkins.

Out there was an army of Stanley Atkinses, spluttering over their racing bets, dancing on a Saturday night, spinning, grinding, or cutting a widget during the week, and occasionally being called upon to defend the realm. And maybe occasionally hearing a tale of imperial adventure in the Serengeti, the Veldt, the Gibson Desert, the open spaces of Saskatchewan, the bazaars of India, or perhaps even the jungles of Malaya. No wonder the Empire always had a steady supply of men wishing to make their name in distant lands. Who would want to stay here? But I loved it, as the rag-and-bone man loved his horse.

My fellow passengers in my compartment did not disturb me. A middle-aged gent puffed on his pipe while doing his *Times* crossword puzzle, an angular woman with an equally angular hat was knitting what looked like a scarf, and a goatee-bearded student read a book. All were scrupulously keeping to themselves in order to avoid the awkwardness of negotiating barriers of class and in my case, race. It was all terribly English, and I was mightily relieved to be left alone.

As the train took me northward through London the view began to change a little. The drizzle had stopped, and the sun was returning. The streets were becoming wider, the houses more orderly, somewhat more prosperous. This, I imagined, was more the land of Jim Plaistow, or it could have been if he didn't find himself yearning for something else. And then, surprisingly suddenly, we left London.

A fence at the end of a Jim Plaistow garden marked the frontier between a city that had been my entire world and an unknown countryside that stretched out before me. We passed out of the smog, and I could actually see a wall of the vile stuff receding behind us, encasing London in a vast brown dome. This opened a whole new world to me. There were green fields, scrubby and greyish at first, but gradually getting bigger and greener. And there were trees and farms, all bathed in winter sunlight and gloriously clean air. I must have been entering England.

My fellow passengers did not appear to notice our transition, but I couldn't help thinking that somebody should be checking our passports or that we should be doing one of those rituals that sailors do when they first cross the equator. I had seen this land before when on the train from Southampton, where my ship had docked, but back then I was impatiently passing through and I could only think of getting to London. This time, I was journeying into this land, a country that must be Tom Pelham's. From the train I could see people going about their lives, but I could not really understand them, because, I realized, I didn't really know Tom, not like I knew Jim Plaistow.

Our train chugged along an embankment raised above the countryside so I could search the landscape for anything that might help me to better understand its inhabitants, how they lived and how they were governed. There was no gleaming white Residence set on a high-point overlooking the natives and there were no jungle-covered mountains.

Because of the jungle, I was familiar with living in a land of green, but the grass of these pastures was almost gleaming. It was also clearly rich enough to make the black and white cows fat and content, unlike our cattle who seemed emaciated by comparison, being herded along from one scrap of grass to the next. Our water buffalo on the other hand, of which England appeared to have no equivalent, were always very fat, healthy, and happy in a bovine sort of way.

We soon crossed a river. Our train followed a small winding river with winter sunlight glinting off its every turn—and where in Malaya, water buffalo would have been wading.

This was the first English river I had ever seen, other than the filthy Thames, and I will never know its name. The rivers of my country can be very wide but are relatively short. If they were in the Amazon jungle, they might not even warrant a name, but for us they once determined all life. The enormous quantity of rainfall in our mountains meant they head for the sea in a straight line with barely a chance for a twist or a turn. But this river had the time and space to go wherever it wanted to go. The steam engine gave a shrill whistle, turning my attention to some children who were playing beside the river, throwing in stones and fishing. They turned and waved excitedly to me in my passing train. These were the first people I had seen that I understood. Although here it was far too cold to swim, I too, used to play undoubtedly the same games—like tormenting a musang, scaring each other by pretending to see a python, and waving at passing trains. I surmised that the people of this land must be agriculturalists or plantation workers.

We approached a small town on a slight hill in the middle of this sea of farmland. The train slowed down and the woman with the angular hat prepared herself to leave. This surprised me, because I had not imagined her to be a farmer's wife. When I saw she had a bag from Dickens & Jones of Regent Street, I assumed that this must be very rich farming land indeed.

As we entered the town, I could see it had a castle perched at the highest point. Nobody else in my compartment gave it the slightest glance and I had to exert every effort to hide an intense boyish glee. An English castle, for heaven's sake! I couldn't help but imagine Robin Hood sliding down its walls after an illicit night spent with Maid Marian. It was a romantic ruin now, but this must have been built by the local raja in order to tame the unruly Saxons. As the train came to a halt, I caught a glimpse of a white solid building calling itself The Town Hall. This must be where the Resident sits, overseeing local grievances. The angular woman got out of the train and a shout from the platform announced that the next stop would be Bramlingham.

Then it was more fields, some green for pasture, some lying fallow, and some of turned earth, but all filled with rabbits that scattered when the steam train passed by. Thick hedgerows lined the fields and snaked around the land, trapping narrow sunken roads, and heading towards scattered copses of bare trees. In Malaya, I would have needed a very good reason to persuade me to enter the forest, but here, the woods did not frighten me one bit. This land had been thoroughly domesticated.

I was, I am almost embarrassed to admit, completely captivated by this new landscape but it was not, I was beginning to realize, entirely new to me. I had grown up reading about it in Thomas Hardy, Jane Austen, Emily Brontë, and many more. The school library was filled with nothing but English literature, and I read voraciously. From the England I had read of, I was expecting some trudging peasants, horse drawn carriages, and a few brooding Heathcliffs on distant hills. In my Malayan mind's eye, Oliver Twist's unfortunate pregnant mother had stumbled across a landscape that was also dotted with more familiar coconut trees and paddy fields and the rainfall that killed her was a veritable monsoon. It was difficult to see how anybody could succumb to an English drizzle.

Now I could remove the tropical features and fill in the gaps with the reality of solitary oak trees, church steeples, and a stone bridge being crested by a brand new and delightful little Austin-Healey. But alongside the simple act of physical recognition, I found another part of myself connecting with this landscape. I felt that something inside me knew this place more deeply, but I didn't know how. The sound of somebody chuckling in my compartment awoke me from my journey.

The tie-less student was now reading a slender volume of poetry, and he was evidently finding it most amusing, but this was disturbing the peace for the middle-aged gent. I could not see whose poetry this was but clearly the gent could, and he was not amused by the student's amusement. When the student made one guffaw too many, the gent could no longer contain himself.

'What is so funny, young man?'

Both the student and myself were shocked that the English code of silence had been broken.

'This poetry,' the student managed to stammer.

'You're reading Rupert Brooke, are you not?'

'Yes.'

'So why are you finding one of our nation's finest poets so amusing?'

'Well, it's ridiculous.'

'Ridiculous, is it? I carried that very volume of poetry in my knapsack wherever I went during the war. I found his words to have been deeply consoling. I suppose you consider that ridiculous?'

'Well, whatever works for you, but old vicarages, teatime, bugles blowing, it's ridiculous.'

'That's what we fought for.'

'Teatime?' said the student, now finding his feet.

'England! And for the likes of you, heaven help us.'

'I thank you, but did you honestly think you might make some corner of a foreign field forever England?'

'I was simply hoping to get back alive, but, yes, if I should die, then, yes, some corner of a foreign field would have been, yes, forever England. And a richer soil for it. Stop laughing!'

'I'm sorry. But chestnuts shade, elm clumps, "And laughs the immortal river still, under the mill, under the mill." This isn't a country, it's a biscuit tin.'

'It's England, and it's right there,' the gent declared, waving his hand towards a startled cow outside our train.

'Even if it is,' said the student, 'Is it enough? Better red than dead is what I say.'

'"Stands the Church clock at ten to three? And is there honey still for tea?"' That was me suddenly speaking. Both the gent and the student looked at me aghast, presumably as shocked as I was that I had spoken, and that this young brown man was quoting Rupert Brooke. I knew it well, and it stirred within me.

'There, you see,' said the gent, vindicated. 'He understands, and he's a foreigner.'

'I'm not a foreigner,' I wanted to clarify, 'I'm Malayan.'

'Well, as you wish, the point is that you understand an Englishman's calling,' said the gent, very pleased with himself.

'You must be joking,' the student said to me, incredulous. 'You agree with him?'

'I don't know if I agree or not,' I said. 'It just is, isn't it?'

The gent was happy as could be that the argument had been settled in his favour and he reached out to shake my hand.

'Major Stothard, retired Queen's Own. What's so funny?' he snapped at the student who found the regimental name amusing. 'We were about to be shipped to Malaya but were sent to Crete instead, which was a cock-up of another sort, but I can tell you that Malaya would never have fallen if the Queen's had been there. Stop laughing!'

'Hamid, MCKK.' I couldn't think how else to describe myself.

'Well, right you are, jolly good.'

I could see that the gent, Major Stothard, did not know what else to say to me (army generally only knew how to shout at *punkka wallas* in Hindi), but I think he felt obliged to continue because of the part I had played in the downfall of the student.

'Studying in these parts, are you?'

'No, I'm studying in London. I'm visiting some friends in Atherington.'

'Who might they be?' asked the Major, enunciating every word very carefully for my benefit. 'I might know them.'

'The Pelhams.'

'Ooh,' said the Major with an air of respect.

'You know them?' I asked.

'I know of Thomas Pelham. A hero.' The Major glanced at the student, who merely shrugged his shoulders. 'Please send him my regards. He doesn't know me but it's Major Stothard, we were the yeoman battalion in these parts. Ah, Bramlingham. You need to change here. The station master was my batman, good chap, Saunders. I'll have a word with him, make sure you get to Atherington.' The train came to a hissing stop and we three alighted.

The student left the platform quickly, but the Major took me to Saunders who promised to make sure I caught my train to Atherington.

'Well, take care, young man. Remember, Major Stothard, Queen's Own.' And the Major departed.

'There are three platforms,' Saunders told me. 'One goes north, one goes south, and this one only goes to Atherington. So, you wait here, you follow me?'

'Yes, sir.'

'It'll be along shortly. There's a fire in the waiting room if you get cold.' Saunders removed a watch from his waistcoat and studied the time.

For some reason, studying the time gives a man a look of importance, as if something essential depends on him knowing the time. It is never necessary for a man like Atkins to know the time, other people will always determine his time for him, but Saunders was clearly important because he needed to know the time. Maybe during the war Major Stothard had told him what the time meant. As soon as he was convinced that I was impressed by his independent stature, Saunders snapped his watch shut and walked away.

Now that the sound of his footsteps and my old train had disappeared, I was struck by the silence—the first time I had experienced such quiet since leaving Malaya. London can be eerily quiet at night, but it is a quiet where you are aware that slumbering bodies lie in buildings all around.

Here, I was alone. A solitary winter bird sang a persistent song, a breeze rustled through a bare hedgerow, and a group of insects hovered in the sunlight. This landscape had been completely tamed for man and it was so very silent. In Malaya, there would have been at least three different bird songs, a gibbon's distant whoop, monkeys chattering in the trees, and insects clicking and biting. Here, there were no leeches in that stretch of damp grass, no scorpions or snakes under the pile of dry wood, nor any tigers or bears in those trees beyond—none of the things that made you think twice. Here, you didn't have to think about the land. Here, you could contemplate the scenery.

Chugging smoke in the distance announced that my next train was arriving, backwards. Saunders briefly appeared, blew his whistle at me and waved to indicate I should get aboard, thereby completing his duty to Major Stothard and to time. Nobody got off the train and nobody apart from myself got on. I could hear water being poured into the engine's boiler, but I couldn't see anybody.

Eventually, my private train pulled away and passed through a narrow defile of steep rocks that blocked out the sun, making my compartment quite cold. We emerged into a new valley that had been laid out for my pleasure alone. There were more trees than before, only occasional pastures, a high and bare ridgeline loomed over it all, and at the top, there were the grassy outlines of an old fort, probably once held by Bronze Age warriors.

The train crossed the valley on a long brick aqueduct that looked like it had been built by the Romans. This was when I saw on the side of the ridge, a strange and, frankly, terrifying sight. A huge figure of a man had been cut into the hill itself, chalk white and pagan, carrying a club and exhibiting the signs of what can only be described as unabashed sexual excitement.

This land did not look quite so tame, which I found to be exciting. I started whistling about going where fashion sits and putting on the Ritz. I could see we were approaching Atherington station. This land must be Tom Pelham's.

Part II

Atherington, England

Christmas, 1952

Chapter 7

I didn't even see the engine driver get off the train. I appeared to be completely alone at the station and the only sign of life was the engine, which hissed at me as I walked past.

I was relieved to see Tom chatting with the station master, who was gazing back at Tom with a mixture of reverence and deference, an attitude that seems nowadays to have been entirely lost from the English vocabulary of manners (it is, thankfully, still occasionally available in more civilized parts of the world). All the railway lines I took that day have also been forever lost, closed down in the 1960s. How could they remain? None of them made any money.

Tom looked happy to see me. 'Hamid, you've made it safely.'

He reached out to take my suitcase, but the stationmaster grabbed it first.

'There's really no need, Saunders,' said Tom.

'Saunders?' said I, surprised. 'That's the name of the man at the other station.'

'No relation,' said this Saunders. 'And it's really no trouble.'

It obviously was some trouble because this Saunders grimaced when he took the suitcase, so Tom took it instead.

'I am sorry, sir. I've still got a bit of shrapnel in my shoulder from Palestine in '17. Makes it difficult to lift sometimes.'

'But it helps you tell the weather?' Tom joked.

'Yes, sir. Goodbye, sir. My regards to Sir Alfred and Lady Pelham, sir.'

'Naturally.'

Tom threw my suitcase into the back of a delightful little Morgan and revved up its throaty engine.

'I'm so glad you decided to join us for Christmas, Hamid. Everyone is looking forward to seeing you again.'

I wanted to know if 'everyone' included Clare, but I didn't know how to ask without asking.

'Thank you for inviting me. Malaya Hall is completely empty.'

'Well, you're here now, and you're just in time for tea.'

'Is there honey still?'

'I expect so.'

We hurtled down the empty country lanes towards my Christmas with the Pelhams.

Tom drove the Morgan with the top down, and I did not dare wear Salim's trilby in case it flew off, so it was bitterly cold, but this did not trouble me either, I was enjoying being driven along the English country lanes. Besides, there was only one thing on my mind. Tom wore a faint smile while braking the Morgan into a sharp corner, double de-clutching the gears, then roaring out again. My heart was pounding, and my stomach was in my throat, but not from fear of the car crashing. It was because I was desperate to know one thing, and I did not know how to ask without asking, which I was convinced would not only be terribly rude and utterly un-English, but also childlike. Any hint of an incipient adulthood I may have felt in talking to Jim Plaistow had evaporated now that I was with a man I could potentially idolize and follow.

Tom was not like my overbearing and distant father. Tom was a man of action and an adult who alone in the world seemed to take an interest in me. I desperately wanted to know what Tom had done during the war. My merry friends at The George had told me all about Tom Pelham, the hero. He had shot down Stukas with his pistol, had tricked a platoon of Germans over a cliff (according to the landlord they fell to their deaths shouting, 'Aargh! *Gott im himmel!*') and he had rescued several damsels in distress, for which they were all most grateful (Atkins had told me so privately, and somewhat sweatily). All this had made Hitler so enraged that he beat his head with his fists while shouting, '*Vo ist Tom Pell-ham?*'

In fact, Tom had tied down so many German soldiers that he probably shortened the war by six months. Granted, the recipients of Tom's heroics were Yugoslavians and not the more deserving Malayans, but it was thrilling heroics, nonetheless. I needed him to tell me but didn't know how to ask.

While I pondered this, I admired his skill racing his car against himself. The Morgan had dipped down into a small valley hidden from the sun and then lurched over a hump-backed bridge—that made my stomach shoot up into my head—before ascending to a softened crest of a hill.

'Look at that view, Hamid,' Tom shouted. 'I think of this view whenever I am away. I carry it with me always.'

It was a fine view, across and along the length of a wide, slow valley. At the time, it struck me as looking proud and true, but now I think of it as having been smug.

'A beacon was lit on that hill in 1588 when the Drake defeated the Spanish Armada,' Tom told me proudly.

1588, that felt so unimaginably long ago. In Malaya, the rain, heat, and insects had long since destroyed the wooden houses from that time and in the absence of any remains, even the stories of a grandfather's exploits would become in the re-telling, a fable as mythically ancient as the legends of Troy.

'Many have tried to conquer this land, but none have succeeded,' Tom continued. 'Well, apart from the Romans, the Saxons, the Vikings, and the Normans. And the Welsh.'

'The Welsh? I don't remember reading about that.'

'You surely remember your Shakespeare, Richard III. The Pelhams came from Wales with Henry Tudor in 1485. We came, we saw, we conquered. And we were given most of what you see.'

What does it do to a people to have a memory like this?

'How is London?' Tom asked. 'Did the smog get worse?'

'It didn't bother me.' In this bright and clear air, I had forgotten all about the deadly fog.

'Have you thought any more about your future?' he asked, casually.

I hadn't thought about it all because the future was simple. 'I will become a civil servant.'

'Naturally, but for whom?'

I didn't understand what he meant. 'For Malaya, obviously.'

'But which Malaya? Today it's part of the British Empire, but one day it might be independent. Where do your loyalties lie—the present or the future?'

'I suppose I will serve whichever Malaya is in front of me.'

This was becoming infuriating. I wanted to know about Tom's past, but he only wanted to know about my future.

'Don't you think about the future, Hamid?'

'I don't like to interfere with it. Let the future sort itself out.' I have been told that I tend to concentrate on the present.

'But don't you think that what we do today can affect the future?'

I suspected that Tom was revving up to one of his lectures, but I was older now and determined to make a show of holding my own.

'The future is not in our hands,' I said, sagely.

'You are very Malay,' Tom chuckled, 'fatalistic to the end. But I would like you to think about the future. We can make it safe for everyone.'

What on earth was he blathering on about? This was altogether too infuriating, and I could no longer keep quiet.

'Tom, what did you do in the war?'

'I told you, back-room staff, nothing special.'

'But I was told that you went to Yugoslavia.'

'That was nothing. Exaggerated out of all proportion.'

'But I was told you shortened the war by six months.'

'Do you think it's possible for one man to do that?'

'It depends on who he is, but I think so.'

'Maybe I'll tell you about it one day. But for now, here we are.'

I hadn't noticed that we were driving alongside a long brick wall until we came to an opened gateway where a sign told us we had arrived at a place called *Tanamerah*, the ancient name for the red earth of Malaya. I wasn't expecting to see a reminder of my homeland among the green fields of England. Tom sensed my surprise.

'I know. We tried to persuade father to call the house anything else, but he insisted. He did live in Malaya for most of his life, you know.'

Tom swerved the Morgan off the main road, and we entered the grounds of Tanamerah. We drove along a curving avenue lined with tall, bare trees and soft grasslands sloping up on either side, dotted with docile sheep and their playful lambs.

'They'll be ready for slaughter soon,' Tom informed me. 'We used to own all the land around here, but we've had to sell it bit by bit. Don't worry, Hamid, we sold the last piece a hundred years ago. There's still fifty acres around the house.'

We turned one final corner and there was the house that would become my pleasure ground for the next few days. The house was beautiful, serene despite its obvious weight and age. Although by no means huge, it was bigger than The Residence in my hometown, but somehow less important. This house was situated at the bottom of a valley and not at the top of a hill, as if trying to understate its grandeur for the local peasantry. This house was three floors of old, dark bricks and not gleaming white. This house had towering ornate chimneys. In Malaya, I had only seen chimneys in the hill-stations.

I did not recognize or understand anything about this house, it was of a style and age that I had never seen before, and there was nothing like it in Malaya or in London. I could only think that it reminded me of the house called Mandalay in the movie *Rebecca*, which I had watched as a boy in a hot cinema in Kuala Kangsar, never imagining that I would one day be outside a similar house. But Mandalay was a sinister house, whereas this house looked decidedly contented.

'What do you think?' Tom asked as he stopped the car.

'It's beautiful.'

'Well, it's not Blenheim Palace but it's home. It's been in the Pelham family since 1486, although most of the house is Elizabethan. There are some older and newer bits dotted around, which I'm sure Clare will show you.'

Clare was here, at the house, now? I instantly forgot all about the house with its Elizabethan bits, and of Tom holding out my suitcase. I was busy looking around for Clare. I saw her then, standing at the door of the house and smiling, a young woman. Her hair was blonder than I remembered, and her skin was whiter than the sun-burnished nine-year-old I had known. My stomach was churning. Framed by a trellis for a winter-dormant rose bush, this was no 'bookish' old maid, she was the delightful epitome of an English rose, and I knew that one day I would marry her. I saw Tom grinning as I walked towards her.

'Clare?' I asked.

She laughed sweetly and tilted her head slightly to one side. 'No, silly, I'm Hermione. I'm a friend of Clare's, but you must be Hamid, we've heard all about you. Come inside, it's cold out here.'

Hermione? A friend of Clare's? What did this all mean? I didn't care, Hermione was wondrous to behold, and I willingly followed her into the house. It was hardly surprising that she might be feeling the cold, she was only wearing a polka dot skirt that ballooned out over layers of chiffon with a pale blue sweater draped over her shoulders. Under that was a tight top and one of those pointy brassieres that made the 1950s such a delight. It was, perhaps, fractionally warmer inside the house. My body had been chilled by the drive but now it was pumping with blood, and I was feeling very fine indeed.

'Clare,' Hermione shouted up the stairs. 'Hamid is here.'

There was a sound of scampering feet on the wooden floorboards upstairs travelling quickly across carpets and then more tap-tapping as they moved towards the top of the stairs. Then Clare's footsteps stopped, perhaps so she could compose herself, and then more sedate footsteps brought her down the stairs. So, this was Clare. She wore spectacles and her brown hair was tied up. I could understand why her brother would call her 'bookish'.

Clare, unlike Hermione, had the sort of looks that needed a second glance. I gave her a second glance, and I was richly rewarded. She had a beaming smile; she was perhaps more pleased to see me than anybody had ever been before. Tom may have been interested to see me again, but Clare was pleased. As she walked towards me, I saw again that sharp little nose and the freckles on her soft skin. She hugged me, which I was not expecting and which we had never done when we were young. Now, she was a woman, and I was a man.

'*Selamat tengah hari*,' she said into my ear.

'Good afternoon to you too,' I said, a little surprised to hear her welcome me in Malay.

She pulled back from me and we looked at each other. A ray of winter sun coming in through the door illuminated some dust in the air and the finest down on her neck. Despite my activities over the last few months in London, I was still unused to being this close to a woman.

'It's really wonderful to see you again, Hamid.'

'Yes, it is,' I managed to say, somehow.

'I see you've met Hermione.'

'Yes, I have.'

'Come and say hello to the parents, they're dying to see you.'

And just like when we were nine years old, she took me by my arm and dragged me away.

'You go on, I have to make a phone call,' Tom said.

'You and your secretive phone calls,' Hermione chided, very sweetly. 'Will you ever tell us who you are calling all the time, Tom?'

Tom merely laughed and left us.

Arm in arm, Clare led me away. Glancing behind me, I could see that Hermione was following us . . . and was she slyly watching me?

'How long has it been, Hamid?' Clare asked. 'I haven't seen you since before the war. Malaya feels like a dream. Do you remember when we were attacked by those ants? They were vicious.'

'Yes, I remember. You were very brave.'

'And you started crying,' she laughed.

'No, I did not.'

'Yes, you did. But don't worry, Hamid, you're safe here.'

'I'm sure Hamid can take care of himself,' Hermione said. She was definitely watching me.

Clare stopped me at a doorway, straightened my jacket and spoke to me in a more serious tone while Hermione slipped the Crombie off my shoulders and took my hat.

'Papa is well, but don't be surprised if my mother does not remember you. She doesn't remember very much these days.'

'She'll probably think you're Jack,' Hermione added. 'She thinks every man is Jack.'

'Who is Jack?' I asked, nervously.

'My uncle, Jack,' said Clare, who didn't find the situation to be as amusing as Hermione did. 'Mother's brother. He was killed in Gallipoli in the first war. Mother has changed, but Father is the same. Come and meet them.'

She opened the door.

'You go and meet my father. Hermione and I will prepare dinner. We're having *kedgeree*. Go on. You have plenty of time to catch up.'

I was left to walk alone into a very large room. In a small, middle-class home, this might have been called a sitting room, but the term was far too prosaic to describe this large, yet cozy, room. The furniture was very fine despite being old and worn, in colours that had surely once been bright but were now faded by the sunlight that streamed in from the windows all around.

Clare's mother was snoozing next to a gigantic fireplace and Sir Alfred Pelham was standing up to greet me. He was as tall as I remembered, but perhaps rounder, and what little hair he had was entirely white. I had rarely seen his hair anyway, because in the past, it had invariably been covered by a white solar topee that had made him look even taller, towering over us Malayans. It was with such simple visual tricks as this that the British had managed to maintain such a vast Empire for so long, and with so little. This was the moment I had been dreading. I was happy to meet Sir Alfred again, but I had still not decided how I should address him, and I did not wish to make a diplomatic faux pas.

'Hamid,' he said warmly. 'It is good to see you again, how are you?'

'I am well, Your Excellency.'

He laughed, but in a kindly manner. 'I'm no longer The Resident, and we're not in Malaya. There is really no need for that.'

'Sir Alfred?' I offered.

'Surely not. You are a guest, a friend of the family.'

'Uncle Alfred?'

'Yes, Uncle Alfred will do. How is your father? I like to think that we were very good friends, you know.'

'He is well, and he sends his regards.' This was not entirely true. I hadn't bothered to tell my father that I was visiting the Pelhams.

'And how is Malaya? You know, I spent forty years of my life in the MCS, but I suppose it has all changed now.'

'Things have changed, things are changing.' Where could I begin trying to explain how things were changing? Even I didn't understand how.

'I left Malaya just before the war, you know,' Sir Alfred said. 'I am sorry about the war, by the way.'

'Yes, we're all sorry.'

'Many of my friends died in Changi. Poor old Carter-Ruddock was deliberately starved to death, you know.'

And I saw my friend Wong beheaded, you know.

'Yes,' I said.

'Well, it's over now. Water under the bridge. Speaking of which, would you care for a drink? I'm having a scotch.'

'Yes, thank you.'

This was back in the days when it was perfectly natural to offer a Malay a drink. But even a delicious single malt would not take away the taste of how we, in Malaya, had been let down in the war, although it might help.

Sir Alfred and I were neither friends nor contemporaries so I was hoping that Clare would return quickly and rescue me from an embarrassingly strained conversation. But decades of diplomatic training in the Malayan Civil Service meant that Sir Alfred could spin a conversation on the merest of threads.

'Tom tells me you are studying in London. What are you studying, Hamid?'

Fortunately, at that moment, something in the ether awoke Lady Pelham from her slumber, and I was saved from having to talk about my disastrous studies.

'Ah, Lady Pelham arises,' Sir Alfred said, with an air of disappointment. 'Please do not be alarmed if she thinks you are her brother Jack.'

'Clare told me already.'

'Good. Celia, my dear, we have a guest. He has come all the way from Malaya. You remember Malaya, don't you?' He spoke to his wife quite tenderly, as one would talk to a puppy.

Lady Pelham looked up at me. Her eyes were dead at first, but they suddenly came to life, and she even raised herself a little in her chair. She spoke with a trembling, hopeful voice.

'Is that really you, Abdullah?'

This came as a bit of a shock to myself and Sir Alfred. Abdullah was my father's name and there was no reason why she should remember him. I turned to Sir Alfred hoping for guidance, but he just stood there holding two glasses of scotch, looking surprised, to say the least.

'No,' I ventured. 'I am Hamid, Abdullah's son.'

'Abdullah, you've finally come,' the misty-eyed old woman continued with breathy excitement. 'Take my hand, sit beside me.'

Abdullah is a common name in Malaya, but there was no escaping the fact that I looked a lot like my father, albeit slimmer, and much more handsome.

'I, er, I'm Hamid.'

She was holding out her hands, yearningly, beseechingly. She looked younger, a little more as I remembered her, and I remembered that she had been a handsome woman. Sir Alfred was speechless as she continued.

'Abdullah . . .'

'. . . Hamid.'

'Hold my hand, Abdullah.'

I decided to hold her outstretched hands. I didn't know what else to do. Her skin was soft, yet waxy.

'Sing to me, Abdullah, sing to me again.'

This was a horrifying moment for me as I knew that my father was a keen singer, especially of romantic Malay songs.

'I don't really sing.' I demurred. 'I like to whistle a tune, but I'm afraid singing is not my forte.'

'Sing for me the song about the river, and about love.'

This was perhaps too much for Sir Alfred, and he slumped into his chair, still clutching the scotches. I decided it was the right time to make an escape.

'I should see if I can help Clare.' I managed to pull my hands away from hers.

'Don't leave me, Abdullah. Alfred won't be back till late. Don't go, I'm so lonely.'

I did not know what to do.

Sir Alfred was lost in his chair, looking and yet not daring to look at his wife. I walked away from them, backwards, like a minion at The Residence. I needed to get away from that room in a hasty, yet dignified, manner.

'It has been delightful to see you both again. Clare says we're having kedgeree for dinner. Tom wants me to think about my future. Goodbye.'

I was turning the handle of the door when Sir Alfred finally spoke, quietly yet sternly.

'Hamid, let's keep this between ourselves, shall we? There's a good chap.'

'Yes, Sir Alfred.'

As I left the room, I saw a man trying to re-understand his long marriage and a woman tapping her head, angry with herself.

'I will remember that song. I must remember,' she said.

Now that was a bit of a surprise, I pondered to myself as I stood in the empty hallway collecting my thoughts. Perhaps it meant nothing. Perhaps it was just the fantasies of a demented old woman. Perhaps she had been an irresistible siren luring in my helpless father. Whichever way you looked at it, there was no proof that any misdeed had been committed. But if I could think of my father as anything other than my father then I had to admit that he was a man with a twinkle in his eye. And he did like to sing.

I honestly didn't know how I felt about this turn of events. Obviously, it was hideously embarrassing, and I knew I should keep my interactions with the older generation to an absolute minimum, but it wasn't as if I had done anything wrong. I was thankfully entirely blameless on this occasion and if my father and her ladyship had had a bit of a kneetrembler whilst his lordship was outstation inspecting some drains then, well, so be it. It had nothing to do with me. In fact, if you think about it, I was an aggrieved party as well. If my father had been a cad, then he had been disloyal to his family as much as he had to his good friend Sir Alfred.

I decided that the correct course of action would be to do the Malay and English thing—to never mention it ever again and to bury all thoughts and feelings as deeply as possible until it all came bursting out in the rage of an amok. It was the only healthy thing to do.

I also decided that I should spend as much time as possible with Clare and Hermione because being in the company of attractive women might help me overcome my disappointment at my father's disloyalty. And, erm, etc.

Now, where were they?

Chapter 8

As I listened intently for clues of the girls' whereabouts, I became aware of the sound of a low mumbling voice, emanating from a tiny room under the stairs.

I crept forward and saw Tom talking on a telephone, but his conversation made no sense to me. The words were like the answers to a crossword puzzle or moves in a chess game. The only sentence I could understand was, 'No, not Berlin. Not yet,' after which he put the phone down—he must have sensed my presence.

'Ah, Hamid. There you are. Were my parents delighted to see you?' he asked, quite cheerfully.

'Yes, thank you.'

'I think the girls are in the kitchen with the cook. They're making kedgeree. Why don't you find them, I have to make another phone call.'

Tom closed the door to his tiny cubicle and started dialling again, and I followed the sound of feminine laughter, mixed with the scent of cooked fish wafting from the kitchen. Before I could find the source of the delicious laughter, another sound from outside the house caught my attention. It was like a growl, or was it a purr? It was the sound of a car, but the likes of which I had never heard before.

I pulled open the heavy front door and witnessed the arrival of an astonishingly bright red sports car with such sleek lines that it made the Morgan suddenly look as ancient as Queen Boadicea's chariot. I had never seen anything like it before in my life and it took my breath away. It looked like it should be on a racetrack. It looked like the future. A girl got out of the car. She removed her hat, releasing thick, lustrous black hair that cascaded down in rivulets. Curiously, she was dressed in a military uniform, and I realized that I had seen this uniform in movies about the war. It was a RAF uniform. She wore her skirt shorter than I had seen in the movies, or perhaps it looked like that because her legs were so long.

She turned and looked at me. She had an unflinching gaze, and I was terrified because she was so astonishingly beautiful. I wanted to run away, but I had been told that in the event when one is confronted by a tiger and all else has failed, you must stand your ground and show your face. She walked towards me, crunching gravel beneath her feet. She wore lipstick as red as her car, but unlike Clare and Hermione, she wore no smile. She looked like Hedy Lamarr, but perhaps even more beautiful, and with better teeth. I saw her perfect teeth when she spoke to me.

'Do you like it?'

'Yes,' I managed to say.

'It's a Ferrari Europa.'

'I've never seen one before.'

'It's brand spanking new.'

Was it my imagination or did she stress the word spanking?

'Daddy bought it for me. It's the first one in the country. It hasn't even been launched yet. Who are you?'

'I'm Hamid.'

'I think Clare said you were coming.'

'And who are you?'

'I'm Margaret de Vere.' She stressed her surname, and then she seemed to be waiting for me. 'You've probably heard of my father.'

'No, I'm sorry.'

'News must travel slowly to Africa.'

'I'm from Malaya.'

'Be a darling and fetch my luggage from the car.'

Margaret de Vere walked into the house leaving me in the wake of her heady, dark perfume. It was like the scent of a black rose. I fetched her luggage from the boot of the Ferrari. It was a small but surprisingly heavy leather valise, and I doubted she ever had to carry it or anything else herself. By the time I got back into the house, Margaret was in the hallway talking to Clare. Clare seemed shocked by something when she saw me.

'What are you carrying, Hamid?' Clare demanded.

'Margaret's valise,' I managed to say.

'I can see that, but why?'

'She asked me to.'

'Margaret, why did you ask Hamid to carry your things?'

'Well, I couldn't exactly carry it myself,' said Margaret, self-evidently. 'And, besides, he doesn't mind.'

'I don't mind,' I agreed.

'Be a poppet and would you take it up to my room,' Margaret asked. I think she was asking.

'Stop,' Clare ordered. 'Put the bag down, Hamid. And, Margaret, shame on you! Hamid is my friend and the first thing you do is get him to carry your bag like one of your lackeys.'

The bag was now sitting alone in the middle of the room, and for some reason we all looked at it. I noticed that my suitcase had already miraculously disappeared.

'I suppose the maid can take it up,' said Margaret.

'No, she won't. You know she doesn't do that here. We Pelhams practise a strict regime of self-reliance. You'll carry it up yourself.'

'Honestly, Clare, we're not at school any more.'

'If we were at school, I'd put you over my knees and spank you, young lady.'

They both seemed to find this notion extremely funny but, good heavens, I really wanted to know if they actually spanked each other when they were at school. Perhaps it was on a winter's evening such as this, flesh illuminated by the flickering embers of a fire, an opened hand swishing through the air . . .

'. . . Hamid!' Clare was practically shouting at me. 'Didn't you hear what I said?'

'Sorry, I was thinking about something. The hydrogen bomb. It has been on my mind.'

Clare continued, 'I said that we're having tea in the library. Tom told me you wanted some honey with your tea.'

'Yes, thank you, Clare.'

Clare walked away, but Margaret stepped towards me. 'So, Hamid likes some honey, does he?'

'I am, er, partial to honey, I suppose. Yes?'

Clare called out from a distance. 'Margaret, stop tormenting Hamid.'

We dutifully followed Clare into the library, leaving the valise alone.

Goodness, Margaret terrified me—much like the fear I felt when I first saw Jane Russell in *The Outlaw*.

Chapter 9

There was a fire flickering and snapping in the largest private library I had ever seen.

Old books were stacked on floor-to-ceiling shelves on both sides of the tall room and ladders led to walkways half-way up. I could see that the sun was already setting through the windows, sprinkling its rays onto Hermione's blonde hair, who was sitting on a sofa smoking a cigarette and fascinating me. They were all fascinating me. Clare was pouring the tea. This room was heaven.

'I'll be mother,' said Clare, confusingly. In those days I could speak English fluently, but I didn't know all their strange idioms, which would sometimes lead me to panic. *Was she a mother?* 'Don't worry, Hamid. Whoever pours the tea is mother,' said Clare.

Every room in this house seemed to exude warmth and coziness. But this room was enlivened by these three women, and I had never been alone in a room with three women my own age before.

'Must we always drink tea?' Margaret complained.

'Hamid wants tea, don't you, Hamid?' Clare asked.

'Yes please.'

'He can drink tea, but I want something stronger,' said Margaret. 'I'm having a gin and tonic. Anybody want anything?'

'Can I have a sherry?' Hermione seemed to be asking Clare.

'Of course you can,' Clare confirmed. 'I'll have one too. Hamid?'

'Yes please.' Actually, I needed a scotch.

I had only entered two rooms in this house so far and both had an excellent selection of drinks within easy reach. Margaret poured the drinks and handed them out, except for mine, which I had to get for myself. I sat down in a chair that was so uncomfortably far away from the three women that it felt like I was not part of the assembly. With Margaret in her military uniform standing behind the sofa and swirling her G&T, pretty Hermione sipping her sherry, and Clare stirring the tea, they looked like a family. Sitting so far away and sipping my sherry, I felt like I could be a hopeful yet nervous suitor being interviewed for a daughter's hand in marriage, presumably Hermione's.

Clare stepped away from the strange family configuration and briefly entered my world to bring me a cup of tea, in a teacup that I recognized from the old Residence. Looking up at her, I could not see even the merest trace of that nine-year-old girl I had once known, until she spoke to me.

'So, Hamid, what are you studying?' Clare asked, as if she genuinely wanted to know.

'Yes, Hamid,' said Margaret, 'what do you do and why are you here?'

'Well, that's hard to say.'

'Don't listen to her,' said Clare, protectively.

Fortunately, I was saved from having to talk about myself as Tom chose that moment to walk into the room. He went straight for the drinks. I was never in the habit of talking about myself, because nobody had ever really wanted to know.

'Good afternoon, ladies. Cook tells me there's tea.'

'Have you finally finished your mysterious phone calls?' asked Hermione.

'Yes, thank you. Why are you wearing an RAF uniform, Margaret? Or should I say WAAF? Have you joined up?'

I was glad that Tom had asked the question. I desperately wanted to know, but I didn't know how to ask without asking.

'We've been bombing Germany,' Margaret said flatly.

'Really? I didn't think we did that these days,' said Tom, pouring himself a whiskey.

'No, silly,' Hermione said. 'Margaret is in a movie being filmed at Appleton Studios down the road. How was it today? I'm so jealous, it must be so exciting.'

'It isn't.' Margaret extinguished Hermione's enthusiasm. 'I'm just a background extra and it's terribly dull. Today, while some of our brave boys were knocking out some dams with some bouncing bombs, and thereby shortening the war by six months, I was pushing a little aeroplane across a giant map of Germany.'

'Didn't you say you were getting a close-up today?' asked Clare.

'I had two, and it was most exhilarating,' Margaret said, sarcastically. 'Before the assistant director could even tell me how I should act I said, don't worry, dear,

I know the drill, look anxious and think of the brave lads who are risking their lives for me. And later, I got to anxiously hand a piece of paper to a wing commander. I was not told what was on the piece of paper.'

'If it hadn't been for those brave boys you'd be speaking German now,' said Tom, not taking Margaret particularly seriously.

'You speak German, Tom,' Clare pointed out.

'Yes, I suppose I do.' Tom laughed.

'But you played a chorus line girl the other day?' Hermione asked. 'That looked like great fun. I wish I could dress up like that. It seems so daring.'

'Yes, showing myself off to our brave boys before they risk their lives for me. War is just for men, there's nothing for women to do, except look anxious or show off our legs. They're either fighting in defence of our bodies or for our bodies. I wish they'd make up their minds.'

'Careful, Margaret, you're beginning to sound like Clare,' said Tom.

'Am I?' Margaret asked. 'War can do that to a girl. I just want them to give me one bloody line of dialogue! Then they'll see that I'm a star and they'll make a movie for me where I'm a secret agent that gets dropped behind enemy lines. Then I can take the fight to the Hun.'

'Like Tom did,' I said.

'I certainly wasn't as cinematic as secret agent Margaret de Vere.'

'It's true,' Margaret agreed. 'I would look devastating with a machine gun. One bloody line of dialogue, then a starring role and then I'm off to Hollywood.'

'I thought you were going to use your feminine charms on the producers?' Clare asked.

'It's not working. Nobody will even flirt with me. They've got their grubby hands all over the other girls but they're all too petrified of Daddy to even speak to me.'

'Well, he does own the studio,' Clare reminded her.

'I just wish Daddy would leave me alone and let me live my own life.'

'Don't worry, Margaret,' Hermione gushed. 'I'm sure they'll see how talented you are. You've certainly got the looks.'

'I know,' said Margaret, sadly accepting the truth of her ravishing beauty. 'But I think they would love you in the movies, Hermione.'

'Oh, surely not,' said a rapt Hermione.

Margaret circled around the blushing Hermione. 'I'm sure they would. My looks are too obvious, but you have delicate, well-bred features and alabaster skin hiding the fire that lurks within, like an English Grace Kelly.'

'Really? Do you think so?'

'I'm sure of it. Especially if you played a chorus-line girl, kicking those athletic legs of yours. There would be something deliciously wrong and forbidden about that. Yankee flyboys would definitely paint your picture on their plane.'

'That sounds too daring. Do you think I could?'

'Don't listen to her, Hermione,' said Clare.

'Actually, come to think of it, Clare is what they're looking for,' said Margaret. 'She looks like a movie star. Beautiful but unusual, like Bette Davis.'

'Looks are unimportant, Margaret,' said an unamused Clare.

Margaret was undaunted. 'Clare looks like the dowdy spinster secretary who then one day lets down her hair, and the widower chairman realizes he's been in love with her all along, thereby saving her from a life of penury.'

Margaret reached out and quickly removed Clare's hairclip, allowing Clare's hair to be released. In the blink of an eye, I suddenly saw the nine-year-old girl again and I simultaneously saw all the intervening years until she had become this woman. With her hair released, she was captivating. But she didn't seem happy being so exposed and she pushed her hair around her head without purpose.

'I don't require any chairman to save me, Margaret. I will do just fine on my own.'

'Really?' Margaret asked. 'What are you studying?'

'Ants,' said Clare.

'I think you'll be needing all the financial help you can get. Don't you think so too, Tom?'

'Don't involve me, Margaret,' said Tom from behind his newspaper. 'She's my sister and she's never listened to a word I say.'

'What about you, Hamid?' Margaret suddenly asked me. 'Wouldn't you pay money to see Clare in a movie? Or would you rather see Hermione? Or me?'

I was not prepared to be asked such a difficult question. How could one possibly choose between them? But I did find myself quickly surveying the three women. Hermione was sitting forward eagerly, surreptitiously pulling up her skirt slightly to reveal more leg, Margaret lit a cigarette, placing it in the middle of her mouth as they do in the movies and allowing the smoke to linger. And Clare stood there with her head bowed slightly, as if she were unwillingly on auction. They were all delectable.

'Why should I choose?' I asked. 'You're all charming in your own way.'

'Because that's what men do, silly,' said Hermione. 'They choose.'

'This is ridiculous,' scowled Clare, peeking up at me a little.

'Don't do it, Hamid,' said Tom, swigging back his whiskey. 'It's the Judgement of Paris. Paris had to choose who was the fairest between the goddesses Athena, Hera, and Aphrodite. It can't be done and choosing one over the others will only lead to trouble.'

'Then I'd be Aphrodite,' said Margaret.

'Oh, this is fun,' declared Hermione. 'Choose me!'

'We didn't really have a classical education at MCKK,' I said to Tom. 'But didn't Paris receive Helen, the most beautiful woman in the world?'

'Yes,' said Tom. 'And it led to ten years of war and the destruction of Troy. Now wasn't that a happy ending.'

Still, she was proclaimed the most beautiful woman in the world, I pondered to myself.

'He's not going to choose anyone,' said Clare. 'Everyone is going to get dressed for dinner. We're having kedgeree. I'll show you your room, Hamid.'

Clare came over to me and offered me her hand, which surprised me, but I took it. She smoothly hooked her arm into mine and spoke quietly to me as she led me out of the library.

'Don't listen to Margaret, she's completely spoilt. Her father is immensely wealthy and gives her anything she wants.'

'I'm sure he was going to choose you, Margaret,' I could hear Hermione saying as we left the room.

I didn't really want to leave the room. Being there with those three women had been extremely exciting but I had to console myself with the thought that there would surely be more of such occasions during this Christmas holiday. Even the fact that Tom had treated me as an equal had been exciting, but of secondary importance.

Margaret truly frightened me. She seemed to be using her obvious beauty as a challenge to dare others to approach her world. And when I had been near Margaret, her body had hummed with a threat. I think it was the threat that she would laugh at me. There was no mystery to Hermione. She was just a healthy, beautiful, beckoning girl, and every man who would ever talk to her would only be thinking about how much they want to touch her. But Clare was a mystery. Unlike Margaret, physical proximity was not the issue. I felt that even if you were physically close to Clare, you would never be in her world unless she allowed it to be so. I had not seen her since we were nine, and I couldn't say that I knew her, and yet as we walked arm in arm up the stairs, I felt that I had been allowed into her world. I knew that she had been in mine since we were nine. Here, in England, I could play the game of looking like I naturally belonged, but I was a Malayan, and she, too, was from Malaya. She knew the sunlight and the rain, and she knew the ants.

'Are you really studying ants, Clare?'

'Yes.' She smiled sheepishly. 'I know it sounds silly.'

'I have to admit it does. Why ants?'

'Because of Malaya, of course. I've been fascinated by ants ever since you and I were attacked by them.'

'But it was a horrible experience.'

'They were just defending themselves. You need to defend yourself to survive, but I think that anything that feels painful must also be able to do good.'

She wasn't looking at me as we walked up the stairs, so I was looking at her.

'I don't know, Clare. Painful things are painful for a reason. It's a warning.'

'Chillies are painfully hot but don't you like eating chillies?'

'Yes, I do,' I agreed a little excitedly as I thought about chillies. I had not eaten any chillies for too long, and I missed it so. Like any Malay, I need chilli in my bloodstream.

'Haven't you ever been frightened but also excited by something?' she asked.

'Yes, I have.' I was thinking of Salim's dangerously hot *sambal tumis pedas*, but I was also thinking of Margaret, or was it Hermione, or was it Clare? Like any true Malay male, I can think about food and women at the same time.

'You don't have yellow fever in Malaya, do you?' Clare asked.

'Thankfully, no.'

'It's like malaria, or dengue fever.'

'I've had dengue fever.'

'You poor thing.'

The sound of genuine concern in Clare's voice made me feel nice inside, and I would have liked to have milked her compassion a bit more, so I was a trifle disappointed when she continued talking.

'Most people survive dengue fever. The man who has just received the Nobel Prize for medicine found that a small dose of yellow fever virus can effectively immunize you for ten years. And most people who catch yellow fever die. Soon, yellow fever will be completely eradicated in Africa.'

'That's nice.'

I did not know it at the time, but yellow fever would not be eradicated, and I would one day catch it in Africa.

We had reached my bedroom. Somebody had already emptied my suitcase and placed the contents neatly in the wardrobe and drawers. I was thankful that I had not packed my copy of *Lady Chatterley's Lover* and brought Joseph Conrad's *Youth* instead.

Clare lingered by the bed and spoke with deliberate care. 'Do you think that sometimes if you expose yourself to danger then it can save you in the long run? I mean, medically speaking, of course.'

'Of course. Yes. Like a vaccination.'

'Yes. Like a vaccination.'

'But you can't vaccinate yourself against everything, Clare.'

'Of course not. But I don't want to get hurt.'

'Nobody ever wants to get hurt.'

'Of course not.'

She seemed vulnerable with her hair loose and her head slightly bowed. She looked up, her hair covering one eye, biting her lower lip. You didn't have to be a chairman to fall in love with this girl.

'Come down for dinner in half an hour,' she told me. 'There's a bathroom down the hall on the left.'

And then she turned and left the room. What on earth had we been talking about? Once upon a time, a thousand years earlier and back in Malaya, I had been caught between Clare and Irma, and I had enjoyed it. I was no doubt flattering myself, but now I had been asked to judge between three ladies, and it was even nicer. *Girls can be surprisingly competitive*, I thought to myself. This was not what I had been expecting when I left London in the morning. I had never before been left alone with three girls.

I vaguely remembered Jim Plaistow telling me to behave myself as I anticipated an interesting Christmas with the Pelhams and as I opened a bottle of beer that was on the window ledge. There seemed to be alcohol in every room in this house.

Chapter 10

The water pipes echoed my thoughts as they made an almighty banging and chugging noise every time the bathroom was in use, which it constantly was as the girls prepared themselves for dinner.

Mine and the girls' bedrooms were on the same side of the house, so we had to share the same bathroom, which meant that every time I heard the bathroom door open, I would grab my towel and make a dash for my door, only to hear somebody else beat me to it. So, I would return to dressing in my dinner jacket and drinking some more beer, which sat uneasily with the sherry in my otherwise empty stomach. Instinct told me to wear the same shirt but to change to a wing collar while I listened intently to the sounds of female chatter as they slipped from one room to the other, zipping or tying each other's outfits.

All my young life, I had desired so deeply to enter what was for me the forbidden and mysterious female world. My glimpses had been few: women washing in the river, the Chinese coffee shop owner's lovely daughter who would serve us with bare arms, or tales of ancient Malay Sultans with their legends and court intrigues, which was all very interesting but what was that bit about his harem again?

As I, with nervous hands, attempted to tie my bowtie, I still could not actually see the many unravelling dramas of this female world, but I could hear its music. Now, after more than six decades of life, a woman's toilette holds very little mystery—and yet, the memory of that sound of chatter and laughter obscured by only a few annoying walls still burns my ears and thuds my heart.

I had been hoping that Clare would be home for the holidays, but the addition of Hermione and Margaret was a thrilling, perhaps frightening, bonus. *What if,* I wondered to myself, *I really could choose one of them? Who would I choose?*

I decided to ignore Tom's advice to not get involved and preferred instead to listen to Salim's voice of discord that was exhorting me to choose because, some part of me was agreeing, such a choice could make me complete.

Eventually, I heard the girls walk along the corridor and down the stairs, which surely meant the coast was clear. I breathed in the serene and overwhelming bouquet of scents that hung in the air where they had passed: jasmine, bitter mandarins, and lashings of lavender. Which scent belonged to whom? Individually the perfumes would have been delicious, but they combined to smell like an over-ripe Ottoman's boudoir. In fact, it reminded me of His Highness. And so did the bathroom, which was steamy and littered with a mess of cold creams and powder poufs, as if the over-ripe Ottoman had exploded in there.

My few years in London had already taught me that girls can present themselves delightfully in public and yet be atrociously messy in private. With the little time that was available to me, I tried to clean myself up, but I became embarrassed every time I turned on the taps. The plumbing thundered so loudly that I felt I must be inside a steam engine, and when I flushed the toilet, it sounded like the agonized death throes of the Industrial Revolution. My bowtie was still lopsided, but I couldn't do any better, so I took a deep breath and made my way to dinner.

Tom was coming out of his room, which was at the other end of the long corridor.

'I see you brought your dinner jacket with you,' he said. 'You needn't have bothered, this isn't The Queen Mary.'

'I like to dress correctly.'

'MCKK and your father taught you well. But your bowtie is at a funny angle. Do you mind if I help you with it?'

Tom stepped towards me and unravelled my bowtie. He placed it around my neck correctly and tied the intricate knot for me. It was a brotherly, fatherly, or avuncular thing to do, and yet I didn't know how to act being this close to him. I kept my gaze fixed on the knot of his tie as he teased my bowtie through itself. I was drawn close enough to be able to smell his shaving cream, which I could tell was 'Burma-Shave'. It was the same American brand that the avowedly 'American' Ariff enjoyed, but they said the ingredients came from Burma and Malaya.

'There, now you are presentable,' Tom told me.

'Thank you,' I said, stepping back from him.

We walked together down the stairs to the dining room without talking. He was just about to open the door when he spoke to me.

'Hamid, please don't make the mistake of getting intoxicated.'

'It's a relief to hear you say that. I really don't drink much.'

'I don't mean alcohol, I mean these three girls, and they are just girls, and you're still just a boy. It must be intoxicating. You're all at that age where you're looking to make mistakes. I don't want you making a mistake under this roof where you are my guest. You're on the cusp of adulthood and you should be asking yourself the question: do you want to be Paris, Achilles, or Odysseus?'

I blinked uncertainly.

'Paris was an idiot, he chased beauty and destroyed his own city. Achilles lived a short but glorious life. But Odysseus, because he was smart, he eventually got back home alive.'

'Didn't he get his liver eaten by an eagle every day?'

'That was Prometheus. Youth is wasted on the young.'

'Shakespeare.'

'No, George Bernard Shaw. Didn't Mr Hargreaves teach you anything?'

'Irony. He taught us about irony.'

'Well, maybe that will come in useful. Let this Christmas be your exam."

Tom opened the dining room door.

'Ah,' he said. 'The Three Bemuses are already here.'

Goodness, they took my breath away. The three girls were all facing away from me, and later I wondered if they had been waiting in that position because it gave them the opportunity to show their backless dresses and to look at me over their shoulders, which is always nice. Intellectually, I know that beauty is ephemeral, even trite, but I do so like nice things. I tried so very hard not to stare at them as they smiled, pouted, or tried to look severe.

If one believed the universe of the movies then one would expect to find beauty in every sitting-room, railway station, or lonely jungle outpost and yet one never actually does. Meeting actual beauty is very rare, and having three examples in the same gaze is a statistical impossibility. I knew even then, at that young age, that this was a moment I must remember. It wasn't just lust—I was impressed. They deserved a round of applause, and I was grateful to be their audience. The girls were unable to maintain their studied poses and suddenly burst out laughing, as if they knew something I did not. People always seem to know something I do not. I noticed that Tom was lurking in the background, and he also seemed to know something I did not. It was as if he, too, was studying me.

'Would you like an aperitif, Hamid? We're having Camparis,' said Clare.

'Yes, please.'

'You look very debonair, Hamid,' Hermione said. 'Like an Oriental David Niven.'

'Thank you. I think that's the nicest thing anyone has ever said to me.' I was quite bowled over by the compliment but also annoyed that I had not followed Salim in growing a thin moustache like our idol David Niven.

'I've met David Niven,' said Margaret. 'He is very charming.'

'But Hamid is quite charming,' said Tom, perhaps more to himself than to us.

'Perhaps,' Margaret mused. 'But David is very charming.'

'Really? Do tell.' Hermione gushed. 'When did you meet him? What did he say?'

'Well, it was when we were filming *The Elusive Pimpernel*.'

While Margaret told the star-struck Hermione about her extremely brief conversation with David Niven (something about sandwiches), Clare came up to me. She was looking lovely and surprisingly at ease in her black halter-top dress. I would never have imagined that the tomboy I had once known could ever wear such an elegant dress, but she had truly grown up. In this dress, her figure was now beautifully expressed where her clothes earlier in the day had merely suggested.

'You do look nice, Hamid,' she said.

'So do you.'

'I don't wear clothes like this very often.'

'You look like you do, or you should.'

'You're sitting next to me, and mother, when she arrives, that is.'

We sat down at the table, it was an elegantly laid table, with an array of silver cutlery, which I recognized from The Residence. I thought this to be odd because surely it was government property.

'Honestly, I'm sorry I told you now,' Margaret was saying to Hermione.

'Was that it?' said an astonished Hermione. '"Sandwich, my dear?" That's all he said to you?'

'Yes, but it was the way he said it.'

'The way you built it up I was expecting a tête-à-tête at Claridge's.'

'I can't help your expectations. Now can we change the bloody subject!'

'Certainly, we can,' said Hermione. 'Bread roll, my dear?'

Clare and I looked at each other, both amused by Margaret's discomfort. As I looked at Clare's smile, I lost mine. I realized I was sharing a moment with somebody for the first time, and I sensed that it was something I had always wanted. I'd had moments with women before, many times, but those were never shared moments. They had been my moments, and the girl's task had been to succumb. This was a shared moment that would become a shared memory, part of a collection of shared memories, something we could look back on, together.

'So, Hamid,' Clare said to me. 'What are you studying?'

'Well, that's hard to say.'

Fortunately, at that moment, the door opened, and Sir Alfred and Lady Pelham entered the dining room. She looked a bit confused as Sir Alfred guided her in, but this was a royal entrance, and everyone stopped talking. I even stood up, as I would have done at school or The Residence, and when I noticed that nobody else had stood up, I deftly pulled the chair out for Lady Pelham.

'Thank you,' she said, her air of confusion dissipating when she saw me.

'Yes, thank you, Hamid,' said Sir Alfred, stressing my name.

As we sat down, I noticed that Lady Pelham was gazing at me, so I turned away from her and tried to shield my face with my hand.

'Is everything all right, Hamid?' Clare asked.

'Yes, everything is fine.'

'We're having Camparis,' said Clare. 'Would you like one, Papa?'

'I'll go straight to the wine,' Sir Alfred stated, a trifle wearily.

Tom uncorked a bottle of wine and filled our glasses, except his mother's.

'Can't I have some wine, Jack?' Lady Pelham asked. Tom looked to his father, who nodded his assent and Tom poured a small amount. I had eaten nothing all day and was concerned that somebody would hear my gurgling stomach, but nobody seemed to notice as conversation started bubbling again. Where on earth was the food? Don't these people eat?

Finally, a door opened, and a surprisingly small and young maid entered, carrying a very large soup tureen, which was also from The Residence. Everyone was concerned as she was walking extremely slowly, trying not to spill the soup.

'It's all right, I've got it,' she said.

'She's a bit familiar,' muttered Margaret.

'They are these days,' whispered Hermione.

Tom poured me some wine and placed the glass next to my unfinished Campari, and dinner began. The food was not as bland as I had imagined it would be, and the kedgeree in particular was quite delightful. The Anglo-Indian dish with its hint of curry powder gave my tastebuds a glimpse of home. It must have been difficult for the Pelhams to have found curry powder not only in the depths of austerity Britain, but also in a Britain where most people, apart from returning colonials, reacted to curry powder as Count

Dracula did to garlic. Indeed, as most British in those days reacted to garlic. Despite the protestations of Hermione and Margaret, who were unused to Oriental intoxicants, this corner of England was thriving on slightly exotic flavours and was getting very merry on copious amounts of wine.

I do not have a terribly clear recollection of the evening; I only remember snapshots of laughter and conversation that seemed at the time to be the most enthralling ever in the history of human conversation. One has a tendency to imagine that the words spoken by a beautiful woman are somehow more important and wonderful than they actually are, but one does listen more attentively when one wants something from someone.

Years later, I would listen with rapt attention to Tun's mindless drivel about his golf-swing as if he were telling me that an Iron Curtain was descending from Stettin in the Baltic to Trieste in the Adriatic, so maybe it's just me. While Tom spoke quietly to his father, I immersed myself in the world of the girls and we shared so many amazing things about their lives, absolutely none of which I can remember (although I think I finally admitted that I found Harris Tweed to be unbearably itchy, I'd never admitted that to anybody before).

Lady Pelham was gazing at me the entire evening and looked as if she were about to speak to me, but I always managed to turn away from her. I was lost to the girls. I think they were flirting with me.

But then, late in the evening, over the blancmange and sauternes, Lady Pelham touched my hand. Everybody saw this surprising gesture and conversation fizzled out. She started to sing, quietly. It was a Malay song about the river and about love. I knew it well—it was a favourite of my father's. Malay songs, the best of them, have a lilting melancholy where love is perhaps more about the pain than the thrill, and everything is loss—lost time and lost love. There is an imprecise moment in the past that will always be better than the prosaic now, and singing in tune is of less importance than being able to emote, choking on the words and the bittersweet memory. The river flows past, it never stops.

As Lady Pelham sang quietly, somehow remembering all the words, I fancied I could see her standing in the shade of the veranda of The Residence looking at the moonlit river below, feeling alone and incomplete, hating everything around her, watching and waiting, possibly for my father sneaking out of the bushes. I was mortified. I did not dare to look at Sir Alfred's reaction. Fortunately, Clare started singing the song as well, and she even added a harmony. Now the song became a nostalgic reminiscence, possibly a compliment to myself, and it had nothing to do with my father. A polite ripple of applause welcomed the end of the song, and Lady Pelham squeezed my hand.

'I remembered it,' she whispered to me.

'Well, good for you,' I said, while extricating my hand.

Mercifully, Sir Alfred scooped up his wife and pulled her away, and I was subjected to a gratuitous brandy and truly awful coffee. In the end, Tom had to assist me up to my bedroom. Before I entered my room, the girls stood at their bedroom doors, and all bade me an alluring goodnight. I collapsed onto my bed.

It had been, in every sense, an intoxicating night. I thought about the girls, I thought about the river, and then I was asleep.

Chapter 11

Youth.

A copy of Joseph Conrad's *Youth* slid off my bed as I awoke in the early morning darkness. I wondered where I was and why my stomach was churning with such intense excitement. Conrad wrote about his intoxication at seeing Asia for the first time, a wall of jungle rising above the shoreline, a sight with which I was easily familiar.

This day, I would discover England and the English on what would be the first and perhaps last day of my youth. I suddenly remembered the three startlingly attractive young women asking me to choose the fairest, a combination of beauty that only ever happens in the movies. Was I living in a movie scripted by the witty and adult Noël Coward? It did not cross my mind that the guiding hand could be a sadistic Alfred Hitchcock and that I might be what the Americans call a 'patsy', the innocent fool. But I was not innocent. I was a grown-up as I played with the steam that came out of my mouth into the cold of the room that could not penetrate the warmth of my bed. I revelled in England's coziness. I should have listened to Conrad's warning, with his ship of youth on fire surrounded by the Asian waters that could have saved him.

Instead, I thought that I might be on the cusp of something wholly new. I may have found the answer to Tom's repeated questions about my future, and it could be Salim's answer.

As I looked forward to my future, I considered the past I would be losing and Irma. She was actually a wickedly funny girl and a Malay beauty with a naughty, round face. She was the belle of my hometown, and I, too, should have found Irma captivating. Yet I wanted to be rid of her. She had chosen me when we were both only five and had stuck true to her choice with the tenacity that only Malay girls can achieve, seeing off all rivals except one: Clare Pelham. Irma must have confidently assumed that I would never dare cross the racial divide and, besides, Clare would leave. Yet, here I was, at Christmas with the Pelhams, reunited with Clare, and now, possibly on the cusp of something wholly new.

I could achieve independence from Irma and from the predictability of a future that my father had mapped out for me if I married Clare. Even in the safety of a warm bed on a chilly morning, I realized that Clare might have her own ideas. But I was too busy enjoying the notion that the daughter of the British Resident would out-rank anything that Salim could ever possibly achieve to consider this.

Clare could be my greatest trophy, my future, and my purpose. And if not Clare, then some other English girl, and then mine could be some kind of English future, hopefully one with the nicest things.

There were the faintest murmurings of movement in the house as I slipped out of the front door, determined to explore this unknown land of my future called England. Turning up my collar, I enjoyed the cold, breathed in the clean air, listened to the birds chirping, their forms veiled by the mist, and began my circumnavigation of the house.

In the thinning mist, I ignored the warnings of a distant cuckoo and followed the sound of feminine voices on the driveway. I turned a hedgerow and spied one of those snapshot moments that has always remained with me. The imperious Margaret de Vere dressed in her RAF uniform putting her valise into her Ferrari, talking to Hermione, who was on a horse.

I am afraid of many things, but in my brief youth, beautiful and, most especially, comfortably confident women frightened me the most. So I decided to keep my distance and study these graces from afar. Hermione's horse was enormous, a beast circling the car impatiently. However could she control such an animal? Margaret's skirt was short enough to win the Battle of Britain on its own and I was disappointed to see her get into the car. With much ostentatious revving and a spray of gravel, she raced away forcing poor Hermione to calm her startled horse. At the sight of her distress, some bizarre and completely unknown protective spirit arose from within me, and I found myself stepping forwards like a gallant Sir Lancelot, who then, just as suddenly remembered that he was utterly terrified of horses and women. Hermione pulled aggressively on the reins and spurred away at a gallop, clearing a gate along the way. The horse had gone, but there remained the sound of panting, which I realized was coming from me. It masked the sound of crunching gravel behind me.

'She's very pretty, isn't she, Hamid?' Clare asked as she emerged from the house.

'If you like that sort of thing.' Which I did, very much so.

'What are you doing up so early, Hamid?'

'I wanted to look around the house.'

'I'll take you on a tour. And then after breakfast, you need to buy some presents. Your arrival has made mother curiously animated, and she wants to make this a Christmas to remember, so we must go into town, and you must buy some presents.'

With slightly hesitant intent, she stepped forward and slipped her arm into mine and showed me this old house. She told me about how the house had grown around its 12th century tower, built to keep nuns safe from rampaging warlords. A Pelham ancestor (Clare called him 'the Impaler') had been given the property by a grateful King Henry VII. Over time, the chunky stonework had given way to delicate slim bricks as this magnificent house emerged.

'I still feel bad for the nuns. This was their home. They were safe here.'

'But that was seven centuries ago, Clare.'

'What are seven centuries in England?'

Centuries merged into each other with stories of various kings throwing up here and there after too much sherry. Of an overly pious Oliver Cromwell delivering a lecture under the same tree where the pathetic Lady Jane Grey had wept when enroute to London, to take the throne she never wanted, and which cost her her head. If only, remarked Clare, she could have remained and become a nun.

Although I liked the sensation, I was unused to standing this close to a woman. I looked at Clare. Her freckles drew attention to her skin that was soft and young. As I slipped my fingers into hers, I marvelled at how my naturally brown skin contrasted with her paleness that was overlain with a slight tan. No Asian has freckles, and nobody I knew would wish to be seen with a tan, because it would suggest labour in the field or a tin mine.

'You have a tan,' I remarked.

'Hunting ants.'

There was surely nothing natural or familiar for me about her, and yet, with our shared long-ago history, she was perfectly natural and familiar. If this woman became a nun, it would be a tragic waste. She knew I was looking, and she smiled at the attention, a little embarrassed but not coy. Unlike Hermione, I don't think Clare knew how to do coy. She turned the topic of conversation to me.

My only experience with being the object of conversation was listening to diatribes from my father about my wastrel ways, but both Clare and Tom appeared to be genuinely interested in me. Whereas Tom's interest was limited to enigmatic questions about my future, Clare wanted to know about my present wants, likes, and ambitions. It was difficult for me to form a passably dignified answer because even I didn't know if a fondness for nice things amounts to ambition. Fortunately, at that moment, Tom appeared from the house carrying an axe, which is not something one sees every day.

'Good heavens,' said Clare.

Tom looked at his axe as if he had forgotten about it. 'Mother demands a Christmas sacrifice.'

I looked around nervously. Was this why I had been invited?

'Don't worry, Hamid. It's not to be a Mohamaddean this year. I have been sent to chop down a Christmas tree. You two should have breakfast. There's much to do if we are to make this Mother's "Christmas to remember". Curious that Mother keeps using that phrase when she remembers so little.'

Chapter 12

I shared the day with Clare in a blur of activity.

With Christmas a mere two days away, the nearby town was as excitedly festive as Austerity Britain could be during a winter that was so cold. However, that day, I hardly noticed the inclement weather because Clare and I were being warmed by the heat exuding from our bodies as we were progressively drawn into each other's orbits.

A thousand years ago, in the heat of Malaya, we had discovered my kampong together. And now, in the cold of England, she was introducing me to hers.

She was treated with polite deference in each shop, as if she were local royalty. *No wonder the British instinctively knew how to play the game in Malaya,* I thought to myself. They were as happily feudal as us. My mother would have been treated in exactly the same way in similar shops.

We made our way to a shop selling coffee, where the smell of roasting beans was absolutely intoxicating.

'This is my friend Hamid,' she told the shopkeeper. 'He's from Malaya, which is where my father was serving.'

'We do have some coffee from Malaya. It's not our most popular bean but it does have a handful of very loyal customers. I'm sure Sir Alfred knows them. A Mr Hargreaves?'

Clare did not know him, but I did.

'Mr Hargreaves was my old English teacher at MCKK,' I said forlornly.

'Then we must invite him for Christmas.'

'Please don't. I still owe him an essay on Julius Caesar.'

Clare smiled, which warmed me to my core. Much to my chagrin, Clare ordered far too much of the Malayan coffee. I must admit that I do not like Malayan coffee and was truly looking forward to something Italian instead, but I kept quiet.

Full of caffeine and some tea cakes, we moved on. Clare chose for me the innocuous presents I should buy for her family, but when it came to presents for her friends, she studied the choices like a chess grandmaster. I noticed out of the corner of my eye, some frilly undergarments that would have been quite delicious on Hermione and Margaret, but instead, Clare chose some books that were excessively boring and utterly unsuggestive. I bought them without question.

'But what do I get for you, Clare?'

'You already have something for me. I'll show you later.'

This simple day spent with Clare was quietly charmed. It was a cold day that yielded some of my warmest memories, even if tainted by ultimate regret. In the car on the way back, we talked and talked. She told me how she wondered if she actually liked her friends or if they were just an old habit from her schooldays.

'I certainly don't trust them. We're all so competitive,' she concluded.

She told me that she was quietly resentful that Tom would eventually inherit the house.

'It's as if my memories only have a temporary lease in my own home.'

And she told me how distressing it was to be a witness to her mother's drift into senility.

'We all put on a brave face and pretend it's not happening. The other day she didn't realize that she had wet herself and I had to clean her. Can you imagine? My own mother.'

Back home, in those long-ago days, we had a small army of servants who helped shield us from anything unsightly.

'And my mother keeps talking about your father.'

'Well, I, er, he is quite memorable.'

Inspired by Clare's confessions, I amazed myself by talking about myself and my innermost thoughts. Like how I didn't actually like tweed because it's itchy, and that I didn't like Malayan coffee and wanted something Italian instead. I wanted to tell her that I always felt so alone but not now, not in her company.

'You should have said something.'

'I didn't wish to appear rude.'

'Perhaps we miss out on too many things because of politeness.'

'It's a Malay thing.'

'It's an English thing.'

Back in the house, we were greeted by the scent of pine and the magnificent sight of a Christmas tree being decorated by Hermione, who was standing on a chair and reaching for the topmost branches.

'Hamid, could you be a gentleman and steady me?'

I instinctively and nervously placed my hands on her hips.

'I think she meant the chair,' said Clare rather sternly.

'Yes, I'm sure I did,' responded Hermione, winking at Clare.

Clare led me away to the kitchen, past Tom who was already having his mysterious telephone conversations. I sat and gazed upon Clare as the low winter sun streamed through the window and illuminated her, haloing around her as if she were an angel. The scene was domestic but serene. It made me wonder if I could really do as my roommate Salim had suggested.

Could I really marry an English girl? And would this be how we would live? Would Clare leave this place and return with me to Malaya? I couldn't stay in England. What work could I possibly do? I'd end up being a waiter in Veeraswamy, which sent a shiver down my spine. Salim's opening gambit to impress an English girl was taking her to London's only Indian restaurant. The thought of me wearing a turban and serving him extra mango chutney made me feel physically sick. Hordes of MCKK Old Boys would be queuing up along Regent Street to view me like I was some kind of circus freak. In Malaya, I would become a senior civil servant whereas in England, I would be nobody.

What would people think if I brought back an English wife?

1952 was before Malayan independence and Imperial racial codes of separation were still being strictly observed. Malayans did not hate the British, but they were them and we were us, and never the twain should marry.

My mother would be horrified, Irma would kill me, and my father would be deeply embarrassed to see the daughter of Lady Pelham. And yet, it dawned on me that others might well be impressed. It would make me look like a red-blooded Malay warrior conquering the heart, mind, and bed of The Empire. But how could Clare possibly exist in Malaya?

My thoughts were interrupted by Clare talking to me in Malay. Her Malay wasn't very good, and it sounded awkward and a little embarrassing to me, so I responded in English. But this was her gift to me, and it warmed me as much as the Aga stove did.

I decided that I would marry Clare and that nothing would stand in my way. She would be my mission, and then she would become my purpose.

Chapter 13

I am glad to say that no alcohol was consumed in the Pelham household until lunchtime, at which point there was a veritable dam burst of aperitifs, digestifs, whiskey and/or whisky, beers, Boudeaux, Chablis, sherry, port, dessert wines, and champagne ('because it's Christmas'). The precise order in which the drinks were rolled out gave a veneer of civilized politeness, but this was alcoholism, pure and simple.

In Malaya, whenever there was a flood, the British always managed to find higher ground, but I was swept away like a helpless villager. Fortunately, I found enough courage to shake off my deeply ingrained desire to be polite and accept everything that was placed before me. Instead, I found myself turning away drinks before I could make a complete fool of myself. I don't know how much the rest of them had drunk by the time Margaret returned from a day of filming. She found us in the drawing room, where we were playing a new boardgame from America called Scrabble. Margaret slumped into the chair behind Hermione.

'How was the filming today?' Clare asked Margaret.

'Frustrating. A man finally managed to pluck up enough courage to flirt with me. A very dashing Wing Commander. Is there a more attractive uniform?

Anyway, obviously, it's a film set, and he turned out to be nothing but a house painter from Solihull.'

'Where is Solihull?' Hermione asked.

'Somewhere between I don't know and I don't care.' Margaret leaned forward to look at Hermione's Scrabble letters. 'You know you can do "ravaged"?'

'Yes, but it seems awfully risqué.'

'Go on, Hermione. You know you want to.'

And then, presumably, to prove some point, Margaret actually smacked Hermione's bottom. Good heavens, if these girls could just stop spanking each other for one moment.

Perhaps it was the alcohol or being in the only male in the company of three attractive women, but my brain was addled, and I was struggling to create any Scrabble words. All I could see were Malay words and nothing terribly decent at that. The more meaningful and polite Malay words are quite long with their prefixes and suffixes. And while short words certainly exist, they can seem childish and even blunt when viewed in isolation. The girls had allowed me to use Malay words so that they might learn the language. Clare did look at me with slight suspicion when I placed some of the words, but her Malay really wasn't good enough to question their veracity or understand any alternative meanings.

I was just about to put down a word, 'I have another Malay word. It means . . .' when Sir Alfred and Lady Pelham entered the drawing room. '. . . but I've changed my mind.'

I knew that Sir Alfred's Malay was absolutely flawless, at ease in The Sultan's palace, the town, the *padi* fields, or even the gutter.

'Hamid has been teaching us Malay with this new game, Sir Alfred,' chirped Hermione.

Sir Alfred stood behind me and looked at the assembled words.

'This word means stick, and this one means itchy,' Hermione explained. 'And Hamid says he's feeling itchy right now. Isn't that right, Hamid?'

'No, I said I don't like wearing tweed because it feels itchy. That's what I said.'

Sir Alfred knew that although it does mean itchy, actually *gatal* means, well, itchy for something else.

'Yes, I don't think your father likes wearing tweed either. May I have a word with you, Hamid?'

Sir Alfred took me to the hallway where Tom was still making his mysterious telephone calls. He did not look happy with me.

'You are a guest in this house, Hamid, but if your *kayu* or your *batang* makes one appearance during these holidays then I will be very, very angry. Do I make myself clear, Hamid?'

'Yes, Sir Alfred. I am terribly sorry, Sir Alfred.'

Sir Alfred had vast experience at conveying things to Malayans in no uncertain terms, and I was horrified because I felt like the whole weight of the British Empire had come crashing down on me, as if the gunboat HMS Pelham had just steamed up my river.

'I don't want to have to ask you if you know how to spell *kurang ajar*.'

His guns were turned directly at me because kurang ajar is the most soul-destroying insult that can be hurled at a Malay. He was asking if I was rude and ill-bred.

'There'll be no need, Sir Alfred. I am terribly sorry, Sir Alfred.'

'Good. I don't want to have to call Mr Hargreaves. I understand you still owe him an essay on Julius Caesar.'

'Thank you, Sir Alfred. It won't happen again, Sir Alfred.'

We re-joined the others. This was the worst castigation I had ever received, and I've had quite a few so I know how to judge these things. But Sir Alfred's gunboat diplomacy in combination with the threat of overdue MCKK homework gave me a newfound respect for my father who had to face salvoes such as this on a regular basis.

'What did my father want?' Clare asked.

'Nothing. He was just asking how to spell something.'

'Did you use rude Malay words in Scrabble?'

'I suppose some of them could possibly have been construed as such.'

'I thought so. You are a naughty old *kambing*.' It means goat but, well, I think you get the idea.

'Yuck,' spat Margaret. 'What is wrong with this coffee?'

'It's Malayan coffee. We bought it today.'

'It's disgusting,' countered Margaret.

'Has it gone off?' asked Hermione.

'I did tell you, Clare. It's an acquired taste.'

'We're going to drink it, and we're going to like it.' Clare stated.

Although most pushed their cups away, I could see that Lady Pelham was staring at me and glugging her coffee thirstily. Oh no, she was recalling memories again. My father loved this stuff, and I'm sure he tasted of coffee and Woodbines. My fingers were crossed that she wouldn't start going on about the river and love and etc, etc. Sir Alfred was obviously of the same mind and was glaring at me.

'So, what is your Julius Caesar essay about?' he asked menacingly.

'Betrayal.'

'Interesting. And what are your thoughts on the subject?'

'It's a bad, bad thing.'

Fortunately, at that moment, Tom entered the room.

'Did I miss anything?'

'I'm not sure,' answered Clare.

Chapter 14

My apologies were worthless.

As I was preparing myself for dinner, I had already forgotten Sir Alfred's warning. I had decided that I would make my move on Clare, make some gesture, some statement of intent.

What would Salim do? I asked myself.

By the time dinner was served, the assembled English people—though they would never admit to it—were all blind drunk, except, perhaps, for Tom, who appeared to be quietly nursing a single malt throughout the whole day. I had stopped drinking and had even gulped down most of the coffee in order to sober up and make sure I didn't make any more mistakes. But the rules of civilized politeness were difficult to understand when most of the participants were becoming increasingly loud, slurring their words, and swaying their way to and from the drinks cabinets to the accompaniment of an old Fred Astaire record playing on the gramophone. Conversation was becoming less a to-and-fro banter and more a succession of unrelated statements and my responses were becoming limited to 'of course not' and 'yes, I'm sure'.

As the only sober person there, one would expect things to become quite dull. However, the alcohol was making the girls increasingly competitive and flirtatious, which was nice but confusing. On whom should I focus my attention? What were the rules?

Hermione was an expert at eliciting compliments.

'Riding makes my legs too muscular. I think it's unattractive.'

'Of course not.'

Margaret was aggressive and delighted in putting me on the spot.

'I know she hides it well, but don't you think Clare is very pretty?'

'Yes, I'm sure.'

Clare did not speak so much. She was enjoying the music; but she did place her hand on my arm when Astaire sang 'The Way You Look Tonight'.

'I wish we could listen to some jazz,' Margaret complained.

But I knew this record had significance for the Pelhams and I dared to venture a statement. 'I remember how you used to listen to Fred Astaire at The Residence, Sir Alfred.'

'Yes. It was a favourite of Lady Pelham's,' Sir Alfred replied, in the past tense.

'Do you remember, Mummy?' Clare asked hopefully, but Lady Pelham just looked lost. A silence descended as the song changed.

'Heaven. I'm in heaven . . .' sang Astaire.

Tom rose from his chair and extended his hand to his mother.

'Could I have this dance, Celia?'

Lady Pelham seemed to awaken and looked almost bashful as she took her son's hand and rose to dance, searching his face with confused recognition. Tom did look very much like his father, and we all watched them.

'Come on, Hamid,' said Clare, 'Let's dance. You do know how to dance?'

'Of course I do.'

How dare she! All of us Old Boys knew how to dance. I was trained at the tea-dances in Ipoh, when we would sneak out of MCKK and drive down in Salim's hidden MG. I knew I could show Clare that the fifty-cents-a-dance with the sometimes-lovely Chinese girls had been my most successful schooling investment. I instantly twirled her onto our impromptu dancefloor to a ripple of applause.

'*. . . When we're out together dancing cheek to cheek.*'

I remembered Hyacinth Chow's advice at one of my first tea-dances. She told me to slow down and not be so excited, so I mellowed my moves and determined to slowly build up to a crescendo. But I couldn't resist a quick little shimmy taught to me by Orchid Lee, which seemed to delight Clare. And then I held Clare, and we swayed to the music.

'*. . . And the cares that hang around me through the week . . .*'

I was concentrating on my dancing but, heavens, she looked lovely tonight.

'*. . . Seem to vanish like a gambler's lucky streak.*'

'Look at Mummy.'

Lady Pelham was smiling, but I am certain it was because of some private delusion that she was reunited with her long dead brother or, worse still, my father. Or perhaps, it was because she was dancing with her son and enjoying herself. Tom had handed his mother to his father, and as they danced, Sir Alfred looked at his wife a little coldly.

'Do you remember Colombo, Alfred?' I heard her say.

'Yes.'

'We danced and danced.'

'Yes, we did.'

'Can we go back there?'

'I wish we could, Celia. I'd like that.'

'. . . *I want my arms about you.*'

Tom was standing with Hermione and Margaret, making a display of deciding whom to ask to dance. Hermione sat forward expectantly, but Margaret looked away with cool disdain.

'Margaret, shall we dance?'

Margaret rose, took Tom's hand, and danced with a look of studied disinterest but I understood what it really meant, and I was surprised. It was fear. I didn't know that Margaret knew the meaning of the word. They were a strikingly handsome couple, though.

'. . . *And my heart beats so that I can hardly speak.*'

I knew that Astaire was about to stop singing and that the musical finale was about to begin, which would be my big dance moment. Surveying the dimensions of the room—where space was rapidly decreasing, factoring in the carpeted as opposed to wooden floor, and that Clare was no Ginger Rogers—I adjudged that my moves would have to be minimal but telling.

'. . . *When we're out together dancing cheek to cheek.*'

This was my cue. Aiming for the gap between two drinks cabinets, I held Clare's hand and executed Astaire's signature back-step flourish, which satisfyingly caught her by surprise. She did find it slightly comical, but I had expected that. I would deal with it by executing one of my favourite moves. Still holding her hand, I placed it on my shoulder, and I slowly turned towards her, so that her arm was around me and we were very close. The unexpected intimacy wiped the smile off her face.

'Goodness,' she said.

For a brief moment, I wished that I had a pencil moustache like Salim, but there was no time to linger. I had work to do. I glided behind her, placed my hands on her hips and our bodies swayed together, not in a crass Latin way, but it was still a very daring move. She looked back at me over her shoulder. She looked confused—confused by her own reactions. I forced her to spin to face me.

'Goodness.'

The song was coming to an end, and I had to control myself for the hardest move. I stepped slightly to one side, placed my hand behind her head and gently leaned her back, all perfectly timed to the final cymbal crash. We looked at each other, her eyes flitting around my face. She was lost, somewhere. This dance routine had even flustered Rose Chung back in Ipoh, and she was a seasoned professional, so what chance did Clare have? As Clare awoke, I led her back to her chair.

'Goodness,' she said, recomposing her hair. 'Where did you learn to dance like that?'

'My mother sent me to Madame Wong's Dance Academy. A highly respectable institution.'

Obviously, my mother only ever sent me to religious classes, but Madame Wong's could be quite respectable—if she had been forewarned that the police were coming.

'You have hidden depths, Hamid,' said Margaret, returning to the table. 'You hardly say a word but then you start dancing and you're Rudolf Valentino. It makes me wonder, who are you?'

Nobody wanted to drink the Malayan coffee, so after the cheese course, which was merely an excuse to drink brandy, the party came to an end. I was given the opportunity to watch three staggering beauties attempt to ascend the stairs. Before I could capitalize on my sobriety and help them, Tom asked to speak to me. Clare stunned me by giving me a quick kiss on the cheek.

'I'll see you later,' she said. And then the three girls giggled up the stairs.

Tom was considering his words. From my vast experience in these things, I could tell I was about to receive a lecture.

'You're an adult, Hamid. And I do not wish to tell you what to do. You've lived through the war, so you know how to survive. But I'm not sure if you have much experience in, shall we say, affairs of the heart. The girls may give the impression that they are worldly women, but I know that they are not. And I definitely know that my sister is not.'

'Yes, I'm sure.'

'I just want you to be careful. Don't do anything you might regret. Anything we will all regret. Goodnight, Hamid. Please be sure to get plenty of sleep tonight. Tomorrow is Christmas Eve.'

As far as lectures go, this one hadn't been too bad. A little longer than some, but quite succinct, if equally unintelligible to me. As with most lectures I have received, it was only much later that I understood.

If I had heeded Tom's warning, then I would never have gone to Berlin and my life would have been completely different. But no such thoughts were in my mind. I was remembering Clare's kiss. And what did she mean by 'see you later'?

I ascended the stairs whistling 'Dancing Cheek to Cheek'.

Chapter 15

I lay on my bed. I stood up. I paced the room. I considered opening a bottle of beer. I couldn't possibly sleep. Clare's kiss and that 'see you later' were consuming me.

A young man's stomach churns, and his brain is a scrambled mess of noise when he imagines he has the interest of a beautiful woman. No rational argument or exertion of willpower can calm the primal noise—and you may not believe this, but my willpower is not reliably strong.

What did she mean? Does she want me to visit her room tonight? I vaguely remembered Tom telling me a very long time ago that Clare was not yet a woman, but I knew she was. I had known her as a girl, and now I could see that she was a woman. Her face, the nape of her neck, and her hands were all the flesh I had seen, but I was skilled enough to be able to discern the shape of her body hidden by her modest clothes, and I was consumed. The noise in my body was so overpowering that it hurt. It was telling me that every question would be answered and every ill would be cured if I could just touch her, and then touch her just a little bit more, and then I'll stop, I promise.

I think she wants me to visit her room tonight. In fact, I know she wants me to visit her, and I know I was right because the noise was agreeing with me. What harm could there be if I just went down the corridor and had a look to see if there was some sort of signal? With fear and lust gurgling in the pit of my stomach, I left my room and entered the corridor.

I saw that there were three doors to three rooms, and I didn't know which one was Clare's. Even the noise had to admit that the mission must be aborted. But then, the noise spotted that one of the doors had been left slightly open. This was the signal. I approached the door and moved to open it. Again, I regretted for a moment that I didn't have a pencil moustache like Salim, but I decided to look a bit more rakish by undoing my bow tie. The noise made me push open the door.

'Hamid!'

'Margaret?'

'What are you doing in my room?'

'Your door was open.'

'So what if it was?'

'Good point.'

There followed a strange silence. Margaret de Vere was sitting at her dressing table removing her make-up in the glow of a single lamp. Neither of us moved. She was wearing a silk peignoir, which left little work for my skilled imagination. I should not have been in her room. I should have left immediately. But there was the problem of her astonishing allure. There was the problem of the strange silence.

'You shouldn't be here.'

'Yes, I should leave.'

And still, the silence. She sat up straight as if gathering her strength, but it patently failed to materialize. This, I regret to say, excited me. It was difficult to remember that I had left my room in search of Clare, but I did remember. And yet, I found myself moving across the room towards Margaret. The noise was commanding me. It was telling me to exploit this woman's moment of weakness.

Goodness, I was closing the gap between us, which, from the moment I had entered her room, had never been a gap of politeness but one of sheer folly—as sheer as her peignoir. Now, I was standing above her and she was looking up at me, not with her face, but with her eyes. Without her make up and her military uniform, she looked fragile and young, soft and feminine. I know that the worship of beauty is shallow, but I truly do like nice things. I was being invited to gaze upon a work of art, and not of some gaudy painted lady but of unadorned marble, framed by cascading dark hair.

'What are you doing in my room?' she asked, impossibly quietly.

I didn't know.

'What do you want?'

I didn't know.

'You can't be in here. Do you know who my father is?'

'No.'

'He's a very rich man.'

'Good.'

'You're nothing but some funny brown man.'

'Am I?'

'My father is very powerful.' She glared at me. 'And he makes jokes about brown people.'

I wasn't sure if the anger was directed at me. The silence returned.

'I suppose that back in mongo-bongo land you think you're some kind of lord.'

I was from a family of good standing and some influence but only The Sultan had lordly powers, so the term had no real meaning in Malaya.

'It's called Malaya.'

'And you have lots of servants, or slaves?'

It was a peculiar question, but my grandfather did have a slave when I was very young. He had been from Africa and would carry me on his shoulders.

'You shouldn't be here.'

I took the risk.

'Shall I leave?'

How did I know how to do this? Nobody had ever taught me. This was my own skill. I had given her a question that she needed to answer. But we both knew what the answer would be. Her hand slowly took mine.

'So, should I leave?'

I needed her to say it.

'No.'

I think she was marvelling at the contrasting colours of our skin. This was not the cold and imperious Margaret de Vere. This Margaret was not a world-weary woman, but a faltering girl. She looked up at me, trying to find words. It was as if she wanted to speak—to speak honestly for once. I shook off the sudden awareness that I also harboured this need, because looking up at me with such vulnerability, she was offering me the gift of power.

'Hamid, I don't know who I am. I'm a grown-up but I don't feel like one. Grown-ups do bad things. I think you know what I mean, Hamid.'

I had no idea what she was talking about.

'Yes.'

'I look at you and I think, are you a civilized gentleman, or are you a savage? You can't be both. Are you good, or are you bad?'

'Yes.'

I tilted her face towards me and closed the final gap. She did put up some resistance, but I knew it was just theatre and my final test. I wasn't thinking about the future but of the present. If she wanted me to be the noble savage, possessor of white women, then, well, jolly good. She returned my kiss. Looking back, it was not my proudest moment, but then again, it sort of was.

Chapter 16

I did feel very bad the next morning.

I had consumed far too much alcohol the day before and my head was really hurting. And, of course, I felt very bad about my night of passion with Margaret de Vere. In my barely slept-in bed, I berated myself for being a worthless, weak-willed, and vile little worm. But this worm was glowing because it had had an extraordinary night. It was an explosive night of guilt, punishment, anger, power, and complete surrender. I think that there were moments in her rapture, when Margaret did achieve a clear understanding of who she was—and it did not look to be a happy understanding. I hate myself for saying this, but her unhappiness simply drove me on.

She had an instinctive understanding that she needed to keep quiet as we repeatedly surged ahead to new heights of passion I had never experienced before. I had been a Malay warrior not just being allowed, but commanded, to claim his prize. And she? Well, she had been something altogether lesser—and the knowledge had been only temporarily satisfying.

It had been extraordinary, but it had not been love. When I was tiptoeing back to my room, she told me that this should be 'our little secret'. I wanted to see her nakedness one more time, but she wouldn't let me. She pulled the sheet up tightly to cover herself, and then her gaze disappeared from me and went to somewhere far away. I think she felt guilt, and when back in my own room and away from the noisy distraction of her body, I was suddenly overwhelmed by the same emotion.

What had I done? What had I been thinking? I had ignored both Tom's and Jim Plaistow's warnings to behave and I had betrayed Sir Alfred because, despite his clear instructions, I had gone and unsheathed my kayu. But mostly, I had betrayed Clare.

I did try to console myself with the notion that my original intention had been to do with Clare whatever it was that I had just done with her friend Margaret. But even I was unconvinced by the logic of that argument. There was no way around it: I had betrayed Clare, but if Margaret could keep her mouth shut forever, then I might just get away with it. I was consumed by guilt and the fear of being found out (are they the same thing?) but at least the noise had gone.

And yet, back in 1952 I was in my early twenties, and my powers of recuperation were startlingly rapid. For young men in their twenties, there is only the noise. I discovered that when the stars are aligned correctly, the same can be true for women as well.

Despite it being the morning of Christmas Eve, Tom was still working and was about to enter his mysterious telephone booth as I tentatively descended the stairs. He stopped and looked at me quizzically, as if he didn't recognize me, or perhaps he recognized me too well.

'You look tired, Hamid.'

'Do I? I feel fine, nothing happened, everything's fine. Jolly good.'

'Well, glad to hear it. A telegram came for you.' And then he disappeared into his booth.

Who could have sent me a telegram? Nobody knew I was here. As soon as I felt the acidic heat emanating from the Post Office envelope, I knew who it was. It was from my father.

WHY ARE YOU AT PELHAMS? LEAVE THIS INSTANT. THEY ARE TROUBLE. RETURN TO LONDON NOW.

The telegram was the familiar blend of disapproval and disappointment, and yet, for perhaps the first time in my life, I felt a sense of warmth and kinship with my father. It was as if he alone actually understood my present situation. I should heed his words of advice. I must run. It made perfect sense. The only responsible course of action was to abandon the mess I had created and pretend it had never happened. But then I saw Clare walking down the stairs towards me, looking lovely. And Margaret had said that our tryst would remain a secret, so when you really thought about it, everything was fine. Jolly good, in fact.

'Who is the telegram from?'

'Nobody. My exam results. Everything's fine. Jolly good.'

I must admit that as I looked at Clare, I did indeed suddenly feel jolly good indeed. I also felt something new. Boldness.

'You're looking lovely, Clare. Can we spend the day together? I want you all to myself today.'

I was being very forward, even aggressive, which was as surprising to me as it was to Clare. But sexual conquest is youth's most powerful affirmation, and after last night—when Margaret had abdicated her power to me—I was brimming with a newfound confidence.

What a fool I was.

'Yes. Of course. I'd like that too. Let's go for one of our walks.'

It pleased me to hear Clare say that she and I now had a tradition. We now had our walks, which was perfect, because this way, I could avoid being alone with Margaret, and therefore, everything would be fine. And if I did end up bumping into Margaret, then that would just be my fate.

The time that Clare and had I spent together on Christmas Eve was intoxicating but looking back on that day from over half a century later, I must admit that I was already a very different man from the one of just the day before.

A beautiful relationship was blossoming with Clare, but I had betrayed her even before anything had actually begun. Whereas just the day before I think we both felt that our glances, smiles, and the slightest of touches were electric with delicious uncertainty and anticipation borne of innocence, by Christmas Eve I was wanting to know what she looked like naked and how she would perform in bed. I was still delighting in her company but on Christmas Eve I was wanting to seal the deal and be given my present. I knew with absolute certainty that the final moment was extremely close, and all I had to do was find the right combination of words.

It was when we were walking through the rose garden that I had a moment of inspiration. I would compliment her looks. Women like it when you compliment their looks.

'You really do look lovely.'

'You've said that already. But you say it like you're surprised.'

'You must forgive me, but I am. The last time I saw you we were nine years old, and you were a skinny tomboy. But now you've truly blossomed, like a ripe flower.'

'A ripe flower? You mean like Rafflesia?'

Rafflesia is the largest flower in the world, and it smells like rotting flesh when it blooms in the jungle, so that was obviously the wrong combination of words.

'No, I meant like a frangipani flower,' I said, maintaining an exotically Malayan theme.

'Aren't frangipanis associated with death? That's right, Malays grow frangipani trees in graveyards. And did you know that they're originally from Mexico?'

'All right, not the frangipani either. How about the hibiscus? You have now blossomed like a hibiscus.'

'Thank you. We were feral children back then.'

'Yes, but now you are a woman, and I am a man.'

I was very pleased with this combination of words and if I had that pencil moustache then this would have been the perfect time to stroke it. But I didn't have one so I attempted a combination of rakish smile with a curling of the eyebrows, which I assumed would say, 'We both know where this is heading.'

'Is there something wrong with your eye?'

'No, I . . . never mind.'

It was when we were walking through the glasshouse that I had a moment of inspiration. I would make a joke. Women like a man with a sense of humour.

'Gosh, look at all these bloomin' flowers. You know, bloomin' flowers?'

'You're not going to go on about flowers again, are you?'

'No . . . obviously not.'

'With the glasshouse we can grow tropical flowers all year round. But we have to inseminate them by hand.'

'Insemination. That's an interesting word,' I said, sexily.

'Is it?'

'Obviously not.'

'My father brought this orchid back from Malaya.'

My mother was my hometown's unrivalled genius at growing orchids, and this deep purple orchid was her favourite. The sight of it instantly quashed every romantic bone in my body and even induced twinges of guilt. My mother, of all people, had suddenly appeared in the wintry English garden to chide me for my unfaithfulness to Clare.

'Are you all right, Hamid?'

'I'm fine, it's hot in here. Can we go outside?'

It was by the time we were approaching the stables that I had exhausted my small repertoire of seduction techniques. I had tried complimenting her looks, being funny, gallantly guiding her across the mud (sacrificing my brogues in the process, I may add), and yet, the apple had still not fallen into my lap.

If Clare had been any other English girl, then I could have romanced her with exotic tales of Malaya (palm trees, elephants, etc) but Clare knew my home, so that wouldn't work. Clare and her enticing body were so close, within touching distance, but for all the progress I was making, she remained a thousand miles away. How could I bridge that final gap?

The sound of a snorting horse broke my impatient contemplation as Hermione emerged from the stable atop her giant horse. The two girls exchanged pleasantries, and I got the impression that Hermione would rather have joined us than ride the horse, but Clare guided her away. This information was exchanged in the subtle, but clear, language of the English.

'What are you two doing?'

'I'm taking Hamid for a walk,' said Clare, taking my arm.

'Oh.' And Hermione trotted away.

'Poor Hermione. I think she's been very lonely since school. Her parents are in Kenya so that's why she's here for Christmas.'

'Do they live in Kenya?'

'No. They're just getting drunk and shooting wild animals most likely. Hermione will choose a husband soon and then all her problems will be solved, or so she imagines. She has plenty of suitors because, as you can see, she's very beautiful.'

Women find it so easy to comment on each other's looks. I would never have said that Salim was a handsome man, although he was, damn him. But even at that young age, I had guessed that such compliment should rarely be read as merely a compliment.

'But you're beautiful, Clare.'

'Hamid, why on earth do you keep going on about my looks? There's more to me than just that.'

'I know, but right now, you're driving me crazy.'

'Hamid?'

She was driving me crazy, and I was out of ideas, and something about the proximity to an empty and secluded stables was charging me with an erotic jolt.

With the full expectation of compliance, I grabbed Clare and kissed her. I found myself pushing us into the stables. However, that expected compliance felt like it was not forthcoming.

'What are you doing?'

'We both want this to happen.'

'Hamid, no.'

I was smothering her face with ugly kisses in an attempt to cover her words.

'Stop it!'

Even I could tell that Clare's hands pushing me away was not mere theatre. I was as close to her as I had ever hoped to be, and yet on her freckled face was not the rapture of love, but a look of confusion that was fast turning to horror and then to rage.

She hated me, and my world collapsed. One moment, she had merely been to me the object of my desires, but now she was a person who hated me. I stepped back, trying to un-cross a line I should never have crossed. I don't think either of us in our young lives knew what the appropriate grown-up response should have been to my betrayal of trust. She disappeared into herself as she walked out of the stable without looking at me.

'I'm sorry, Clare.'

I did not know then that this would be the most oft repeated phrase I would make to the woman who would become my wife, but it felt as hopeless then as it would a million times later.

Chapter 17

The rest of the day was a living hell.

My stomach was churning with guilt and the fear that the full enormity of my behaviour would be discovered. Although this was already a familiar set of emotions in my life, this occasion did feel particularly bad. I knew my actions had been utterly disgraceful, and I avoided all company while I stewed in my own shame. I wouldn't have been so ashamed if my lunge at Clare had worked—as I had hoped it would—but it didn't, so here I was.

Oblivious to my turmoil, the kitchen was bustling with activity in preparation for Christmas Day. So, when I tentatively appeared for lunch, there was a mercifully reduced number of us—just me, Sir Alfred, and Margaret.

While Sir Alfred talked about the Persian roots of many Malay words (obviously he was fluent in both languages), I tried to avoid any eye contact with Margaret. I could tell that she was glaring at me with expressions that seemed to instantaneously flicker between a shockingly intense hatred to remorse, and then, perhaps, to longing. I was probably transposing my own helter-skelter of emotions onto her lovely face.

I scuttled away as soon as I could, but I had learnt that almost all Malay words to do with towns and their administration have Persian origins. I returned to the house after five desultory circumnavigations and entered the empty library, drawn to the warmth of the fire.

I realized that Margaret was there too, nursing a brandy. Leaving now would mean doing away with all manners and courtesy. We sat in silence. She took the opportunity to glare at me. The sense of boldness that Margaret had bestowed upon me through our night of passion still lingered in me, so I decided to take the initiative and break the ice.

'Lovely weather we're having.'

'No, it's not.'

'No, it's not, you're right, it's bloody awful. A complete disgrace.'

She swirled her brandy like a man, attempting her old trick of intimidation, but it quickly flickered down, like the embers burning weakly in the fireplace, to something like sadness.

'Why did you do that last night?' Margaret asked. 'Why did you come to my room?'

'It was a mistake.'

'A mistake?'

'Yes, but a good one.'

'Well, that makes me feel much better.'

'No, you don't understand, I didn't mean it like that. You see, I was looking for Clare's room.'

'What? How dare you, you bastard!'

'But what we did was absolutely terrific. Really top notch. I mean that most sincerely.'

'Are you stupid?'

'I think I might be.'

'Is this how you savages act in mongo-bongo land?'

'It's called Malaya, and we most certainly do not.'

'Because I'm not like that. I'm not a slut. I am not a slut.'

'I never said you were. Well, perhaps I did a few times, but that was different, you told me to say it. But I know you're not.'

She leaned forward as if nursing an ache, and her dark hair collapsed across her face. She really was astonishingly lovely, certainly the most beautiful woman I had ever held in my arms, and yet even as my eyes were taking in her body, I was discovering a new sensation. The noise that usually overwhelmed my youthful mind and body when in the presence of such a decidedly nice thing was absent. I didn't want her again. I wanted to be with Clare. Our night together had been terrifically good fun, but I had used Margaret, and she had wanted me to use her. But after the awful incident in the stables I knew that it wasn't me. I didn't want to be overpowering women. You may not believe this but I'm rather more used to it being the other way around.

'Gosh, you really are beautiful.'

'That's what they all tell me,' she said tiredly.

'But there's so much more to you than that. You're intelligent and funny.' It took less courage than I would have imagined, to lean forward and brush her hair to one side. 'And I've seen that you're incredibly delicate and sweet.'

We were close as we looked at each other for quite some time, which was something I had never done before with anyone.

'Are you going to kiss me again?' she asked.

The temptation to abuse this beautiful girl's trust was intense, just as it was, I think, for her to be used again.

'I truly hope not,' I found myself saying.

I was having to remind myself to breathe as we continued looking at each other. That tiny remaining gap was so easily bridgeable. Goodness, we were going to do it again. We were going to kiss, and then we would become overwhelmed by lust right here in the library, and then we would be caught and thrown into our own separate pits of shame. But I never think that far ahead, and instead, the excitement from the intimacy of searching her face and seeing the flush of her cheeks told me that we were about to experience a tremendous two, maybe three, minutes of unsurpassed ecstasy.

And then I saw Hermione trotting past the window on her horse and I leapt away from Margaret and back into my chair. Had Hermione seen us? She expertly reversed and looked at us quizzically.

I have been caught many times doing something I shouldn't have been doing, so I summoned an old school ruse to deflect attention.

'Quick, laugh like I just said something very funny.'

We both forced laughter, which actually came as something of a relief.

'And then she stepped on the ball!' Margaret added as a punchline to our imaginary joke, which we both found to be stupidly funny. We were genuinely laughing and hardly noticed Hermione's departure.

Margaret looked at me, finally, with a smile on her face.

'My father would hate you so much.'

'Now, why doesn't that surprise me?'

'He's in the South of France, so I'm here for Christmas.'

'And where is your mother?'

'I have absolutely no idea.'

I did not love this girl, but I could, and it would be hell.

'Staying exactly where you are,' she said with determined, if fragile, confidence, 'tell me about Malaya. And you can tell me something of Clare. But be gentle with my emotions.'

I did tell her something of Malaya. Not my usual exotic *Thousand and One Nights* nonsense. Instead, I told her of the prosaic stuff—about small towns on rivers, tin mines, Malays, Chinese and Indians, Communists in the jungle, my mother and my father—and I realized that I was feeling strangely homesick. I also told Margaret about Clare, about our adventures together when we were nine, and how she reminded me of home and of that time. Margaret asked if it was Clare I loved or Malaya.

'Perhaps I do love Malaya, but Clare is much more attractive.'

'Careful, Hamid. Remember what I said about my emotions.'

'Obviously you're very attractive too. Please help me, Margaret. I don't know what to say. I've never been in this situation before.'

'Neither have I. I'm essentially a virgin. There, I've said it. You should go and speak to Clare.'

'Would it help?'

'I don't know. Clearly, I'm not an expert in these things.'

I got up to leave.

'Will you be all right?' I asked.

'Perhaps.'

Chapter 18

I left the library feeling simultaneously pleased and aggrieved that I had not repeated my mistake with Margaret.

But—I am somewhat ashamed to say—I was satisfied that the door was still open to several delirious repetitions of said mistake. Margaret clearly had many demons that I could only guess at, but the naivety and arrogance of youth is such that one imagines one can tame demons with ease, or ride them.

Once again, Margaret had bestowed confidence upon me and I went looking for Clare, only to be stopped by Tom, who was relaxing in his telephone booth. I could barely see or understand Tom through the haze of cigarette smoke when he spoke to me.

'I can't decide if you are attracted to women or if they are attracted to you.'

'Well, I, er, I like to keep fit.'

'Are you familiar with Mata Hari?'

'Of course, I know the sun.'

'No, not the Malay word, I mean Mata Hari the spy.'

'Vaguely. Something about the First World War, wasn't she shot?'

'Actually, she wasn't a spy at all, just an exotic dancer with an interesting mix of personal clients.

But if she had been a spy today, we would call her a "honeytrap".'

'Would we?'

The phone rang and Tom answered it before the second ring. I wasn't sure if I should leave so I just stood there, waiting to be dismissed. Tom listened to the voice on the other end and then quickly leafed through a book he had on hand, it was Goethe's *Faust* in German. Having found the page he wanted, Tom counted down the lines and words and then he said, much to my surprise, 'Besut', which happens to be Salim's hometown. Tom put the phone down and leaned back, looking very pleased with himself.

'We still haven't spoken about your future, Hamid. But perhaps we will very soon.'

'Yes, I'd like that, but do you mind if I go, I need to speak to somebody.'

'Of course.'

I took one last look at the mysterious Tom Pelham. I was actually saying goodbye. Tom Pelham had invited me to join his family for Christmas, but everything had changed since that long ago time, and I was now no longer interested in his mystery and manliness. The sheer predictability of my future continued to terrify me, but where once a dream of living under Tom's guidance offered vague promises of career excitement, I now only wanted the promise of Clare Pelham and a life of love.

Every single Malay song that my father had sung smugly, or my mother had sung mournfully, had been about love. Nobody ever sang a song about the beauty of a life in the civil service as the rat destruction officer in Parit Buntar, or doing whatever it was that Tom did.

I had imagined that Tom could liberate me from my father and the responsibilities of adulthood, but now I knew that Clare could give me my youth—an eternal youth that would make me whole. She could release me from a life with Irma, a woman I did not love.

I hate to think ill of Irma. I would break her heart, but I know that I would also set her free. Over the decades, she has beguiled and fascinated me and exacted her revenge many times over. I wanted love, a career would take care of itself.

Naively unaware that Tom's reach was so long, I walked away from him to hunt down Clare.

I finally found Clare whispering with Hermione in a corridor that was cold despite the sunlight. I didn't dare approach. I needed Clare to be alone for me to make my apology and declaration of love, so I hid in a shadow and watched.

My world fell out from under me. Clare was upset, dabbing tears from her eyes as Hermione listened and whispered words I could not hear, but I could tell were tinged with hate. Clare replied with words that might have been in my defence, but Hermione was adamant, and Clare was agreeing. I was losing Clare, and my future, and there was nothing I could do as it would have been impolite to step forward and claim her. I made a compromise of sorts by accidentally knocking over a giant elephant foot umbrella stand that clattered to the floor.

'Hamid? What are you doing there?' Clare demanded.

'Clare, I need to speak to you.'

Clare looked at me with an expression I did not know she possessed. It was of anger or disappointment. I was not sure which, but it hurt either way.

'Not now. Maybe later.'

She walked away.

Hermione looked at me and stood up straight. With her whiteness and blonde hair, she looked powerful in the sunlight. It would have been impossible to push past her. She looked at me with absolute disdain and then the slightest smile crossed her lips before she swept away after Clare. I followed them from a distance, until they disappeared into Clare's bedroom.

If the opportunity still existed, then I would have to wait for my chance to say the right combination of words to unlock Clare's affections. In the meantime, I went to my room and waited for Christmas Eve dinner, which I knew was a big deal in Christian circles.

Chapter 19

Christmas Eve's Midnight Mass was an important and colourful date in my hometown. Many of the town's Indians would dress in their finest clothes and best saris, and along with Eurasians and Europeans, would gather at the church.

As young boys, we used to enjoy sitting outside the church and hailing friends as they celebrated one of the town's few late-night events in a time when most things ended after the evening's Isha'a prayers. In the cold of my English bedroom, my recollection of a Malayan Christmas now had snow on the roof of our grand mosque. I was dressed like a Dickensian urchin, watching the beautiful Clare Pelham proceed to church, while I promised myself that I would one day meet and marry this girl.

Whereas once, I had imagined a far off, mythic England with palm trees and water buffalo, I could now only remember my Malaya with oak trees heavy with snow.

Where did I belong?

In both, I supposed.

In both worlds, a life with Clare made perfect sense. She knew both my worlds. The sound of a Malayan gong signalling dinner merely added to the music of gamelan in my dreams of my future, and my past.

I arrived for my first Christmas Eve dinner bearing gifts to an atmosphere quite different from the night before. The cast of characters in the dining room was the same, and I was dressed exactly the same (save for a new collar), but now, there was a sense of gloom.

In later years, I was to discover that for those who celebrate Christmas, it is far from being the season for good cheer and is instead the time when long suppressed family grievances bubble up to the surface, fuelled by plum pudding and too much booze. But at the time, I took the oppressive atmosphere personally, and perhaps for good reason.

The room was full and yet everybody was absent, lost in their own worlds and not playing their ascribed roles for keeping the peace. Margaret was silent without her usual cynical wit, which made it easier for me to try to avoid her without looking like I was trying to avoid her. Clare was surprisingly curt when giving instructions to the maid and nobody would look me in the eye apart from Hermione, who was pointedly staring at me, daring me to look at her and her unhidden knowing smile. Lady Pelham was there in body but was otherwise absolutely not present, which clearly filled Sir Alfred with a deep frustrated sadness as he was forced to play nursemaid to his wife. Only Tom and I watched the gathered crowd, but a few too many whiskeys and witnessing the discomfort of his family had made him cranky.

'Why on earth are you carrying Christmas presents?'

'Don't you open your presents on Christmas Eve?'

'Of course not,' he scoffed.

'We're not Catholics,' Hermione joined in.

'Aren't they Christians?'

'No,' she condescended. 'They're Catholics.'

'Oh. And you're Christians?'

'Better than that, we're Anglicans.'

'Apart from Tom,' said Clare. 'He's an atheist.'

'Actually,' Tom spoke, as if steeling himself for an admission. 'I'm thinking of becoming a Catholic.'

'What?' Sir Alfred awoke suddenly. 'No, you are not. No child of mine will become a Catholic.' He started waving an angry finger at an old painting. 'Remember that it was our forebear who lit Thomas More's pyre. Only alcoholic whoopsies become Catholics. You're not Evelyn Waugh, that little shit.'

'Graham Greene is very charming,' Lady Pelham pointed out.

'Oh, for god's sake, Catherine. Not now! And you use the soup spoon for soup!'

'Sir Thomas More was not burned at the stake. He was beheaded,' Lady Pelham muttered.

'She can't remember which spoon to use but she remembers Tudor history,' Sir Alfred exclaimed. 'Damnable Yorkist.'

'Lancastrian.'

'A pox on both your bloody houses,' Tom muttered.

And so, I enjoyed my first Christmas Eve dinner, which was a mixture of bland food with the occasional hot eruptions of the War of the Roses, but mostly, cold silence. Only Margaret showed me any kindness.

'Don't worry, it's just Christmas,' she leaned over to tell me. 'Put the presents back under the tree and we'll open them tomorrow.'

Perhaps I recoiled from Margaret a tad too obviously and my glance at Clare was altogether too guilty. Fortunately, Clare was leaving the dining room and didn't see anything, but Hermione saw me, and her smile was unsettling. I quickly gathered my presents and chased after Clare.

'Clare, I need to speak to you.'

'Not now. Maybe later.'

'But when?'

'Later. And then I'll give you your present.'

In one's youth, the fear induced by being in trouble is especially stomach-churning, but on the bright side, the leavening brought about by the merest hint of hope is especially gleeful. I was now happy because Clare had said that we still had a thing called later, and that later I would have the opportunity to talk my way out of trouble.

I put my presents back under the Christmas tree while planning a tactic of doe-eyed abject grovelling that would lead to pity. I looked at the Christmas tree surrounded by presents and beside the glowing fireplace. It really did look pretty. I was certain my plan would work.

Sometimes, it is good to be alive.

Chapter 20

'Twas the night before Christmas and I was in my room waiting for nobody in the house to be stirring—at which point I would tiptoe down to Clare's room.

I could barely contain my excitement as I anticipated receiving her 'present', assuming she would be more catholic in her Yuletide timetabling. I rehearsed my lines a few times.

'I am really, really, really sorry.'

Then I took a deep breath and entered the corridor. I now knew which room was Margaret's, and I wouldn't be going in there again despite the fond memories. I had seen Clare and Hermione enter Clare's room earlier in the day. Now, the door to her room was slightly open. My heart was racing as I nervously placed my hand on the door handle and assumed the correct expression of pathetic contrition. For once, I was glad that I didn't have a pencil moustache, as it would have been outré. I stepped into Clare's bedroom.

'Hamid!'

'Hermione? Isn't this Clare's room?'

'No, it's not!'

'Dammit.'

'What makes you think you can just walk into anybody's room?'

'The door was open.'

'So what if it was?'

Things were starting to feel like déjà vu.

'That really is an excellent point. I'm very sorry, Hermione. I'm leaving now.'

'No. Wait. Now that you're here I want to talk to you about Clare. Come inside. Close the door.'

I did as I was told. It would have been impolite to have done otherwise. And I admit that part of me was bewitched by the sight of Hermione at her dressing table in her pale peignoir.

'Sit down. Not on my bed. Sit on the floor next to me.'

I sat on the floor, which was demeaning, and yet, looking up at Hermione as she removed her make-up did stir a familiar noise from not too deep within me.

'Are you looking at me? You can't look at me. Look at my feet. That's all you're allowed to do.'

I am not particularly interested in women's feet, or anybody's feet for that matter, but Hermione's feet were attached to Hermione's athletic legs, and in those, I may have found a stronger stirring.

'You really are a vile man. Is this how you people are in mumbo-jumbo land?'

'It's called Malaya.'

'It's called mumbo-jumbo land if I say it is. Do you really think you can just walk into Clare's room after what you have done? She told me what you did in the stable, or tried to do, you savage.'

'I made a terrible mistake.'

Hermione looked down on me, from much the same height as if she were on her horse.

'That might be what you do with your native girls in mumbo-jumbo land, but this is England, and you do not lay your filthy hands on an Englishwoman. Do I make myself clear?' She was waving her hairbrush at me. 'Are you looking at my legs?'

'No.'

'You're disgusting. I know what you've been up to with Margaret.'

This revelation came as a shock, but I remembered Salim's Golden Rule: Deny everything.

'I haven't been up to anything with Margaret.'

'Liar. I saw you two in the library. Do you really think it is acceptable behaviour to grab Clare and declare undying love one minute and then be smooching with Margaret the next? And that you can then just barge into Clare's room after all that? Except that this is my room and now you are staring at my legs. Animal.'

Although it sounded like she didn't know about my night with Margaret, there was a lot of truth in Hermione's admonishments. I had acted abominably, and now I felt depths of guilt and shame I had never felt before. And I was staring at Hermione's legs as if they could offer answers. And was she letting me? Of course not, she's Clare's friend.

'Do you love Clare?' Hermione asked, quite gently.

'Yes, I do. Does she love me?'

'I can't tell you that. That would be betraying Clare's trust. But if you do love Clare, then you have a funny way of showing it.'

'What should I do?'

'What can you do?'

Hermione thoughtfully stroked a riding crop as she pondered her own question.

'What can you do? How can you prove yourself worthy of Clare?'

'Yes, what can I do? Just tell me, I'll do whatever it takes.'

'Because you love Clare.'

'Yes, I do.'

Hermione stood up. She seemed to tower above me. I never knew a woman could look so powerful, and that noise in my body seemed to suddenly click into an altogether new and unfamiliar higher gear. She picked up her riding crop and touched it to my face, warily at first but then more boldly when I offered no resistance.

Generally speaking, we Malay men do not go in for the ridiculous macho posturing that European men so enjoy, but we know where we stand. Between Malay men and women, we know the rules of the game: she's the boss but, bless 'em, they do everything they can to make us think that we are. But when the game is being played between two different races, the rules can become confusing.

'Do you think I'm pretty?' Hermione asked coyly.

How do I answer that question? Yes, she was the most terrifyingly gorgeous creature I had ever seen, one that I had assumed had been trained to primly perform dressage but, which, I was beginning to see, might be an untamed wild horse. But we were meant to be talking about Clare.

'Yes.'

'Prettier than Clare?'

Gosh, now how do I answer that one?

'Yes.'

'Wrong!'

Dammit! I've always been terrible at multiple-choice.

'Hold out your hands,' she demanded. 'Did your teachers punish you with the cane at your ridiculous mumbo-jumbo school?'

'Yes, they did. And it's called MCKK, the Eton of the East,' I whimpered defiantly as I held out my hands.

'Am I talking to myself?'

How on earth should I answer that question? What did it even mean?

'Now answer my question correctly. Am I prettier than Clare?'

'No.'

She suddenly thwacked the riding crop onto the palm of my hands.

'Ouch! Yes. Yes, you are prettier than Clare.'

She thwacked me again.

'Yes, no, I don't know, I don't know. You are beautiful and so is she.'

'The correct answer is that you are a vile, stupid brown man, and you have no right laying your hands on an Englishwoman. It's disgusting. You are disgusting.'

She leaned down and lifted my face with the tip of her riding crop, which afforded me a view inside her top, but this merely confused me even more. I was being punished for my bad behaviour, I was being told that my very race was disgusting and inferior, I felt humiliated and in pain, and yet the sight and close proximity to Hermione's power and barely hidden femininity was making me feel tremendously excited. Everything about this was so wrong. And weren't we meant to be talking about Clare? What was going on?

'You are weak and pathetic,' Hermione explained to me. 'Tell me.'

'I am weak and pathetic.'

'You are disgusting and wrong.'

'I am disgusting and wrong.'

She contemplated me for a moment, as if weighing up her options. I had not been this close to Hermione, I had not truly imagined that I ever would be, but now she was inside my circle. Her pale eyelashes were longer than I had imagined. As she was considering me for a moment, her tight lips broke into a private smile and the pupils of her eyes dilated. And then, just as I thought that we might have been about to kiss she pushed me back with both her hands. As I lay on the floor gasping like, well, gasping like a girl, she quickly sat astride me.

'You are disgusting.'

'Yes, yes I am.'

'And this is wrong.'

'It is. It is.'

'You love Clare.'

'I do. I love Clare.'

And then she started fumbling with my belt, whacking my hands away. Was I trying to help or hinder her? I dare not answer. While she grunted in my ear that I was disgusting and I grunted in hers that I loved Clare, there then followed the most explosive and confusing two, maybe three, minutes of my life. For such an athletic girl, she was surprisingly exhausted after what had been a relatively short workout. She quietly repeated 'wrong, wrong, wrong' and we held each other close for a brief second before she rolled off me and kicked me aside.

'Get out. Get out!'

I crawled out of Hermione's room (because she wouldn't allow me to stand up and walk), and I slumped against the wall in the corridor trying to understand what had just happened. I looked at the door to the room that I now knew through a process of elimination absolutely had to be Clare's. After what I had done over the last two nights could I ever enter that room?

Hermione had given me no assurances that this would be 'our little secret'. I considered Margaret's door because she was, perhaps, the one person in the world I could talk to, but even I knew my crimes had been too great. I collapsed onto my bed thinking about my brief encounter with Hermione that left me feeling worthless. Is this how Margaret had felt? I had a task to rebuild myself as I asked if I really was so disgusting and wrong. Hermione couldn't have found me to be too disgusting, as it was she who had initiated everything. Perhaps if I returned to her now, she would tell me I am a worthwhile human being and absolve me of my shame, and then we could do it again, but this time in a more normal way? But even as a young man, I still needed a bit of time to build up another head of steam, and also, it just didn't sound like the right thing to do.

I didn't know what it had meant, and it didn't leave me feeling good about myself, but it had been bewilderingly extraordinary, both affirming and degrading at the same moment. Hermione, so coy and delicate and yet also so evil and strong. I wanted to go back to Hermione's room and perhaps be invited to sit at her feet again and perhaps this time be allowed to actually touch her if I was good, but as my heart rate began to subside, I also began to think that wouldn't be a very manly thing to do.

It was past midnight. It was Christmas Day.

Chapter 21

Mr Hargreaves had told us the story of the sword of Damocles. Of how the obsequious courtier Damocles had been allowed to sit on the king's throne, but he had to do so under a sword held only by a single horsehair.

I thought of it when an exuberantly happy Clare greeted me in the morning and pulled me under the mistletoe for a Christmas kiss. She looked around quickly and then smiled bashfully as she leaned in to kiss me. Had she ever been kissed before? The kiss was clearly not meant to be short but instead lingering and seeking of my guidance. This should have been the happiest moment of my young life and perhaps it was for her, but I did feel wrong.

I had felt wrong from the moment I woke up from a surprisingly good sleep. Even a brief moment of ecstasy can help give rest to a guilty conscience, but then it all came crashing back. What had I done? What on earth was I going to do? I followed another one of Salim's Golden Rules and packed my bag just in case I needed to make a fast getaway. Would I be found out? Would the girls talk? My fate was not in my hands, it so rarely is, but this time the potential loss was everything. As I kissed Clare under the mistletoe of Damocles, I was consumed by fear. She looked at me.

'I've decided to forgive you.'

Could it really be that easy?

'You were beastly in the stables, but I've decided to forgive you. And now, I want to give you your present.'

'What? Now?'

'No. In the library.'

'Is it empty?'

'No, the girls are in there.'

'Oh, the Christmas present is an object.'

'Of course it is, silly. What else could it be?'

'Yes, exactly, what else could it be?'

She pulled me by the hand into the library and gave me a gift from under the tree. Hermione and Margaret were there too, neither of whom would look at me, both pretending to be doing something important.

'Open it,' said Clare excitedly.

I did the best excited acting I could possibly perform, considering the difficult audience. This was the most excruciatingly embarrassing moment of my life to be basking in Clare's obvious affection in front of Hermione and Margaret. And yet, I was beginning to realize that I might get away with it after all. From the sheer intensity of Hermione's supposed busy-ness, it was clear that she was not going to spill the beans. And Margaret had already said that our tryst would remain our secret.

My future together with Clare would be built on a quicksand of lies and filthy secrets with her best friends, but we would just get new friends. The obvious shame and silence of Hermione and Margaret were turning out to be the best possible Christmas presents, and I began to open Clare's gift with genuine enthusiasm. It was a display box with a glass front and several dead insects pinned inside. I knew all these insects well because I had crushed and swatted enough of them in my life.

'They're the insects of Malaya,' Clare squealed with delight.

'Yes, they are.'

'Now tell me honestly, did you know I was going to give this to you? I tried to hide it, but I'm sure you found out.'

'Clare, I can honestly say that this is not the present I was expecting. But it's bloody marvellous.' I was almost weeping with relief.

'I was hoping you'd like it. Do you remember how I used to torture them on the veranda? But now I love them.' And then she took my hand and came much closer. 'And now I think I love you, Hamid.' She pressed her body against mine, closed her eyes, and leaned forward to deliver an untutored, but loving, kiss.

'Stop it you two,' Margaret uttered.

'No, we won't,' Clare replied playfully.

'Yes, stop it,' Hermione demanded. 'It's disgusting.'

'No, it's not,' Clare asserted. 'I love Hamid. I think I always have. And I don't care who knows. I don't care what you two think, and I don't care what my father thinks either.'

I was so proud of this brave, strong, and beautiful woman. Despite the difficult circumstances of our courtship, that she would never know anything about, I knew we were going to have such happiness together and for the rest of our lives, which we would spend in Malaya and faraway from these minxes. When I held her close, I could feel her body respond to me differently, it yielded to me. Despite the crassness of my behaviour, I had won her heart, and she was mine. Yes, I would give in to the rather drab certainties of becoming a civil servant but now, I finally had a greater purpose as being the possessor of Clare Pelham, and I would try ever so hard to remain faithful to her. I was basking in Clare's smile and the happiest moment of my young life when Margaret spoke.

'Hamid and I slept together two nights ago.'

'What?' Hermione was instantly aghast. 'You slut!'

'Don't play the virgin princess, Hermione,' said Margaret. 'I know you had sex with him last night. My room is right next to yours. I heard you rutting and squealing, "You're disgusting, you're disgusting" like a mare in heat.'

'That's ridiculous, Clare. No such thing ever happened.'

I was too stunned to be able to say anything, but I did think to myself, *Good girl, Hermione. Deny everything.* In my state of fear, I left it to Hermione to continue with her well-reasoned rebuttals.

'Margaret has always been jealous of you, Clare, but I never imagined she would stoop so low just to hurt you.'

Hermione was making some excellent, and to my mind, very convincing points, and yet Margaret persisted.

'You were thrashing him with your riding crop. You must have heard that, Clare.'

'Perhaps I did hear something.' Clare was struggling to comprehend what was happening to her world.

'It's a fanciful story but you have no proof for any of this.'

'Really?' Margaret got up and stepped towards me. Her face betrayed no hint of the warmth we had shared just the day before, even though I was silently beseeching her to leave me alone. 'Hold out your hands, Hamid. Show me the palms. Exhibit A.'

Across both my palms were long red welts with the unmistakable impressions of a plaited leather riding crop. I bruise like a peach.

'How did you get these marks?' Margaret asked me.

'He walked into a door. I saw him do it.'

'Do you think I'm stupid? I can easily match your crop to these marks. But I won't have to because I have a witness.'

'Who? There was nobody else there. I mean, there wouldn't have been if any of this were true, which it's not. Unless you mean . . .'

'. . . Yes, the weakest part of your defence, Hamid.' Margaret turned to me.

'Did you have sex with Hermione last night?'

'Don't answer that, Hamid.'

'All right then. I'll ask this. Did you and I sleep together two nights ago?'

'Why are you doing this, Margaret?' I pleaded.

'Because of Clare. I can't let you hurt Clare. I can't hurt Clare any more than I already have. She's my friend, and you are an evil monster.'

I looked at Clare. Innocent, trusting, loving Clare. Her beautiful face that I wanted to see shine with happiness whenever she caught her insects, the face I wanted to grow old with. Now, I saw that nine-year-old girl again, but she was stunned, as if suddenly exposed to all the lies and horrors of adulthood all at once. Deny everything, Salim had told me. Deny everything, and my future with all its certainties might still be assured.

'Yes. Yes, I did sleep with you two nights ago.'

'What kind of beast are you?' Hermione spluttered. 'But this has nothing to do with me. I told you she's a slut, Clare.'

'And I had sex with Hermione last night.'

I turned my eyes away from Clare and looked at the floor as silence fell across the room. I could sense that Margaret felt no triumph in my confession, but perhaps some kind of release from our shared lie.

'Get out!' Clare told me, her voice wavering with anger and confusion. 'Get out of my house right now. Don't say anything. Don't anybody say anything. Get your things and get out of my house now!'

I stepped back towards the door.

'I'm so sorry, Clare.' I said, not even hoping that it might mean something.

'Get out, and you can take this.'

Clare threw the insect case at me, but I ducked, and it smashed against the wall. Crushing dead beetles underfoot, I walked into the hallway that had been so welcoming just two days before but now hated me. Clare followed me, and her shouts soon became sobbing screams that tore away at me as nothing has, before or since.

'Why would you do this to me? What did I ever do to you? Why me? Why me?'

I continued on up the stairs to retrieve my suitcase as she slumped against the wall sobbing why, why, why. Neither Margaret nor Hermione dared approach her, and she was there alone until Sir Alfred came out of his study.

'What the devil's going on?'

Sir Alfred may not have known the full story but after a quick glance around the hallway at all the guilty faces, I think he understood the gist of it.

'There, there Clarabelle, Papa is here. Let's take you by the fire and have some tea.'

It was a long and lonely walk to my suitcase, which was thankfully right by my door, and then back down to that dreadful hallway where there was now only Hermione.

'You are a stupid, stupid dirty savage,' she hissed before slapping my face very hard indeed. 'Call me.' She stuffed a piece of paper into the pocket of my overcoat and walked away.

It struck me as being highly unlikely that the events of Christmas 1952 could ever become something that the Pelhams and I would one day laugh about, so I was fairly sure that I was walking out of their front door and onto their driveway for the last time. Margaret was standing at a nearby window. We were looking at each other when Sir Alfred called to me.

'I knew you were trouble the moment I saw you. But I want you to give something to your father.' And then Sir Alfred punched me squarely in the face. I collapsed onto the ground with blood spurting from my nose.

'I'll be sure to pass that on, Sir Alfred. Thank you, Sir Alfred.'

'If I ever see you again, I will slit your throat and gut you like a *babi hutan*.'

He proceeded to hurl many Malay, Hokkien, and Tamil insults at me as I staggered down the driveway. I never knew there were so many and almost all of them seemed to involve goats and your mother, but I probably deserved them all.

At the end of the driveway, I had a choice between going left or right, but I had no idea where I was or where I should go. Which direction was the London I should never have left and how could I escape from the England I should never have entered? This was Christmas Day and there would be no trains or taxis. In fact, there was absolutely nothing, there was no sound at all, as if even the birds were enjoying a holiday. I took one last look at Tanamerah. I turned left and started trudging to I knew not where, clutching a handkerchief to my nose.

Just a few days ago, I had come up to the Pelhams by train and had been so full of excitement, delighting in the sights of the English countryside. I had imagined Oliver Twist's unfortunate mother battling through the rain, and now here I was, like Oliver Twist himself, walking to London. And just to complete the poetic symmetry, a violent thunderstorm broke overhead.

A few days ago, I had been asked to judge which of three beautiful women was the fairest. I had judged them all to be winners, and now we were all the losers. But surely, all was not lost. Surely, there had to be a way to do or say the right things, so that I could win Clare over again. Then I would be complete and not alone. I had been trudging in the rain for what seemed like hours when I heard the sound of a car. I watched hopefully as it approached and stuck out my thumb. My hope dwindled when I recognized the car. It was Tom Pelham's Morgan and I had nowhere to hide. The car pulled up beside me.

'Get in,' Tom ordered.

'Please don't hurt me,' I squeaked.

'Just get in the car.'

'Are you going to kill me, Tom?' I said as I obediently got into the car.

'You have hurt my sister very much, but I'm not going to kill you. I'll give you a lift to London. I have to go there myself. A matter of urgency.'

Tom took a look at my nose and wriggled it about aggressively, which sent white flashes of pain into my eyes.

'It's not broken. Did my father do this?'

'Yes.'

'Good. It saves me the trouble of doing it myself. You have been a very naughty boy.'

He revved the car, double de-clutched and then he drove me back to London, away from one disaster and into another.

'Hamid, you need to pay penance for your sins, and I think I might have just the job for you. Do you remember what I said about honeytraps?'

Part III

Berlin, Germany

1953

Chapter 22

Unlike in England, the wind in Berlin often blows from Siberia.

It was only the slightest breeze, but it was enough to chill my bones, which had been steamed in the heat of Malaya. After two months of training in London—where I had singularly failed to understand even the basics of codes and ciphers—I was now, at the end of February 1953, in the American sector of Berlin, receiving my final briefing before embarking on my mission.

'How do you like your clothes?' Tom asked.

'I don't like them at all. I look like a student.'

'Hamid,' said Tom with a tone of exasperation that I had become familiar with during my training, 'that is the idea. You are a student from Asia, fired up with a zeal for socialism, wanting to learn more from your young comrades in the East.'

'*Ja, ja, socialismus ist gut,*' I incanted just about the only German phrase I had managed to learn. 'But why can't I dress like him? He's German.'

There were two other men with us in the room. An American who had sprayed on far too much expensive eau de cologne that morning, and an impeccably dressed German who was definitely an aristocrat. I can always spot an aristocrat, and for some reason, I am always drawn to them, I can't think why. This German was beautifully dressed in the English style, but perhaps his reproduction was too sharply precise, because he had all of the style but none of the wit.

'I am German. But you are not.' The German appeared to be confused by my statement.

'Can I at least wear a hat? I can be a socialist, but must I also be a savage?'

'What is he talking about?' asked The German.

'Tom, you know we don't like this,' said The American.

'Your boy is obviously a Grade A moron.'

'I'm telling you,' said Tom, 'he is a magnet for women.'

'Him? Get outta here.'

'I wouldn't have believed it myself if I hadn't seen it with my own eyes. Even the most beautiful women are drawn to him. It's like magic. I tell you, he has a mysterious but undeniable skill.'

I liked the sound of that, even if it wasn't true. I had merely been caught in the crossfire of competitive women who had seen me as an exotic toy.

'But we want to lure men. Men hold all the power,' The German pointed out. 'And we all know that British Intelligence has many operatives skilled in that task.'

The American found The German's joke and Tom's embarrassment to be very amusing.

'I admit we've had some problems but that's all in the past now,' said Tom. 'What harm can it do, sending Hamid across? Maybe he'll give us another angle we can pursue.'

'I'll be honest with you, Tom. You say it's all in the past, but it was only last year that Burgess and Maclean defected to Moscow, and our faith in you Limeys is not high. Berlin is our patch now, with the assistance of our German friends, of course. But we're willing to give you this one for old time's sake. Just don't involve us and don't expect our help when it all goes wrong. Has he seen his mark yet?'

Tom sifted through a pile of photographs. 'We want you to target this woman.'

'I can't see her, there's a fat girl in front.'

'That is her.'

'What? Surely this would be a waste of my mysterious but undeniable skill?' I desperately sifted through the pile of photographs myself. 'Now this girl looks very nice. Why don't I target her instead?'

They all laughed at the very thought.

'She's out of your league,' The American told me. 'That's Margot Feist, the head of the Young Pioneers. Just had Eric Honecker's child.' I didn't know what he was talking about. 'You've heard of Eric Honecker? Member of the SED's Politburu? Head the FDJ?'

I'd heard of them. 'I've heard of them. The FDJ is the Free German Youth movement. They're the ones I'll be infiltrating.'

'At least he's heard of them, but otherwise your boy doesn't know a damn thing!'

'And that's the way I like it,' Tom said. 'We'll let him find out as he goes along. They won't suspect a thing. You can try it with Margot Feist if you want to, Hamid, but it would probably end with the firing squad. The target we've chosen for you is this woman. Her name is Katrin Schule, and she speaks some English. She's a rising star in the FDJ, and one day it might be useful to have somebody high-up who has been compromised by us, don't you think?'

Tom turned to me. 'If you turn your Casanova gifts to good, then you might be able to bring liberal democracy to half the world. Wouldn't you like to do that, Hamid?'

'This is madness,' said The German. 'And he doesn't speak German?'

'Not a word.'

'Are you sure?'

'Absolutely.'

With that assurance, The American and The German started berating Tom in German. I couldn't understand a word they were saying but I could tell that Tom was defending my value, and he kept repeating a word that I didn't understand but which seemed to appease them both.

'Okay, Tom. This is your show, but we want nothing to do with it,' The American spoke for himself as well as for The German. 'He can never know about anything else we're doing, and *do not* involve the French.'

They all found the mere thought to be most amusing.

'You have my word. And don't worry, he doesn't know your names.'

'Doesn't matter much if he does. They know who we are. But he knows your name. They might be watching the house right now, so we'll go first. Good luck, Tom. Maybe your boy will be useful.'

'I am certain he will be.'

The American and The German went into a courtyard where they got into a waiting car. A second identical car drove onto the road first and turned left, and then theirs exited and turned right.

'You can never be too sure in Berlin.' Tom explained.

'What if they're right, Tom? What if I mess it up?'

'There's nothing for you to mess up. You haven't done anything yet. But I know you will be excellent. Just remember why you're doing this.'

'The trainers told me I'm doing it for England, although I'm not really sure why that argument should work for me. I'm a subject but not a citizen. So, when you think about it . . .'

'You're doing this for Clare. You were a dreadful cad, and you hurt her, Hamid. I spoke to her last night and she's still very upset. I don't know if she'll ever recover, and she certainly won't talk to you ever again. But if you succeed in this, then you'll be a hero, and I am sure she will forgive you.'

'How can you be so sure?'

'She's my sister. I'll convince her. Now then, are you ready?'

'I'm so scared I think I want to be sick.'

'Good. That means you will be alert. The FDJ meeting will be starting soon. Do you have your letters of introduction?'

'Yes.'

'Do you have the gift?'

'Yes. I went to KaDeWe like you said, and I chose a perfume.'

'Really? I would have gone for a scarf but wooing the ladies is your area of expertise. I doubt you'll be able to give it to her today, but anything is possible with your skill. What is it?'

'It's called Betrayal.'

Chapter 23

In early 1953, it was still possible to travel quite easily between the different sectors of the divided city of Berlin.

Just the year before, the entire border between East and West Germany had been sealed completely shut by the Communists, but the divided and isolated city of Berlin remained an exception. What had once been the capital of Germany was now, from a Western perspective, an island in a sea of Communism that stretched unbroken from Germany to China—and the Communists were hoping, soon to Malaya.

For the last week, I had been staying in the British sector of Berlin (there were also the American and French sectors) and now, I was about to embark on my first venture into the Soviet sector. In my training, I had been told to always conduct a reconnaissance before committing, but Tom had kept me locked away in a drab safe house because he wanted me to retain a state of blissful ignorance. My ignorance, he said, would be my shield.

Unfortunately, this meant that I had no idea what I would find in the East when I went to attend a big gathering of the communist youth movement, the Freie Deutsche Jugend. Although the easiest way to cross was to take the U-Bahn because checking was minimal, Tom calculated that I still had enough time to walk to the Deutsche Sporthalle and practise the close observation techniques I had been taught. So, he took me to the crossing point at Friedrichstraße. I was a little concerned about being seen in public with Tom, but he assured me that the moments before I crossed into the East were the last moments when I would definitely not be watched. He waved goodbye to me, like a proud parent sending his child to his first day at school. At least, that is how I imagined it must have been like. My father had done no such thing.

'Don't do anything stupid,' Tom gave me one last word of advice. 'In fact, don't do anything at all. Be normal, boring, and inconspicuous. Do not embellish your stories. No unnecessary extra details. I'll see you when you get back tonight.'

It was difficult to feel inconspicuous when I was probably the only Malay man in the whole of Germany, but I tried my best as I walked towards the border crossing.

Leaving the American sector was easy—the German police and American soldiers barely looked at me—and entering the Soviet sector was surprisingly easy too. The guards were curious to see me, but after checking that I wasn't carrying any Western money or black-market contraband (the perfume was safely hidden in a secret pocket in my bag), I was waved through. And now, I was in the East and inside a Communist continent that stretched all the way to the Pacific Ocean.

The process of crossing into this new world was nerve-wracking and yet, surprisingly familiar. I had, after all, lived through the Japanese occupation of Malaya during the war. As soon as I entered the East, I realized that all the training they had tried to give me in England was irrelevant, because I had already been trained in my childhood. Instead of German border guards, in my mind, I saw Japanese soldiers. I had to stop myself from bowing each time I saw a Russian soldier. Because of the war, I already knew how to be inconspicuous and how to blandly blend in. And because of the war, I knew that they weren't looking for me, they were looking for the Chinese, in a manner of speaking. During the war, I had been a Malay child, which meant I didn't have much to worry about. The Japanese hated the Chinese, and it was they who bore the brunt of Japanese suspicion.

In my hometown, I had seen a young Chinese man dragged away and bayoneted by the side of the road, all because he had a tattoo on his body, which they mistakenly believed meant he was a member of a secret society. Sometimes, when I cycled past the school that had been become the headquarters of the Kempeitai, I could hear some unfortunate Chinese man or woman being tortured.

As I remembered these horrible childhood memories, I realized that I already knew how to be. My skin was drawing attention as a beacon of browness, but I knew that if I walked at a moderate and purposeful pace then people would assume I had a valid reason for being there. Admittedly, they had tried to teach me this in England but now I understood why I hadn't been listening. I knew it already.

From Friedrichstraße, I was soon on the boulevard of Unter den Linden. With its opera house and grand buildings, this had once been the showpiece of old Prussia, and while much of the devastation of the war had been cleared away, the bullet holes were still there—as they were, all over Berlin.

I stopped for a moment to watch some workers hoist the torso of a massive bronze statue out of a bomb crater. With his spiked helmet, I adjudged him to have been an old Kaiser (a Frederick and/or Wilhelm). A Communist official of the interchangeable kind read out some accusatory funeral rites, and as they winched the Kaiser's broken remains onto a waiting truck, I looked to see how the workers felt about the final removal of their old country, but their faces showed no emotion. *I know that look*, I thought to myself. They didn't want to draw the attention of the Japanese. I wished I could have shared that thought with Clare, or Margaret, or even Hermione.

In crossing the most rudimentary of borders, I had unexpectedly returned to the worst time of my childhood—a time when the British and the Pelhams had betrayed us with their defeat, leaving us Malayans with nothing but uncertainty and a future of helplessness and hopelessness. The skills I had learnt in that time made me feel surprisingly calm, but these were not happy memories. We had been as cut off from the world—as I was now—which made the loneliness I had felt ever since Christmas Day, feel even more complete. I had to continue down this path because, as Tom kept pointing out, it was my only possible path to redemption.

I managed to clear Clare and her friends from my mind for long enough to be able to start worrying that I was going to be late for the FDJ gathering. I quickened my pace towards the new communist showpiece of Stalinallee, but as I crossed the river Spree, I was confronted with the absolute destruction that had been visited upon Berlin in the war. I had thought the destruction in London or West Berlin had been bad, but here, vast swathes of land were nothing but rubble piled high, away from the road. Something magnificent had once stood here that the old Kaiser must have perused with satisfaction as he trotted past in his carriage on his way to the opera, but now, both he and his city were gone.

Workers, mostly women, chipped and chiselled away, salvaging bricks. Above them, loomed dozens of portraits of Joseph Stalin, and a slogan, that even with my feeble grasp of German, I knew meant 'We must learn from the Soviet Union'.

During the war, we in Malaya, had little comprehension of what was happening in Europe, but with the Japanese-run newspapers reporting German victories getting closer and closer to Berlin, we had felt that Stalin was a potential saviour. So, I had a warm regard for Uncle Joe. But now, I was beginning to find the sheer abundance of his portraits to be sinister as I entered his new grand boulevard.

Stalinallee was buzzing with workers. The boulevard was exceptionally wide and only some of the buildings had been completed, that too, in an architectural style that was completely unfamiliar to me. The rest of Berlin was built with a dark stone, made even darker by being covered with soot and by being pockmarked with bullet holes. But here, the stone and plaster were new, bright, and shiny—and horribly soulless. This place had not been designed for people, but for human ants.

I was rapidly approaching my destination, one of
the few buildings that had been completed and that
was opposite, yet another, giant statue of Stalin. On the
front of the Deustche Sporthalle, was a huge painting
of young people grasping shovels. Outside it, stood a
young person waiting impatiently.

'Are you the delegate from Malaya?' he asked me.

'Yes. Hamid.'

'You are late, Comrade Hamid.'

'Yes, I'm sorry about that.'

'The meeting has already begun. Show me your
papers and then we will go inside.'

He checked my letters of introduction, which had
been arranged several weeks earlier by Tom's people.
I was feeling very nervous because it was at this
moment that I could be found out. The letters were
not forged, but they were not legitimate either. The
Malayan Socialist Youth Council did not exist, and
even if it did, you can be sure that I would never have
been a member.

'Good. Now we go inside.'

'Excuse me, but what is your name?'

'Karl Schule.'

Chapter 24

The FDJ jamboree was in full sway as Karl Schule led me past thousands of curious eyes to my seat, which, to my horror, was near the front of the auditorium, scuppering my hopes for sitting anonymously at the back.

The fiery speeches had begun, and they would continue to drone on for what felt like an eternity. I briefly reflected upon the peculiar fact that this was my first ever political rally, and it was a Communist one in Germany.

I didn't understand a word because it was all in German, but I was confident that they would have been dull in any language. But the youthful crowd greeted every speech with excited applause, and their faces had a strange, ecstatic look, as if they were gazing past the speakers and beyond, to the promise of the Socialist horizon. I had to remind myself that I was a socialist now, so I adopted that Socialist-horizon gaze myself.

Everything in this Socialist utopia was on a gigantic scale, which might actually have pleased the old Kaiser but obviously, his face was absent. Instead, the speakers spoke below a gigantic painting of some old Communist god I did not recognize, but who had struck the customary pose of grasping his lapel in one hand and a book in the other.

'Who is he?' I asked Karl Schule who looked at me with disgust.

'Karl Liebknecht, our Socialist martyr.'

'I would have expected Karl Marx. He was German, wasn't he?'

Again, Karl Schule looked at me with disgust.

'Comrade Stalin has located a counter revolutionary Jewish conspiracy. The matter is being dealt with.'

Even I knew that Marx had been a Jew, but Karl Schule's statement made no sense to me otherwise. What I did not know at the time was that Stalin was embarking on a persecution of Jews because of a harebrained concoction that Jewish doctors were trying to kill senior Soviet leaders, and therefore Marx was suspect despite being dead for seventy years.

I nodded sagely in agreement, even though I had no idea what Karl Schule was talking about. Besides, I had lost interest in what he was saying because it was at that moment that I noticed a girl a few seats down from me. It was Katrin Schule, the girl I had been sent to romance.

Mercifully, she had lost some weight since her old photograph, and she was not without certain charms, but despite Tom's belief in my skills, I knew I was no Casanova. How on earth was I going to seduce her?

The succession of unintelligible speeches receded into the background of my mind as I tried to remember how and why I found myself in this peculiar situation.

Six weeks earlier, Tom Pelham had given me a very simple choice in Malaya Hall, when he woke me at noon on New Year's Day.

Did I want to see Clare ever again? In that case, I had to do exactly as he said. There would be a high degree of risk, but it would match and recompense the high degree of my sins.

I didn't like the sound of it, but he was prepared to sweeten the deal by helping me out with my exam results.

'How does a 2–1 sound?' he asked.

'A first sounds better.'

'If you push your luck, it will be a 2–2. We both know that left to your own devices you won't even be able to scrape a third.'

I was very affronted by this insult, because I had every confidence that my Bengali namesake, who was going to sit my exams for me, could easily breeze to a high 2–1. Those Bengalis are very clever chaps. To my astonishment, Tom knew all about my Bengali Hamid. He actually seemed quite impressed by my entrepreneurial spirit.

'It's the one thing about you that makes me think you can pull off this mission. I've spoken to the relevant people and your namesake will sit for your exams, but it doesn't matter what he does because you've already got a 2–1 . . . If you want it?'

'What do you want me to do?'

'You have to agree to do it first, and then I'll tell you my plan.'

What were my choices? I had been living with my shame and loneliness in an empty Malaya Hall in empty London, since my return on Christmas Day.

The only highlight had been the New Year's Eve shindig at The George, where I had become something of a regular, and where I had learned the words to classic songs such as 'Roll Out the Barrel' and 'Knees Up Mother Brown'. For those of you who do not know the song, it involves endlessly repeating 'knees up Mother Brown' until the Malaya Hall doorman passes out. I stunned them with my flawless rendition of 'The Bonnie Banks O' Loch Lomond' because every Malayan of my generation knows his Scottish and Irish folk songs. Several of the crowd clasped their arms around me and heartily told me, 'You're all right, you are.' I felt certain that that sentence was usually followed up with, 'Not like the rest of your lot,' but I accepted the earthy compliment, nonetheless.

In the course of the evening, I had even confessed of my Christmas nocturnal activities to Jim Plaistow who had not been impressed, having been cuckolded himself. Being a stolid colonial policeman, he was probably more used to confessions about stolen Sten guns, but he did manage to utter, 'Well, let that be a lesson to you' a few times, which I took to be a mark of friendship.

'Did you mention me to Tom Pelham?' Jim Plaistow had asked nervously.

'I'm sorry but I didn't.'

'Thank God for small mercies at least. Well, let that be a lesson to you.'

Assuming that the pub was open even on New Year's Day, I was planning to return upon waking up, but I felt that Tom's mysterious plan might, perhaps, be a more meaningful and profitable long-term proposition.

'All right then,' I told Tom. 'I agree. What do you want me to do?'

'I want you to be a spy for England, and for Clare, of course.'

I had worked out by now that Tom was some sort of spy, but his statement still confused me.

'We're leaving here immediately for your training,' Tom continued. 'Pack a few things. The cover story for your absence is that your father has sent you for private tutoring in Solihull.'

'Does such a place even exist?'

'Exactly. No Malayan will even know how to look for you in Solihull. Get up. Let's go.'

I didn't like the way I was being pushed into action without being given any information, so I decided to rebel.

'What if I say no?'

Tom stood up, revealing his full height and more than a hint of his displeasure.

'If you say no then neither England nor Clare will be happy with you.'

With my rebellion thus concluded, I started to put on some clothes.

'There's a colonial policeman. He asked me to mention him to you. Ex-army, late of Tanganyika and Palestine. Presently unemployed. Good chap. Very solid.'

'I'll be sure to look him up. Don't bother packing your dinner jacket. You won't be needing that.'

'That's a joke, isn't it?'

It wasn't, and I was whisked away for what turned out to be a pointless period of training where my trainers ending up learning more than me.

'Please tell us,' one of my trainers asked me after yet another frustrating lesson in espionage, 'Exactly how stupid are you? So that we know what we're dealing with.'

'I think it's going to be a journey of discovery for all of us,' I opined.

The journey had taken me to the Deutsche Sporthalle in the Soviet sector of Berlin, where I was pretending to listen to endless speeches while I was actually thinking about Clare and my sins, Margaret and my anger, and Hermione and my degradation. Suddenly, the assembled Socialist Youth roared their excitement for a star speaker.

I nudged Karl Schule and told him, 'Margot Feist.'

He seemed impressed for once.

'You know her?'

'Of course. She's very famous in Malaya. As famous as, you know, all the other famous socialists.'

The crowd clearly adored her as she lectured them on, presumably, the achievements of Communism and for once, my attention was caught. Despite her sexless attire, she was a very handsome woman—the unadorned female embodiment of Socialist zeal glowing like a beam of red-hot steel.

Tom had explained to me why Communism was very bad, and I had agreed with it all, but at that moment, the concept of a Socialist utopia filled with lots of Margot Feists was quite appealing. They would be a lot like Margaret, with an outer hardness belying an inner fragility; or like Hermione, just hard and mean through and through. Either way, I would have been quite happy.

Karl Schule interrupted my reverie.

'Comrade Hamid, may I introduce you to my sister, Katrin.'

Katrin Schule leaned across her brother to give me a firm handshake.

'Karl tells me you know of Margot Feist in your country. She is wonderful, is she not?'

'Yes. We admire her very much. Perhaps you could tell me more about her later? And about the glory of Socialism, of course.'

'We will,' said Karl Schule. And with that, they returned to the speeches, and I, to my Socialist horizon gazing and to daydreams about thrilling Five Year Plans with armies of Margot Feists, perhaps some of whom could be in military uniforms? But this just reminded me of Margaret in her RAF uniform, and of Clare and Hermione. Memories of beauty, pleasure, guilt, regret, and deep shame flooded my mind. I was here, in Berlin, because Tom had offered me a path to redemption. All I had to do was seduce a German Communist and I would win back Clare. It all made sense.

I glanced across to Katrin Schule to see if I could summon up a tingle of excitement. I was young in those days and despite her active suppression of any hint of femininity, that tingle could be called upon with relative ease.

Chapter 25

For lunch, we went to a nearby café where the already stomach-churning Berlin cuisine was made even more disgusting by being cooked in flavourless Communism.

Although I was pleased to find myself sitting next to Katrin Schule, I was not at all pleased to find myself sifting through a truly horrible dish that I think contained some cabbage to add bulk to the salt, and I once again found myself wishing I had some chlilies.

I had already decided to play a long game of seduction with Katrin Schule, and my plan of attack was to dazzle her with flashes of my winning smile, sprinkled with a few exquisite bon mots and some intoxicating tales of old Malaya— endless sandy beaches, elephants, crocodiles, etc—all while maintaining a polite physical distance. I wasn't sure which tales I would tell. I was going to play it by ear, but I knew that Malaya would do the trick.

'What are the worker's conditions like in Madagascar?' Katrin Schule asked.

'I don't know, I'm from Malaya. But we both have endless sandy beaches.'

'I do apologize, I meant what are the worker's conditions in Malaya?'

I had never stopped to ask myself this question before. I thought about our dozen or so family retainers, and they appeared to be happy enough. If they remained loyal to us, then we took care of them into their old age. Now I that I took the time to think about it, I realized that Megat had been subtly asking for an electric fan for his bedroom.

'The worker's conditions are bad.' Karl Schule joined our conversation.

'So, Comrade Hamid, how is the class struggle in Malaga?'

'I don't know, I'm from Malaya. We have elephants and crocodiles.'

Katrin castigated her brother in German and then spoke kindly to me.

'We must apologize for our ignorance in geography. Our educations were interrupted by the war. We were taught other terrible things but nothing about your land.'

'Yes, my sister is correct, but now we wish to know. Is there class struggle in Malaya?'

Now this was an issue with which I was intimately concerned. I would have to go all the way to Kuala Lumpur to visit a decent department store, and Whiteaways was often outrageously tardy in re-supplying basic staples such as new collars and cufflinks. It was a genuine struggle to maintain a sense of class and elegance in Malaya. However much I liked my tailor, Ah Liew, I did find his cutting to be heavy handed, and I had to wait until I got to London's Savile Row before I finally had a double-breasted suit that I could take pride in.

'The class struggle is terrible. Really quite awful.'

'And the lumpen proletariat?' asked Karl Schule.

'Well, they're not helping, are they.'

'I'm sorry,' said Katrin Schule. 'I do not follow your meaning.'

I realized that perhaps we did not share the same views on the sheer lumpeness of the proletariat and that I needed to change tack.

'I mean, the proletariat have become blind to their slavery in the feudal capitalist system, which is why we are required to guide them as cadres of the revolution,' I said, summoning up some of the phrases Tom had taught me, and hoping I had said it correctly.

'Ah-so,' said Katrin Schule. 'All is clear. There is not enough salt in my food. I will ask for more.'

'Please, let me ask.' I jumped at the opportunity to appear gallant, and to take a break from being a socialist. 'What is salt in German?'

'Salz.'

I went to the café's busy counter. I couldn't find a gap to squeeze in and instead hovered behind the crowd while pathetically whispering 'excuse me' and 'salz'. I had to be bolder, so I fought my way in, accidentally pushing a woman wearing a stylish hat. She turned around slowly to glare at me, and then she hissed something in a European language that was not German. I was taken aback by her anger and by the suddenness of her beauty. She looked a lot like Margaret, except this woman's anger was not pretence.

'I am sorry. I didn't mean to push you. I was trying to get some salt.'

She turned to the waiter and demanded the salt. 'Next time be more careful.'

She took her drink kand sat at a table alone. I know it is shallow, but I am drawn to nice things and after a morning spent in the broken drabness, interspersed with the shocking newness of Socialist Berlin, I was stunned by the silent and sad beauty of this woman. I had spent the morning with young people gazing at the Socialist horizon, but suddenly, there was this woman who was also our age, but appeared to see no horizon at all. I took the salt back to Katrin Schule.

'Thank you. That is very kind of you. You were saying that Malaya has sandy beaches and elephants. That sounds wonderful.'

'Yes. Yes, it's very nice.'

I tried to concentrate on Katrin Schule's words, but I was thinking about the woman who was sitting alone and wearing a stylish hat. At that moment, a large car pulled up outside the café, and at its front were Soviet flags. A handsome Soviet army officer stepped out, and as he strode into the café, his presence was preceded by a wave of silence and the occasional nervous nod. He sat down with the woman in the stylish hat and kissed her hand, to which she replied with a weak smile. The sound of conversation steadily returned to the café, but Karl and Katrin Schule seemed a bit quieter than they had been earlier.

'Who is he?' I asked them.

'Don't point,' Karl told me. 'He is a Soviet commander.'

'So, he is a friend,' I pointed out.

'Yes, he is. We must learn from the Soviet Union. And now we must go back to the Sporthalle, the afternoon plenum will begin soon.'

'The delegate from China will be speaking. Perhaps you know him?'

Chapter 26

I cannot tell you the number of times I have met Europeans and Americans who assume that because I am from Asia, I must therefore be able to speak Chinese, and that there even is a language called Chinese.

In my hometown, Hokkien was the main Chinese dialect spoken, and while I had picked up a few words, enough to be able to joke with my friends, I was nowhere near fluent. I firmly believed that all Chinese dialects were impossible to learn after the age of five. The imperceptibly tiniest difference in tone is enough to change the meaning of a word from 'have' to 'frog'. On the other hand, Malay and English share the robustness to be understandable with even the most atrocious accent.

So, when the Chinese delegate droned on in Mandarin and his associate translated into German, I was at a loss. I failed to understand anything—twice over. Karl and Katrin Schule kept asking me if the German translation was correct, and I grew tired of telling them that I also did not understand. So, I told them that although the translation lacked the lyricism of the Chinese original, the speaker clearly had an exquisite appreciation of dialectical materialism. That seemed to satisfy them, and I was free to drift off into thought about the woman wearing the stylish hat.

Her decidedly glamorous appearance amid the greyness and rubble of the East, had taken me by surprise. I imagined that she, unlike the fervent young Socialists in the Deutsche Sporthalle, did not wish to submit and conform to the reality that lay all around her. But my imaginings of this woman quickly became memories of Margaret and Clare, which made me feel desperately alone again.

I had grown up in a household full of people, which had made me yearn for some degree of solitude. But now that I had nothing but solitude, I yearned for company. Those feral childhood days spent with Clare had been the first time I had felt the intoxicating togetherness of solitude with one other person. And then, during Christmas at the Pelhams, I had experienced it again, albeit in a more adult form and with three different women. For the briefest of moments, we had allowed each other into our circles, and I had discovered that the deepest part of me needed to always be that close.

But did I want to be close to Clare or to Margaret, or even to cruel Hermione? While the Chinese delegate presumably described the revolution that had released 800 million peasants from their British-imposed 'unequal treaties' and subsequent 'century of national humiliation', I was thinking about how it did not matter. I had no choice, I had destroyed everything. I had managed to find Margaret's telephone number when I had returned to London, and with trembling fingers, I had dialled the phone. But I had been told that she had gone to the South of France to join her father.

She would surely eventually return, and I would have to wait until then. I had not called Hermione, despite her giving me her number, but I had stood outside her London house for five nights, watching as she was whisked away by various appropriate suitors, with whom she was probably alternately simpering and destructive. I really wanted to touch her again, but the price to pay was too unequal. I kept her number just in case my resistance broke down.

I did not even try to call Clare because I did not have the words to overcome the humiliation I had created. Besides, Tom had forbidden me and also explained that it would only be through my actions in Berlin that I could possibly redeem myself. Until then, I was to be utterly alone and if I failed, I would be utterly alone forever. I knew this in my head, but the sudden appearance of the woman in the stylish hat had released the most painfully beautiful memories into my entire body.

'We Germans love to sing together,' Katrin Schule told me.

The afternoon session ended with the entire auditorium joining in on a rousing rendition of the Socialist anthem of the Internationale. It really was a wonderfully stirring tune. I didn't know the words, so I sang a list of all the Malayan dishes I was sorely missing, and when I got to my mother's *rendang tok*, I actually cried, and my tears impressed the Schule siblings enormously.

'It really is spectacularly good,' I babbled through my sobs.

The Communist bigwigs led the crowd in some cheers, and then, properly filled with zest for the revolution, we all spilled out onto Stalinallee where the workers were still working on the new city as they had been since the morning.

In the decade after the war, I did get to travel a bit, and I can honestly say that wherever I went I found a feeling of optimism that something new and exciting would be built out of the ruin and rubble of conflict, and this crowd of German Young Socialists were more excited and optimistic than most. After introducing me to some of their comrades, who were all very impressed by the tale of my tears during the Internationale, the Schule siblings walked me to the U-Bahn station, lecturing me on some of the wonders being constructed along the way.

'The National Socialists hated Berlin,' Karl Schule explained. 'Berlin was always a Communist city. Our parents were members of the Communist Party.'

'You all must have been happy when Berlin was liberated by the Red Army.'

'It was a necessary time.'

As we were walking along, I could see the U-Bahn station getting closer and closer. I had not made any headway with Katrin Schule. The FDJ meeting had come to an end. I had no excuse to return, and I could feel the bottle of perfume burning a hole in my bag.

'Here is the U-Bahn. The train will take you back to the American sector,' Karl informed me.

'Would you like to come with me?'

'No. I do not go the West. And I have to go the Leipzig tonight.'

He was going to be out of town. That was handy.

'Katrin, would you like to join me? I've found a wonderful jazz club on Kurfürstendamm.'

'I have no interest in jazz. And I have an appointment with Margot Feist.'

I jumped at the chance.

'Could I meet Margot Feist? I would love to interview her for our paper, the, er, *Socialist Straits Times*. She will be an inspiration for our readers. I have so much more to learn, and if you will help me, then your name will be remembered in Malaya.'

The Schule siblings looked at each other and Karl shrugged as if to say it was his sister's decision.

'I will make some enquiries,' she said.

'Can I meet you tomorrow? You can be my teacher.'

'I will make some enquiries. Tell me how I can contact you, and I might call you.'

It was not exactly the warmest exchange I had ever had with a woman, but I had successfully pursued even less encouragement in the past. I gave her the contact number that Tom had given me for such an eventuality and then bade my farewell as I descended into the U-Bahn.

Walking into the Soviet sector had been a quiet affair while leaving was anything but. Hundreds of people were crammed onto the trains heading to the West. There appeared to be entire families and lots of young people, all of whom were wearing as much clothing as they possibly could and carrying bursting suitcases. Their luggage and anxious expressions told me that they were not going on a happy holiday. They reminded me of the people who had clogged the roads of Malaya in '42, after the British had run away and before the Japanese had arrived. These were refugees. They were all German, but they were refugees, nonetheless. As the stations drew closer to the Western sector, the hubbub of conversation steadily faded, giving way to an anxious silence, punctuated by the rocking of the train.

In this wave of movement towards the West, I suddenly caught a glimpse of a stylish hat. I managed to squeeze my way through the crowded train and spotted her. There she was, the woman from the café. I could only spy brief glimpses of her through a swaying gap between the bodies on the train, but it was enough for me to be able to imagine who she might be, which was a very calming exercise. Her clothes were in the latest style from the West, but had they been chosen by her?

In later years, I would become familiar with what mistresses looked like, the constant acquisition of which would become Salim's addiction. But even back then, I could tell she was not a wife. She wore clothes that a man would like to see her in. If her clothes gave no clues away, then perhaps her absent stare did. It reminded me of Margaret's after our night together, when her thoughts had departed from me and had gone somewhere else—faraway, and in her past.

Perhaps, I was not having any success divining this woman's secrets because she was neither Malayan nor English, rendering me clueless. But I felt that I could know her, if I could just smell her. Was her perfume sweet and girlish or darkly tragic? Her perfume, I knew, would tell me who she really was. But could I get close enough?

As we approached a station, the man sitting next to her looked like he was about to give up his seat. I abandoned all pretence of politeness and started pushing my way towards my target. But then she also stood up to leave. She smiled at a little refugee girl and exited the train at the last stop before leaving the Soviet sector.

As with most things in my life at that time, I had been defeated in my mission, and I knew I would never see this woman again. But I had gleaned one piece of information, something I felt I shared in common with her. She was alone.

The train crossed into the safety of the American sector, but the refugees did not appear to greet their release with any excitement. It looked as if they had replaced the anxieties of the past with new anxieties of their unknown futures.

Chapter 27

Back then, we were discouraged from referring to East and West Berlin as separate because neither side recognized the other's legitimacy nor the permanence of the divide.

The terms were naturally coming into being as was the evolution of two distinctly different cities from what had once been a single Berlin. While waiting to hear from Katrin Schule, I spent several nights in a jazz club on Kurfürstendamm, which was a torment. In the early 1950s, I felt like I was supposed to like jazz, but in actual fact I did not. Just like I was supposed to like champagne, but I really didn't.

Jazz was everywhere in those days and people of my age and of my class were supposed to like it because it was modern and exciting and American. But I wanted something else, something perhaps older and more settled than jazz, and something with a tune. I had come to Europe hoping to find its oldness, not for any newness. But the old was in short supply amid the ruins of war.

The boulevard of Kurfürstendamm was West Berlin's cultural epicentre, which meant bright lights and shopping districts. Before the war, Potsdamer Platz had been the teeming heart of Berlin, but that was now a bombed-out wilderness in the Soviet sector. The more gentrified Kurfürstendamm had risen to take its place.

It was saddening to be a witness to the unique dismemberment of a once mighty city into two such different and diminished halves. If London had been so divided, then it would have been as if Piccadilly Circus was the heart of West London but with its theatres in ruins, while Westminster and Buckingham Palace were under Communist control.

In West Berlin, there were children everywhere, while the East felt empty. The emptiness was more attractive to me at the time, because being stuck with a throng of happy families only highlighted my loneliness. If I could have just eaten some Malayan food, then I would have felt so much better but, shockingly, there was not even a Chinese restaurant in Berlin.

I think that Tom could sense that I was falling into a funk of depression, so he took me to the British army's Officer's Mess for dinner one night. Under a photograph of the young Queen who had not yet been crowned, and gulping down some peppery mulligatawny soup, beloved of British colonials in India, this was the nearest thing to home I had experienced for weeks.

'We're very pleased with your progress so far, Hamid. The information has been most useful.'

'But I didn't do anything.'

'But you did. I'm sorry I can't give you much information, but you should know that you are doing valuable work for England.'

'I hope so, I think.'

'Don't you want to help England?'

'I think so, I think. There has been a lot of talk of independence for Malaya, so I think I should probably be doing valuable work for Malaya instead.'

'Perhaps Malaya will have its independence, but it will always remain under the protection and guidance of Great Britain, and you can be on the inside, have a front row seat, have your hand on the driving wheel.'

Tom's uncharacteristic mixing of metaphors suggested to me that he was trying a little too hard to sell something, but these were in-between times for a Malayan like me. We were not yet independent from Britain, and I didn't even know what independence might mean. Who would be my new masters? Would I be the new master? Perhaps, Tom had realized that his sales pitch had not been entirely successful, so he took a different approach.

'Malaya is fighting a war for its very survival against Communist terrorists as we speak. Granted, you are not fighting them in the jungle but you're fighting against the threat of Communism at its very source. You can achieve more here to protect Malaya than an entire battalion in the jungle of Malaya.'

'I'm just not sure if the fate of Communism lies in Katrin Schule's underwear, and to be honest, I'm not entirely sure I want to know.'

'Rome wasn't destroyed in a day, Hamid. There must be many different angles of attack. Taken individually, they may not appear to amount to much, but taken together, they make the difference between defeat and victory. That's one thing I learnt from the war.'

'Is this what you did in Yugoslavia during the war?'

'Not exactly. I blew up bridges that were rebuilt in a week. That sort of thing. Nothing terribly heroic.'

'The people at my local pub say you're a hero. They say Hitler sent an entire army division to track you down.'

'That's an exaggeration.'

'So, you did do something?'

Tom shuffled the salt and pepper.

'Yes, I did do something,' he finally admitted.

'But in The Residence, you told me you would never fight for King and country.'

Tom was pouring salt into his food. In the dry air of Berlin, the salt flowed freely, unlike in Malaya, where the humidity congeals it into a block.

'People do change, Hamid. I changed my mind because of my father. I admire that man so much. More than you may ever know. I would do anything for him.'

'He told you join up?'

'No, he would never do that,' Tom smiled to himself, but the smile quickly disappeared. 'Do you remember Uncle Jack, my mother's brother? He was my father's best friend and then he died in Gallipoli in the first war. My father had a safe job in naval intelligence, and he never forgave himself. I watched his pain every single time my mother mentioned Uncle Jack. She taunted him with it. Why did he survive and Jack die? So, when the war came, I joined up immediately and volunteered for the most dangerous jobs around. I was parachuted into Yugoslavia to work with the partisans. In retrospect, it was insane because the chances of survival were virtually nil. There's even a rumour that I only survived because I joined the KGB there. Can you imagine, me joining the KGB?'

Tom laughed at the idea. I did not want to imagine it, but I was now.

'But what they don't know is,' Tom continued, 'I didn't want to survive. I think I wanted to die for my father's sake. To stop that woman.'

I was not expecting a confession from Tom, so I didn't know how to react.

'Oh,' I said. 'Your mother seems nice to me.'

'You don't know her. You don't know what she has done to my father. And I'm not sure if I can forgive her, even if he has. I've made a mess with this salt, I must put it away. Anyway, my point is that we all have different reasons for doing what we do. Some do it for King and country, or whatever your country is, Hamid. Some do it just to survive another day. Some as penance for their sins, or to win the hand of their fair maiden,' Tom looked squarely at me. 'But I did it and continue doing it for my father. To protect him and his world. And perhaps that will be your reason? Don't you want to make your father proud?'

'More than anything,' I admitted. 'So how did you get that scar on your face? Was it the Germans?'

'No,' he seemed to find the thought grimly amusing. 'This was done by a woman. I pulled her out of a bad situation and for thanks she slashed my face. It is remarkable, what drowning people will do to survive.'

'And did she survive?'

'For a while.'

'So, my friends in the pub were right. You are a hero.'

'There were no heroes in Yugoslavia. Only victims and monsters. But if your friends think I am a hero, then that's what is important. That's how the mystique of what you and I do leads to victory. We give courage and hope to our people and spread fear among the enemy. The stories told become more impressive than the actual fact. And I know that Clare is impressed.'

The mention of Clare caught my attention.

'Is she?'

'Oh yes. I spoke to her last night, and she actually asked after you for the first time. She doesn't know you're in Berlin, but she knows we're working together and she's very impressed. If you do a little bit more, Hamid, then I think you will succeed with Clare. You do want that, don't you?'

'More than anything in the world.'

Talk of fighting for a faraway Malaya that did not yet exist as a country had left me more confused than moved, as did the notion of fighting against the perils of Communism, but the possibility of winning back Clare was intoxicating. Tom Pelham had his hand on the wheel on the road to that victory and as I slurped down another bowl of mulligatawny, I resolved that I would remain under his protection and guidance.

'Feeling better?' Tom asked.

'Yes. Much.'

'Good, because Katrin Schule called. I think she's ready to receive you in the East. But remember, don't do anything with her in the East. You must bring her back to the West if you're going to seal the deal, so to speak.'

Chapter 28

Unlike the official language of the Western zones, Katrin Schule was very happy to talk of a permanently divided Germany by fastidiously referring to West Berlin as the Western sector and East Berlin as simply being Berlin, the capital of an East Germany that she would only call the Deutsche Demokratische Republik.

She wanted to take me to a concert of Johann Sebastian Bach 'because he was from the DDR'. When I met her outside the concert hall in East Berlin, I found that she had been subtly transformed with an actual hairstyle and a splash of lipstick that offered more than a hint of femininity. She was even wearing some jewellery—a little gold necklace that I could see because she had left her top buttons undone. She, nonetheless, remained the image of Socialist severity and so I immediately launched into my rehearsed diatribe about the horrors of Anarcho-Syndicalism, which I assumed was catnip for Communists. But she stopped me.

'No politics tonight. Tonight, we listen to the music.'

I was happy to comply because I was just repeating what Tom had told me to say—he had seemed quite passionate about the subject. I spent the first part of the concert spying my prey and asking myself if I could really go through with my mission to seduce her. She really was quite short, but then I'm not terribly tall either. Both of us had presumably grown up with the deprivations of a wartime diet—although when most Malayans had to subsist on ghastly yams, my family had never gone without rice.

She may not have been my dish of choice, but I was not averse to some chubbiness, and she was quite pretty, as well as surprisingly pleasant company. There were surely worse ways to fulfil my patriotic duty—although I really wasn't sure what my country was in 1953, I could probably, quite literally, lie back and think of England.

I decided to follow her instructions and listened to the music. I told Katrin Schule that it was apt that we were listening to the Brandenburg Concertos, because we were in Brandenburg.

'Brandenburg was the home of Prussian militarism.'

'But didn't Bach write this for the King of Prussia?'

'No, not exactly. But that is all history, now Bach is music for children,' she whispered.

I adore Bach for his melodic lightness, and I ignore his complexity, so I agreed with Katrin Schule's DDR assessment that Bach was safely for children. It was a delight to be finally listening to some music with a tune and not that modern jazz stuff.

After the concert, I guided her through the stalls in a gentlemanly manner, taking the opportunity to assess the view from behind, which did turn out to be bigger than I had previously calculated. As we left the theatre, I became worried that my evening with Katrin Schule appeared to be coming to an early end. An awkward silence fell between us as we stood next to a familiar Soviet military staff car.

'Is this the same car I saw the other day?' I asked.

'Yes. Probably. The Russians enjoy culture, and we must learn from the Soviet Union.'

The crowd parted for the Soviet officer as he emerged from the theatre, and walking two steps behind him, was the woman with the stylish hat, now wearing a different stylish hat. He opened the car door for her, but she seemed to hardly notice his presence. She entered and he closed the door firmly, making his way to the other side. Once everyone was seated, the car sped off at an alarmingly high speed.

'Do you know her?' Katrin Schule asked me.

'No.'

'You look at her like you know her.'

'No, I don't.'

'Perhaps she reminds you of somebody?'

'No. No, she doesn't.'

'It is still early. Shall we take a walk?'

It was still early, but it was already very dark, and the street lighting in the Soviet sector was far poorer than in the West. We walked deeper into East Berlin and up a hill. I didn't know Berlin had any hills. For a short while, we were walking alongside workers going home after a long day's job, but they soon branched off in a different direction. All the while, there was a steady stream of people carrying suitcases heading in the opposite direction. As we walked away from people, we passed the ruins of war. Eventually, we came to an area that had either been missed by the bombers or had received special treatment since the war. The apartment blocks had been rebuilt and it was quiet. All the life and all the children and all the bright lights of West Berlin were hemmed into an unnatural isolated island but here, where there was room to breathe, there were no people. I had been told that before the war, Berlin had been as busy as London and growing even faster. Now, it was like a ghost ship.

'Can I ask you a question, Comrade Katrin. I don't mean to be impertinent but how do you come to speak such excellent English?'

'I could ask you the same question.'

'I'm from Malaya.' Judging by the quizzical look on her face I realized that my self-evident answer was not self-evident to her. 'Malaya is a British colony, so we speak English.'

'You are a product of British Imperialism.'

'I was educated in English. I mean, I was conditioned by the imperialist running dogs.' That hurt to say, but I needed to play the part. 'What about you?'

'My parents were Communists.'

'I see.'

'No, you don't. My parents believed that English would become the language of international Communism as soon as the Socialist revolution spread to America.'

'That didn't exactly happen.'

'It will.'

'What do your parents do?'

'My father was murdered by the National Socialists before the war. My mother died in Dresden. Can I ask you a question, Comrade Hamid? Why are you a Socialist?'

I quickly summoned up one of Tom's lectures to me. 'I believe in freedom, justice, and above all, equality. I think the Soviet model will be the fairest and most efficient method for the redistribution of wealth in Malaya.' Although I really did believe in freedom and justice, the closest I had ever come to the efficient redistribution of wealth was telling one of my servants to carry my luggage in both hands and not just one.

'That's good to hear,' said Katrin Schule as she searched for something in her bag.

'But I still have much to learn about Socialism, if you will teach me.'

'Yes, yes, of course.' She pulled out her keys. 'I live here.'

This news took me by surprise. I hadn't realized that we had been walking towards her apartment. I didn't know what to do next and even through the darkness, I sensed that neither did Katrin Schule. She was looking at the ground and not at me.

'You live here,' I said.

'Yes. I live here.'

'I see. It looks jolly nice.'

We stood in silence hoping that one of us would figure out what to say next. She took the plunge.

'Would you like to come up?' she blurted out.

This was all very fast for me. I hadn't even been wined and dined, and already she was expecting me to go to her apartment. What did she think I was? I was very excited, that's what I was. And I was extremely pleased with myself because clearly, I truly was a very attractive man who could beat down any woman's defences without even trying. But I also remembered Tom's instructions that I had to take her back to the West.

'Or, here's a thought, or we could go to my place in the West.'

'But I live right here. This is so much more convenient. If you come up, then I can teach you about socialism. About dialectical materialism, means of production, surplus value, even agitation.'

I really wasn't entirely sure where this was heading but, in the darkness, I was beginning to see Katrin Schule in a new light and I was also feeling a surprisingly distinct sensation of an agitation within myself. I imagined that she had not led an amorous life, and that perhaps for her, these Marxist buzzwords actually constituted flirtation. Or perhaps she really did want to teach me about Socialism.

If I went with her upstairs then would it lead to two, maybe three minutes of ecstasy or two, maybe three hours of a lecture on the labour theory of value? I really needed a clear signal, but none was forthcoming as she continued staring at the ground. I remembered, because it ate away at me every single day, my nauseating crassness with Clare in the stables, and I didn't want to repeat that mistake. And when I remembered Clare, I thought that I should stay true to her, even if it was a tad too late for that.

'It is getting late, Comrade Katrin. I should return to the Western sector before the border is closed for the night.'

She made the slightest of sounds. I could barely see her in the darkness, so I couldn't tell if she was disappointed or relieved. But why would she be relieved?

'You don't understand,' she said, grabbing my arm. 'You must come upstairs with me.'

The agitation of an old familiar noise buzzed through my body when she grabbed me, but as I stepped towards her and saw her a little better, I remembered Tom's instructions that I must take her to the West.

'I really must go, Comrade Katrin. But I would like to see you again, so that you can teach me about Socialism.'

'Yes. Of course.'

Again, was she disappointed or relieved?

'We must meet again. But if you must go, then could you deliver something to my cousin? He lives in the French sector. It's just a letter. The address is on the envelope.'

'Certainly.'

'There's no need to tell anybody about it. It's just a private letter.'

'I understand.'

'You can call me directly on this telephone number. And do you have a direct telephone number? It is very inconvenient leaving a message at the number you gave me.'

'Yes, I do.'

I gave her the number of the telephone in my bedroom, and then we shook hands.

'I will see you again very soon, Comrade Katrin.'

'I would like that, and please, just call me Katrin.'

I practically skipped back to the U-Bahn station feeling overwhelmed by an intense excitement because I was obviously utterly irresistible to women. I had even broken down the Iron Curtain of a German Communist so nothing could stop me feeling pleased with myself, not even having to jump out of the way of a speeding Soviet military staff car.

Chapter 29

And then Joseph Stalin died.

This set in motion a train of events that would change all our lives forever. I first became aware that something peculiar had happened when I switched on the East German radio on the morning of 5 March, and instead of the usual propaganda, I heard Tchaikovsky's 'Pathetique' being played on an endless loop.

'Malenkov and Beria are in charge now in Moscow now,' a distinctly anxious Tom told me. 'Maybe this changes everything, maybe it changes nothing.'

'And who are Malenkov and Beria?'

'Malenkov's a nobody, a yes-man, but Beria is the head of the KGB and is Stalin's butcher. Was Stalin's butcher. Now he's his own man. If he stays true to form, then he'll kill everyone, but maybe he'll surprise us all. Funny people, these Communists. They don't have any yesterdays, only a continuous stream of todays. We British only have yesterday. Meanwhile, you carry on as normal. Go and see Katrin and find out what the FDJ are thinking. Ulbricht and his gang must be nervous. And take this watch. For some strange reason, you don't have one and you need to know the time.'

'But I don't want to know the time.'

'Don't be ridiculous. You have a job to do, and you must know the time. If it makes you feel any better, then you can think of the watch as an early graduation present. Congratulations. Now bugger off.'

Tom had given me a Glashütte. It was a good, solid German watch, but I put it on unhappily. My time had always been my father's or my school's, and Irma wanted it to be hers. This watch told me that my time now belonged to Tom Pelham, and presumably his Queen. The watch told me I was no longer a child or a student. This was my first job and Tom was my first boss. I may be an adult, but I didn't feel like one, because surely, an adult owns his own time. I wanted to share that time with somebody. I stared at the watch hoping to see Clare's face, but all I saw was my time running down.

In an ambling disconsolate mood, I delivered the letter for Katrin Schule as she had requested and tried calling her telephone. There was no answer, but I crossed into the Soviet sector anyway.

Over time, the border guards and I had become accustomed to each other. We were not exactly friendly, but we would nod to each other. But today, they didn't seem to know how to treat me. Yesterday, they were curt, but today, was I a friend or the enemy?

Every time I crossed the single painted white line of the border, I could sense the different moods of these two completely different worlds. Today, the predictable stream of refugees heading westwards had thinned somewhat. Today, in the East, I found an unsettling mood of uncertainty. I looked at Tom's watch, peculiarly happy. In the East, Tom's time had immediately lost its power over me. It was as if the watch was running slowly backwards or making great leaps forwards into a glorious future. Neither Tom nor my father or Mr Hargreaves could see me on this side of the border. Here, I was my own boss. In the Communist East, I was a free man.

I was walking fast to Katrin Schule's apartment, which was difficult to find in the light of day. When I got there, I didn't know which building was hers, let alone which apartment. The only place I could think of to find her, was the FDJ headquarters. But I wanted to keep my pursuit of her a secret, so I searched the streets. I didn't know where she could possibly be. Katrin Schule had been swallowed up into an East Berlin that was still watched over by Joseph Stalin wherever the eye turned.

I was expecting to find a crowd of mourners to be gathering at the statue of Joseph Stalin on his Stalinallee, and although I saw two women weeping, everyone else seemed to be keeping their distance—as if uncertain as to whether it was safe to approach. Stalin may have been dead, but his statue still hummed with power, as if there was an orchestra buried beneath playing a tune nobody could recognize.

Stalin had been a constant presence in my life, even in faraway Malaya, where he had inhabited our imaginations briefly as a force for hope during the war and had then immediately reverted back to being perceived as pure evil. He had been the enemy, a friend, and then the enemy again. He had been a presence throughout everything I had ever known, and now, he was dead.

I was passing a Ministry, when I saw a familiar Soviet military staff car pulling in. Several middle-aged DDR bigwigs had gathered to welcome the car as it arrived. They greeted the Soviet officer with a degree of obsequious abasement that I thought only the most feudal of Malays could achieve when meeting The Sultan. With the death of Stalin, this Soviet officer's standing had risen, so clearly something had changed.

Having lost Katrin Schule's scent and having no further legitimate reason to be constantly entering East Berlin, Tom enrolled me in a university course in the East without even bothering to ask me. The course was meant to be on German literature, so I don't know why the lecturer (who looked suspiciously like a German version of Mr Hargreaves) was talking about the works of the Russian author Maxim Gorky. After the first lecture, I decided to rebel. Even I could see that my sense of freedom in the East was an illusion. I needed to go back to London, to Clare, and to my future. It was an adult decision.

'I can't do it, it's all in German,' I complained to Tom.

'Then you had better learn German very fast.'

'Why can't you send me back to London?'

'Even if you have to study Gorky in German, you will still get a better grade than if you sat for your actual exams in London. This way you get a 2–1 by this summer.'

'But I've lost Katrin Schule. What more can I do here?'

'A lot. You're one of the best operatives I've ever had, and I've told that to Clare.'

Tom's constant use of Clare as an emotional bribe was beginning to make me resent her a little, but I had made my decision to get back to London and take my chances with Clare, or perhaps have a springtime with Margaret or Hermione.

'You are going to study Maxim Gorky,' Tom ordered. 'And while you're in the East, I want you to take this piece of chalk and put a small cross on some walls. I'll tell you where in time. And I thought you might like to know that Hermione is getting married. A banker. Very appropriate. You have not been invited to the wedding.'

Although I doubted marriage would put a halt to Hermione's true nature, I was prepared to scratch her off the list. That still left Margaret. I was absolutely determined to stand my ground, but then Tom made a compelling counterargument.

'Stop complaining and get back to work.'

So, it was as a student that I began crossing the border on a daily basis. On my second day, I saw Katrin Schule. I was subtly marking a wall with a tiny chalk cross when I spotted her on the street and started following from a safe distance, as I had been taught. I didn't want to approach her in a crowd. I had to wait until she would be alone. When she entered an apartment building, I leapt forward and caught the door before it closed. She was looking at her mail in the hallway.

'Hamid? What are you doing here?'

'I'm studying in the East now.'

'Yes, but what are you doing here?'

'I saw you in the street. What is this place?'

'I live here.'

'You do?'

'The other place, yes, that was temporary accommodation.'

'I've been looking for you. You wouldn't answer your phone.'

'Joseph Stalin has died.'

'I know. Was he answering your calls?'

'Do not make jokes about Comrade Stalin. Many things have changed. It has been difficult for me.'

'I'm sorry. Did he mean a lot to you?'

'Yes. Everything.'

'He meant a lot to me as well.'

We looked at each other in the privacy and silence of the hallway. Until that moment, I had not realized that I was attracted to her. She had a look that I had never seen before, something like Margaret when she had been at her most vulnerable but with a hint of a pent-up rage and a growing determination. I was gripped by a surge of excitement because I knew that she wanted me to touch her. And then she lunged at me, opened her mouth as wide as she could and attached herself to my face. I instinctively opened my mouth as wide as she had and we desperately attacked each other, as if we were gnawing our way through a wheel of cheese.

I had never thought of myself as having a particularly good physique, but I was being treated like a sexual object, and it was quite nice as she kneaded my buttocks like an eager baker. Because she was so short; I was holding onto her as if she were a bag of flour that was constantly slipping out of my grasp. She pulled away from me and looked up with her big, dilated eyes.

'The death of Comrade Stalin has made me very confused and frightened.'

I had never before thought of Joseph Stalin's potential as an aphrodisiac, but I was quite happy to exploit it.

'Yes,' I whispered. 'He was a powerful leader.' My words appeared to send a pulse of excitement through her. 'He was the Great Helmsman.'

'That's Mao.'

And then she attached herself to my face again. We pressed our bodies together as she pushed me against the wall. It was extremely exciting.

'Can we go up to your apartment?' I asked.

'No. My brother is there.'

'Then come to my place in the West.'

She searched my face for her answer.

'Yes. But not now. Now you must go, Hamid. We cannot be seen together.'

While continuously rubbing against each other like two blind drunkards, I distractedly wrote down my address, and then she pushed me towards the front door, taking a final opportunity to grab every bit of me that she could.

'I'll call you when I can come over,' she said. 'Do not come here again. Leave now, and walk away quickly. Do not look back.'

One final kiss, if that's what it was, and I was pushed out the door. I found it hard to suppress a smile as I walked down the street in an elated daze. *My goodness*, I thought to myself, *I really am extraordinarily attractive to women.*

It seemed impossible that we were simply so foreign to each other that we might be blank pages upon which we could imagine anything, and instead, I assumed it was my air of sophistication or my exotic good looks. I concluded that the magic mustn't be clinically dissected, and it simply had to be all of me— albeit in the case of Katrin Schule, helped by a sprinkle of Joseph Stalin. But if my essence could be put in a bottle, then I could make a fortune.

I remained in a state of blissful smugness through all my classes, of which I did not understand a single word, and beyond, to when I was walking home. Spring was in full bloom, and greenness was even budding in the grey of East Berlin, where every single tree had been cut down for firewood during the war. With the death of Stalin, the cold wind from Siberia had gone and been replaced by an invitingly warm breeze from the Atlantic. No matter how hard I tried I could not successfully imagine Katrin Schule wearing one, but I was pleased that soon the summer dresses would arrive.

It was when I was chalking one of my crosses that I saw fashion's first spring swallow striding down the street. It was the woman in the stylish hat, now wearing a stylish summer hat and a swaying white dress and carrying a bunch of bananas in a string bag. I decided to follow her.

Perhaps my magic would work on her too.

Chapter 30

I followed her through various twists and turns, occasionally losing her scent, but by quickly analysing her potential choices, finding her again.

It was as if I actually remembered some of the surveillance techniques that Tom had taught me on the streets of London, and it seemed that I was quite good at it. She disappeared, but I found her in a shop. Had I been stalking her in London or West Berlin, the task would have been much harder. Here in the East, there were so few shops where I might lose her, and the few that existed were so sparsely stocked, that I could watch her with ease. Her hat obscured her face, but this was the first chance I had had to look at her. Her fashion may have been light and summery, but her beauty had a severe and humourless wintry darkness that broke into warmth when she stopped to chat with a group of young schoolgirls. They clearly knew each other, and when she gave them the bananas she'd been holding, they were all thrilled.

She continued walking without any further evasion until she entered an empty café, choosing a table at the back. I kept watch from outside, judging the situation. This café was far better appointed than any other I had seen in East Berlin. It looked like it had actual

Italian coffee and not the usual ersatz muck that made Malayan coffee taste palatable by comparison. Surely this café was reserved for Communist aristocracy, so the lumpen proletariat was unlikely to enter. Plus, the fact that she was now reading a book suggested that she was not expecting any company.

Was it safe to enter? I felt like I was back in the corridor at the Pelhams deciding whether or not to open what turned out to be the wrong door. *What could be the harm*, I thought to myself. I didn't want to talk to her, she frightened me too much for that. I just wanted to smell her perfume, because then I would know who and what she was. And because the café had Italian coffee, I decided to enter.

Drinking coffee at an unknown establishment is a task filled with danger. So I ordered an espresso to test the quality of the waters and sat at the table next to her. I spied her from the corner of my eye and breathed in deeply. I was confused. She was not wearing any perfume. She offered me no hint of her past, present, or future, and I felt a deep sense of regret that who she was would forever remain unknown to me. She asked for something in Italian from the presumably Italian and presumably Communist proprietor, who seemed reluctant to fulfil the order. But eventually he acquiesced and did it, and it involved him disappearing into the basement. She returned to reading her book.

'Why are you following me?' she asked me in English with some kind of European accent. 'Don't look at me. Keep drinking your coffee. Why are you following me? It makes me nervous that you are following me.'

'I'm not following you. I just wanted a coffee.'

'I gave you many chances to stop following me,' she continued, disregarding my feeble lie. 'Who are you? What do you want?'

I was lonely and I wanted to talk to her. I wanted to tell her about my recent fumble with Kristin Schule and how she reminded me of Margaret and Clare, but I couldn't tell her any of that.

'I'm a student, from Malaya,' I told her into my coffee cup. 'My name is Hamid. What is your name?'

'My name is not your concern. Finish your coffee, pay Franco, and then leave. And do not ever speak to me again or I might kill you myself if The Colonel doesn't get to you first.'

I had been rejected by women before, many times, but none of them had ever threatened to kill me, so I was feeling a bit shaken. I got up to leave.

'Hamid, forget everything about me and leave this place. It is not safe here.'

I gave some money to Franco, who had re-emerged from the basement, and hurriedly returned to the West.

Chapter 31

‘Who is the Colonel?’ I asked Tom in the Officer’s Mess a few days later.

‘There are many colonels, Hamid. Do you mean Colonel Calloway over there?’

‘No. Not a colonel from here. In the East.’

‘There are many colonels in the East as well. Why are you asking?’

‘I’m just curious because somebody mentioned “The Colonel” like I should know who he was.’

This seemed to pique Tom’s attention. ‘Did they mention it in a nice way or a not nice way?’

‘A not nice way. A Soviet staff car drove past, and somebody said, “That’s The Colonel”.’

‘It’s surprising that anybody would actually say that because everybody normally pretends he doesn’t exist. He’s the head of the KGB in Berlin. The official head is somebody else, but The Colonel is the real head.’

‘So, he’s your opposite number in the East?’

‘You could say that,’ said Tom, somewhat pleased with himself. ‘But I’m a pussycat compared to him. He is the most sneaky, vile, and murderous monster that has ever lived. And since Stalin’s death, he has become even more powerful because he’s Beria’s man. I should think he’ll be returning to Moscow soon to take over the KGB. You stay away from him, Hamid. What you do is already dangerous enough.'

I didn't like the sound of that.

'It is?'

'Of course it is.'

'But I'm just putting little crosses on walls.'

'Yes, but in East Berlin. I don't want to frighten you, but I also don't want you to take this lightly. There are tanks facing each other all along the Iron Curtain and bombers circling overhead, and you're behind the lines.'

'I am a bit frightened now.'

'Just do as I tell you and don't play any games and you'll be fine. Don't worry. I understand that Margaret is back in London.'

'Has she asked after me?'

'No. But she might if you return as a hero. And you could be a hero, you know. Have you seen Katrin Schule recently?'

Weeks passed as I waited for Katrin to call me, but no matter how much I stared at my telephone, it did not ring. Did the telephone even work?

Spring took hold of Berlin turning it into a lovely summer as I continued my studies. Even my German improved a little. I made supposed friends with some of my fellow students, but how can you be true friends when both sides are suspiciously hiding what they really are? From the babbles of my childhood home to boarding school and then Malaya Hall in London, I had always been surrounded by people, and now I was utterly alone and completely dependent on Tom for company. He drip-fed me information from England (Clare did not want to see me/Clare was proud of me, Margaret had left London for Kenya of all places, and

Hermione's wedding was marred only by the suggestion that she was already pregnant). I knew I was being emotionally manipulated into staying true to my task, but I was also powerless to resist because I was even more isolated from the outside world than the city of Berlin was.

Meanwhile, the values that Tom spouted became my values and my purpose in life: spying for England was my patriotic duty, and it would win me the hand of the English woman of my dreams. I should have been happy, because he was offering me everything I wanted, an excellent degree for no work that would assure my future, but also a delaying until the last possible moment of all the drab certainties of that future. And he was offering me Clare, who knew who she was and what she wanted to be, which would negate the need for me to ever do the same.

Being Malayan was losing meaning to me. I was an aspect of England, and how could I argue otherwise when I spent so much time with British Army officers who were excitedly preparing for the Queen's Coronation. There were only two places where I could catch a glimpse of a disappearing me. One was in a Turkish restaurant in the Neukölln district in the American sector, where I was finally able to eat some glorious chilli that pumped some Malaya back into my veins, and the other was in the company of Nadia.

I called her Nadia, but I didn't know her name. In her stylish hats and summer dresses that favoured white and navy blue, she was easy to spot on the quiet streets of East Berlin. I would follow her. At first, she would try to evade me, but I would break her down with my persistence and my silent reassurance that I would always keep my distance. We never met, never spoke to each other, but I learned her habits and routines, which were as solitary as my own.

She would return to the same threadbare shops without ever having to queue and drink coffee at Franco's, where I would join her. She would be seated at one end and I at the other. Together, we would read our books with me spying on her, trying to imagine not only who she was but also who I might be.

I knew so little about Europe that I simply could not imagine where she might be from. But I believed I could sense a sadness from her. Her smile was sudden and infrequent, usually seen whenever she met her gaggle of schoolgirl friends and then freely gave them whatever meagre luxuries she had managed to scavenge from the shops.

Sometimes, the Soviet staff car would arrive to take her away, but often we sat, reading together for hours. We went to the cinema together, with her seated at one end and I at the other. We watched the newsreels proclaiming the reconstructive might of Communism in a staccato voice, as if the words were being produced not by a human but by an angry typewriter. We watched the new and uncrowned Tsar in Moscow and a benign looking Lavrentiy Beria waving at the happy May Day crowds and receiving flowers from children. He did not look to me like he was or could ever have been Stalin's butcher as Tom had suggested. Then we watched Hollywood Westerns, and even if I couldn't see how they spoke of class struggle, we enjoyed them together in the darkness.

Fate had decided that I could not actually speak to this elegant woman I called Nadia. Therefore, I couldn't open my big fat mouth and ruin everything by revealing that I was still just a boy. Instead, in our silence, I began to imagine that we might be creating a shared bond in our loneliness and difference from everything around us. In my silence, I was perhaps forging my first adult friendship with a woman, knowledge I could carry back to Clare.

This had become my Berlin, and it was looking like nothing would ever change it, until one June morning, when my telephone rang.

Katrin Schule was on the other end.

Chapter 32

So, it turns out my telephone did indeed work. Its silence spoke not of its disrepair, but of the absence of people calling me.

When the telephone rang that June morning, I was preparing to go to the Officer's Mess to watch television and witness the beginning of a new era: the coronation of Queen Elizabeth II. I was feeling terribly excited because it was going to be a welcome break from my routine, and because this would be the first time I would have ever actually watched television. The British Army had built a series of broadcasting relay stations so that we could watch the BBC transmission of the coronation as it was happening and not, as was usually the case, see it days later in a newsreel. I was going to see a young woman ascend to the throne for which I was working.

'Comrade Hamid,' Katrin said very officially. 'I can deliver the copies of *Das Kapital* that you have requested.'

'Thank you.'

'I do not know when I will be able to make the delivery but please be available for each evening of this week.'

'I will.'

'Goodbye.'

At the Officer's Mess, I told Tom that Katrin Schule would be visiting.

'Good. Finally,' he said. 'You stay here and watch the television broadcast today. Don't go back to your flat until I tell you.' And then he went to the corner to make a phone call.

If any army had chosen to invade whatever remained of the British Empire on 2 June 1953, then they would have captured it with even greater speed than the Imperial Japanese Army had won Malaya in 1942. Everybody was that captivated by the coronation, either watching it on television or listening to its broadcast on the radio. The British Army officers in Berlin (joined by military representatives from the republics of America, France, and West Germany) gave their professional opinions on the display of their comrades in London.

'Bloody Guardsmen, they're so full of themselves,' said a Lieutenant Colonel as he ordered a whiskey. 'They should do some real soldiering. I say, Jones, could I have some hot water.'

'I think they're doing a splendid job,' said a Colonel. 'Makes you proud to be British.'

'Hear, hear,' responded a few.

There was absolute silence in the room when the procession and the camera entered Westminster Abbey. For ten centuries, nobody outside a select coterie of courtiers had ever before been a witness to this moment. I wasn't even sure if we should be allowed to see this, and yet, I was riveted. For me, it was as though I was spying on the epicentre of an Empire upon which the sun had not yet entirely set, that had dominated the lives of millions around the world for over two hundred years. For the British soldiers, it must have been a renewal of something far older still.

I had been very young and confused when I had witnessed the coronation of His Highness to the Sultanship of my home state in Malaya, and I was now beginning to understand how his ceremony had merged Westminster Abbey with the court of Siam in order to be confusing. The television commentary explained the history of various arcane words and gestures, but I didn't need for it to be explained. It was ancient, I was somehow connected to this, and this was connected to the past. That was all I needed to know.

I don't think I would have recognized the exact moment when Elizabeth officially became Queen if the army officers had not suddenly stood up and shouted, 'God save the Queen,' which was terrifying and stirring. Then they moved to the window as their on-duty comrades boomed an artillery salute followed by volleys of rifle fire that quickened my heartbeat further. What was happening to me? I was feeling patriotism, but for where? For my father, it would have been simple. Although much reduced by the shocking arrival of the Imperial Japanese Army, his allegiance to the new Queen remained. But I knew different, because Salim had told me that a change was coming.

'I rather regret not joining them now,' said a Colonel.

I never spoke to these army officers, and they never spoke to me. I was only ever Tom's guest, but I was now in awe of them. They all seemed to know what was happening, what all the symbolic gestures meant. Basically, they knew how to put on a really good show. My grandfather must have been overwhelmed when all those decades ago in Malaya, he first saw this kind of display with warships, sailors, marines, marching bands, and Sikh soldiers. It must have told of dignity, strength, and protection. And now, I was in the heart of it all and my senses were being overwhelmed. But I couldn't help remembering the day when the Japanese soldiers had arrived, something that was not supposed to happen. I wanted to talk to somebody about my confusion, about why I was so moved, but I was alone.

'They look splendid', said a Major, in the rare instance when an officer below the rank of colonel dared speak. 'Troops from the Empire', which brought a snigger from his brother officers. Even they suspected that this might be the last flowering of the once mighty, now waning, Empire.

'Canadians. I was liaising with them during D-Day. All volunteers, you know.'

Canada. The cold of Canada was so far away from the heat of Malaya, and yet I was somehow connected to Canada.

As the ceremony inside Westminster Abbey concluded, a procession led by soldiers from India, Africa, the Pacific Islands, the West Indies, and what was then called the White Dominions, moved along the wet streets of a rainy London to Buckingham Palace. Did I catch a glimpse of the Royal Malay Regiment? It was hard to tell through the unfamiliar fuzzy black and white of the television.

'She must be cold. Who is she?'

In an open top carriage was a large woman, even when seated she was clearly impressively tall as she waved cheerily to the crowd.

'I think that's the Queen of Tonga.'

But what caught my attention was the man sitting in the carriage with the Queen of Tonga, who looked tiny compared to her. Wearing a masterfully peaked *tengkolok* on his head, was the Sultan of Johore. My heart leapt. I have absolutely no connection with the State of Johore, it does not neighbour my home state, and felt as far away as Canada, but finally, not just in the coronation but after months in England and Berlin, finally, I was seeing something of Malaya.

Much later, I was told that Noël Coward, when asked who the man was in the carriage with the Queen of Tonga said, 'Her lunch,' which was extremely rude. But, for me, this was not a matter of jest. It was the moment I saw an allegiance that must be mine. And then, in other carriages I saw the Sultans of Kelantan, Selangor, and Perak. I searched the television screen for a glimpse of His Highness, and therefore of my state, my country. But he was not there.

To this day, I do not know why His Highness was not at the coronation. He bristled with jealous rage if ever it was mentioned, so I never dared to ask him. He always enjoyed a good ceremony, but he may have been thankful to have missed the cold and wet carriage ride that the Sultan of Johore manfully endured. I kept my silence because the British Army officers would never have understood, and I'm not sure if I fully understood, but with the sight of the Malayan Sultans, this was now my procession.

Although I wanted desperately to see His Highness, and although, I was deeply moved by this vision of an ancient England, I had seen a reminder of my homeland, and I asked myself, *Did I serve Malaya? What did it mean to serve a nation that did not yet exist?* For my father, the answer was simple: he served his Sultan and his state. And I remembered the question that was eating away at me: Did I want to go back? It would be so much easier if I just served Clare. But as with most things Malayan for most Malayans, it mainly reminded me of food. Which is probably where lies our ultimate allegiance, and it made me determined to have some Turkish chilli.

A Major gave me a drink. 'Did you enjoy the coronation?'

'Yes, I did. Very much so.'

'Did you see any of your lot?'

'Yes. Yes, I did.'

I copied them as they raised their glasses for a toast.

'God save the Queen!'

Chapter 33

Tom sent word that I must leave the barracks hidden in the back of an army truck when troops were being sent for their sentry duty. I joined the soldiers as they jumped out of the truck and then I slipped into a car that took me back to my apartment, where Tom was waiting for me.

‘You can never be too sure in Berlin,’ said Tom.

‘But any one of those soldiers might talk about me in a bar.’

‘Them? They’re Signals Corp. They do work for me from time-to-time.’

‘Do you think I’m being watched?’

‘I don’t think so. We’ve been watching your flat to see if anybody else is and so far, the coast is clear. Everything is ready for your “date” with Katrin, except for one final ingredient. You. Are you ready?’

‘I think so. She’s just bringing some books. We’ll talk, I don’t know what else you expect me to do.’

‘I expect you to work your magic. We’ve made sure you have absolute privacy and now I want you to complete your mission with Katrin.’

‘But, how?’

‘Don’t play dumb with me, boy. I want you to seduce Katrin Schule. This is why you are in Berlin; this is your only chance to redeem yourself. You have some unholy appeal to women that I don't understand but you inflicted it on my sister, and now I expect you to put it to more positive use in the service of your new Queen.'

'But is she really my Queen? I've been thinking about it and . . .'

'How about this, Hamid. If you don't seduce Katrin Schule, then I will break your scrawny little neck. Does that help you to resolve your political, moral, or ethical problems?'

'Yes, I think so.'

'Good. Now make yourself pretty, wait for her phone call, and then give Katrin Schule the time of her life.'

After his Churchillian speech, Tom left me to prepare for Katrin's possible arrival. I desperately wanted to eat some Turkish food and thoughts of hunger occupied me while I perused my wardrobe for just the right outfit. I didn't want to come on too strong or desperate and frighten her. I wanted something casual yet devastating that said, 'What this little thing? I just threw it on.' But mostly, I didn't want Tom Pelham to break my neck, although I wasn't entirely convinced that he actually would. Tom was the nearest thing I had to a friend, but it was clear that I was only useful to him as a tool in his secretive war.

In the loneliness of my Berlin, my only friends were Nadia and Katrin. One was a woman I had never spoken to and the other, I was about to ruin. I had to believe that redeeming my earlier betrayal of Clare, and Margaret, outweighed any loyalty I might have had to Katrin, who was, after all, an enemy of my nation. But what was my nation?

It slowly became clear, through the mist of my looming personal crisis, that an evening of fun and games with Katrin Schule was precisely the distraction I needed. I began to feel a little frisky as I waited by the phone. Just when I calculated and deemed it too late for her to visit—now I could go and get some chilli—the phone suddenly rang with blistering loudness.

'I am at your door.'

'I'll let you in.'

I ran down the stairs excitedly and opened the door. She had made an effort. She did not look at all like the dour Young Socialist. She was wearing make-up, and her hair had been elegantly styled. She was also wearing incongruous white shoes, which suddenly made me hate her, or rather I hated myself because she had willingly come to me, made herself look special, and now, I was about to ruin her. But I was lonely, and she was here, and she did look quite attractive. I led her to my room.

'How are your studies progressing?' she asked.

'The German is difficult for me but I'm learning a lot about the people's struggle. Please sit down.'

We sat opposite each other in awkward silence.

'I've been thinking about you,' I said.

'Yes.'

'About that moment in the corridor.'

'Yes.'

'It was very exciting.'

'Yes.'

'I want to do more.'

'Yes.'

'And yet . . .'

'Yes?'

'Perhaps we can talk first.'

'Yes.'

More silence.

'You are a Black man,' she said.

'I am?'

'Yes. It is not a problem for me. I thought it would be, but it is not.'

'Good.'

'If we do something here, then next time we must go to the East. I have found an apartment we can go to.'

'Good.'

I stood up, clumsily took her hand, and led her to sit beside me on the bed. Not knowing what else to do, I stroked her arm with my thumb, summoning up the courage to press my hands further, which I calculated would not be resisted.

'Hamid, why do you find me attractive?'

'I just do.'

'But why? Tell me.'

'Because you're very attractive.'

'Tell me.'

'Your eyes are very nice.'

And then she lowered her eyes and gazed at her lap while I attempted to kiss her cheek.

'I do not find you attractive, Hamid.'

That stopped me.

'What?'

'The last time, when we kissed, I did. I would have done everything. I wanted to. It was very exciting.'

'Well, here I am. And here we are.'

'But I am very bourgeois.'

'I'm willing to try anything,' I said as I again leaned in to attempt a kiss.

'You don't understand. Please stop.'

I didn't stop. I felt certain there was a button my lips could press.

'Hamid, no. Not like this.'

Her words were a sudden and sickening reminder of Clare's in the stable, when I had been crassly bold. I stopped and saw that a tear was dropping down her cheek.

'You don't understand,' she said. 'I am a virgin, and I am bourgeois. I wanted to keep myself for my wedding night and you are not my husband, and we will not be married.'

'Why not?'

'What?'

'Why don't we get married?'

'You're crazy.'

Was I being crazy? Probably, but she was a sweet girl, and I was tired of being alone. It made perfect sense.

'We should get married.'

She laughed and wiped away her tear.

'And then you would live in the DDR?'

'Perhaps, or you could live in the West, or in Malaya.'

'And leave everything I know? I could never do that, even if you can. I am German and you are, I don't know what you are, but you are crazy.'

'Katrin Schule, will you marry me?'

As she looked at me, I could tell she was asking herself yes or no, and the fact that she was asking the question meant that I did not have to ask it of myself.

'I can't do this now,' she said. 'This is not how it is meant to be. I cannot do this. I must go.'

She stood up to leave and I suddenly became desperately afraid that I was losing my future wife. I remembered the gift I had been carrying for months.

'Katrin, wait. I want to give you something.' I sifted through my bag, opened the secret compartment. 'It's called Betrayal.'

I gave her the perfume. She gazed upon the luxury and mystery of the bottle, something a genie might inhabit, and smiled a girlish smile I had never imagined she possessed.

'I bought it for you. Try it.'

She gave herself a spritz that filled the room with the intoxicating scent of dark femininity. I could see that she was beguiled.

'It smells like the bourgoisie,' she laughed.

'I know, and don't they smell wonderful.'

'I cannot take it. The border guards will confiscate it. You can give it to me in the East.'

'Yes. But you must first see me here again in the West.'

'We'll see. It's getting late. I must go. I'm sorry.'

'Don't be. We'll meet again.'

'Yes.'

As she left my apartment, we did kiss. It lacked passion but it suggested friendship and companionship, which I knew was the best I could hope for.

Chapter 34

Tom seemed unconvinced when I told him that I had successfully seduced Katrin and had demanded that I find her and, as he called it, 'seal the deal'.

As far as I was concerned, I had fulfilled my task and done my duty. The deal had been sealed. But I had no power with Tom Pelham, and when he told me that I had to confirm the compromise in specific locations, either in the East or the West, I did as I was told.

Why was he so keen on these locations? But searching for Katrin in East Berlin was not an easy task. She had forbidden me from going to her apartment, so I had to search for her on the streets. As I did so, I noticed that the atmosphere had been changing in the East since the death of Joseph Stalin. After the war, the accident of a Berliner's postal code decided if they were to be a Communist or a Capitalist and after seven years, the strain was beginning to show on those who had been blessed with Communism.

The job of reconstruction was hard work with poor pay and without a hint of the little luxuries that make life bearable, unless they could afford the black market prices. Germans, I had decided, were bourgeois by nature and they liked nice things as much as me. If even an aristocrat of communism like Katrin swooned at the scent of a rich perfume, then what about others?

Recently, there had been a rise in hope because rumours and hints had been emanating from Beria's Moscow that there would be a softening in the Soviet Union's traditional hard line towards the West and towards its own people. My fellow students were nervously excited because word was spreading that industry must begin to prioritize consumer goods over reconstruction. Even the masses labouring in Berlin's wastelands were now looking forward to some new clothes and something nice to eat. But the problem with hope is that it can be dashed, and East Germany's Walter Ulbricht had a more old-fashioned vision for his people's future.

As the East Berliner's hopes were rising, mine were being dashed because even after several days of searching, I was not able to find Katrin anywhere.

After over a week of searching for my only friend in Berlin, I found Nadia enjoying the summer sun on a park bench. Even though this was a very public place, I chose to sit on a bench quite far from her. In my mind, I discussed with her my future marriage with Katrin. *Was I being foolish*, I asked myself? Where would we live, what would we do for work? My father would not be happy if I returned married to a diehard Communist, but I was convinced I could cure Katrin of her communism with some Belgian chocolates, my mother's rendang tok, and a dose of the Malayan sun.

Or could I stay in the DDR? It would solve at a stroke my confused allegiances because I would become German instead.

Nadia, I thought to myself, *was like a cat basking in the sun.* And then, like a cat, she uncurled herself as she stood up and walked away. I had no classes to attend, and I could not find Katrin, so I followed her.

We walked very far, and I lost her as she cut through a building and its courtyard. Then I caught sight of her again in the distance and continued my pursuit. It was hard to cut down the gap because I knew I had to maintain a steady pace if I didn't want to attract attention. I had lost her. This was not our usual part of town, so I could not predict where she might be. But then I saw a cinema, which was not showing our usual sort of movie. It was a Russian war movie, but I thought it possible that Nadia might be trying to broaden my education. I had, by now, developed the instinct to look around before committing, but I did not know what I was looking for.

Perhaps that man in the car was waiting for a friend and perhaps the couple were genuinely interested in that poster. I adjudged that it was safe to enter the cinema. In the flickering light of the screen, I found Nadia sitting at one end of the empty cinema, so I sat at the other. I had joined the movie at the precise moment when our hero was joyfully steeling himself to even greater sacrifice after seeing Joseph Stalin himself. I didn't speak Russian, but I could recognize Stalin's name because it was repeated as many times as the word for love is in a Malay song, and with exactly the same meaning. I was settling down to enjoy the liberation of Berlin, when I was shocked to hear a voice behind me.

'They're following you,' said Nadia. 'Don't turn around. Don't look at me.'

'But I haven't done anything wrong.'

'I don't know, and I don't care. You are in danger and you're putting me in danger also.'

'What's your name? I'm Hamid. What's your name?'

'That doesn't matter. Leave Berlin. Go back to where you come from.'

'I'm from Malaya. Where are you from?'

'Listen to me, we only have a few minutes. They're watching everything you do.'

'Then meet me in the West.'

'I think they're here. I will leave first, and you leave in ten minutes. If you get across the border, do not ever come back.'

'But I want to talk to you. I need to talk to you. You're the only friend I have.'

'Saskia.'

'What?'

'My name is Saskia. I am from Silesia. If anything happens, then you will be blamed.'

'Blamed for what? Nothing has happened.'

'Are you blind? Don't you read the newspapers? Haven't you been watching the workers? Cross the border now and do not come back, Hamid from Malaya.'

As she left, she threw two East German newspapers onto my lap. The two headlines appeared to be completely contradictory, but I paid them no heed because I had other, more exciting things on my mind. I stayed till the end of the movie. Watching scenes of the joyous liberation of Berlin, I felt alive for the first time since Christmas at the Pelhams. Partly perhaps because I had been told I was in danger but mostly because I was enjoying saying her name in my head. Saskia from Silesia.

'Where is Silesia?' I asked Tom when I was back in the West.

'It's mostly in Poland now, but until the end of the war it was part of Germany and long before that, it was part of Austria.'

'People from there must be very confused.'

'Not really. All the Germans were kicked out at the end of the war. Why do you ask?'

'No reason.'

Despite Saskia's warning, getting back across the border had been as easy as usual. My papers had been checked by East German security when I was on the U-Bahn but they let me through. And why shouldn't they? I hadn't done anything wrong, except fail to hand in an essay on Pushkin. I had been in a very good mood until Tom called me in for a chat.

'There's no more reason for you to be in Berlin,' Tom said very sternly. 'You have failed in your simple mission with Katrin Schule, so I'm sending you back to London.'

'But how do you know I failed, I mean, what makes you think I failed?'

'I just know. I am extremely disappointed in you because you are an absolute failure.'

How many times has that exact same sentence been said to me?

'I've thought about it, and you serve no purpose,' Tom continued. 'I'm going to save you from any further danger and send you back to London. But because I feel sorry for you, I'm still going to give you a 2–2.'

'But you said I would get a 2–1.'

'You are lucky I don't just fail you. And when you get back to London do not bother to get in touch with

Margaret. She's married in Kenya and expecting a baby. And if you dare to contact Clare I will be very, very unhappy. Do I make myself clear?'

'Yes.'

'Pack your things. I'm sending you back to London tomorrow.'

Chapter 35

Unlike my usual routine, I awoke very early on the morning of 17 June. It was still dark outside and I'm not even sure if I had slept at all.

Today, I was to leave Berlin after five months of having achieved absolutely nothing for either Queen or country, whatever that country may have been. I had gained for myself a 2–2, which is an honourable degree, but I felt an emptiness, because I had failed in my true goal: redemption.

Now that my Bengali namesake had finished my final exams, I would be returning to a final summer in London, before returning to Malaya empty handed. I did not want to be alone any more, but Margaret and Hermione were both married and pregnant, which was surprisingly fast, I would never see Katrin again and any thoughts about the mysterious Saskia had only ever been a ridiculous dream, and Tom had warned me away from Clare. But then again, what was the worst that he could do to me? He could kill me, but surely, he wouldn't if I won Clare first.

Yes, Clare in summer, it suddenly made absolute sense. I had first known her in the sunshine of Malaya and now, in the English summer, we could rekindle that original lost innocence without the distraction of her beautiful friends or her brother. Obviously, I would be returning without being the glorious hero I had hoped to be, but I could beg. I'm very good at begging and have won many battles through squirming and supplication. All was not lost. I would return not to London but to England, not with Katrin but for Clare.

I wanted to leave Berlin. I packed my meagre belongings with desperate speed. Just as I was about to remove the bottle of perfume from its secret pocket, I saw an electrical wire coming out of a tiny hole in the wall. There was still dust on the floor from when the hole had been drilled through the wall. This was recent and I didn't remember asking my landlord for any home improvements. Come to think of it, I didn't remember ever meeting a landlord. I followed the wire from the wall as it led to my bedside table and up the lamp until I found, hidden in the lampshade, a microphone.

Why was there a microphone in my bedroom? Who could have put a microphone in my bedroom? Tom, of course. But why? What had I been doing in my bedroom that warranted a microphone? I thought of my embarrassing exercise regime but then I realized, Katrin, of course. How else could Tom have known I had done nothing with Katrin if he had not heard our conversation?

I now understood the true purpose of my mission in Berlin. What on earth had I been thinking all this time? It was now obvious to me that Tom was not operating a match-making service to pair lonely Malayans with virginal Communists so that the lonely Malayan could win the hand of his sister. I was in Berlin to seduce Katrin in my apartment while Tom recorded the evidence and then for the rest of her life Katrin could be blackmailed into working for British Intelligence, and I also. I felt violated and betrayed by Tom Pelham. Yes, he was being loyal to his sister but what about me? I was angry with Tom, but I also felt proud of Katrin because her bourgeois niceties had stopped us both from actually doing anything.

And yet, what was a sound recording without a film? I looked around the room for where Tom may have put a camera. Maybe my dark suspicions were all in my head? Surely Tom was my friend, but then I spied a dark corner up above. I stood on a chair and found embedded in the ceiling cornice a camera lens. I felt deflated. Katrin and I had not done anything truly embarrassing, but I was probably now England's pawn forever, even before my own nation had come into being. I do like to have the illusion of a choice in these things. And Clare was disappearing from me. It would be very difficult to marry Clare when her brother had evidence that I was nothing but a disgusting cad. I was probably done for, but what about Katrin? I thought of her plump face, experienced in war and hard in her politics but innocent in love, and I felt an immense warmth for her at that moment. Perhaps I owed it to her to warn her that we had been filmed? There would be nothing she could do about it but at least she would know I was not to blame. My flight out of Berlin was not for four hours, and I thought about making one last trip into the East. I had enough time to go to Katrin's apartment and warn her. The thought was ridiculous. I had never done anything so heroic in my life. All I had ever done was let people down and betray them. I was absentmindedly rolling the bottle of perfume in my hand as I considered what to do next.

Now, the bottle of perfume was back in its secret pocket, and I was crossing the border the very first minute it opened. The border guards seemed more tense than usual, but I was feeling elated because I was going to do the right thing for Katrin. As I walked towards Stalinallee, I noticed to my surprise that even at this early hour, I was joining a throng all heading in the same direction. I wondered if there was some Communist festival that I had not heard about, but the mood of this crowd was dark. These were workers and not the wide-eyed young Communists who normally packed a festival. I overheard a few scattered references to 'quotas' and 'pay' but people stopped talking when they saw me and glanced at the FDJ badge I wore on my lapel. When I heard somebody mutter 'Ulbricht out', I knew that this was not a festival crowd because to say such a thing about the leader of the worker's paradise was the ultimate heresy.

I began to understand the importance of the newspaper headlines that Saskia had shown me. One had been a message offering hope from Moscow, but the other was Berlin's dark response. Walter Ulbricht had gone against Lavrentiy Beria's wishes and had chosen not to divert industry to the manufacture of consumer goods for the masses. Instead, he had demanded increased quotas for the same pay. If there was any hope from the Soviet Union that there would be a softening after Stalin's death, then East Germany had dashed that hope. By the time we reached Stalinallee, there was already gathered a large crowd, still dwarfed by the vast emptiness of the unfinished grand boulevard, but it was filling at every moment.

As far as I could tell, the crowd was leaderless and although disgruntled, they appeared to be uncertain about what to do next, so they milled around testing a few chants. Soon, a few of the chants began to take hold, especially 'Ulbricht Out!'

This was the beginning of what would become the June 17th uprising, and I was in the middle of it.

Chapter 36

As a rule, I do not ever wish to be in the middle of any unpleasantness.

I tried hard to work my way through the crowd to get to Katrin's apartment as quickly as possible. But the crowd kept growing and it was hard work despite my repeated '*entschuldigung*' and 'I'm most terribly sorry'. At first, the people merely mocked me for my FDJ badge but as I worked my way through, and as the minutes passed, people became more aggressive and pushed me around a bit, as a pent-up hatred for all things Communist started to flow.

I had never been in such a situation before. I had never been in the middle of such a large crowd and one that was gathering in order to stand up to an authority created by the brutal Joseph Stalin. In Malaya, during the war, it would have been terrifyingly unthinkable for a crowd to have dared gather to protest against the Japanese, which was precisely what these Germans were doing now.

I looked at the faces and saw that these were not the bourgoisie with whom I feel most comfortable, but workers. Men and women, most of whom were old enough to have lived and even fought in the war. Had these Berliners been Communists before the war, or enthusiastic Nazis, had they fought and killed Russians on the Eastern Front, had these women cowered in cellars during bombing raids and then just a month ago gathered to wave garlands of flowers at the Communist May Day rally? An almost desperate mood of excitement was overwhelming the crowd as it grew in numbers and in courage and defiance. 'Down with quotas!', 'Free elections', 'We are not slaves,' they chanted.

Nobody knew where this might end but they must have realized that they had crossed a dangerous line. The air of happy festivity was undercut by a fear of uncertainty. I worried that the rage, fear, and hope might need to unleash itself on an easy target, and what better than the only brown man in East Berlin who happened to be wearing an FDJ badge? I deftly removed the badge and joined in with an 'Ulbricht out!'

Perhaps it is the feudal Malay in me, but I err on the side of order and authority, and when I saw that even the police were retreating, I could tell that this was not the right place for me to be. A crowd is a rare and brainless creature, but this one was united enough in its purpose to be able to agree on a direction, and it decided to head towards the headquarters of the ruling SED party to make its demands. The crowd started to flow in that direction, and I was carried along. I, somehow, managed to edge my way to the side and popped out of its body. Three workers who were standing outside the crowd looked at me quizzically, presumably trying to decide what I might be and whether or not they should join the throng. I ran away before they could come to a decision.

Although I was extremely glad to be away from the crowd, I wondered if this sudden mass demonstration should put an end to my mission to find and warn Katrin. If the crowd did win the downfall of Walter Ulbricht and the SED regime then what did it matter if Tom Pelham held incriminating recordings of Katrin? And what about me? Should I not get back to the safety on the other side of the border?

It surprised me. It was the first time I could remember that I had considered somebody else's needs before my own. It was in this daze of confusion that I unexpectedly found myself on a quiet street and outside Katrin's apartment block. Tens of thousands of angry workers were gathering in Stalinallee, making demands that could lead to the end of the DDR and the creation of a reunified Germany. Yet here, in Katrin's district that had somehow been spared the worst of the wartime bombing and just a few blocks away from the current maelstrom, you wouldn't have known that anything potentially epochal was happening at all.

My heart was still racing from the excitement of Stalinallee, but nobody appeared to know or care here. People were heading to their offices and some children and a dog were playing in the street. Everything was perfectly normal. Before that day, I had always imagined that an entire nation was involved in, and animated by, its epochal moments. I had assumed that all of France was storming the Bastille. But here, just a few streets away from Stalinallee, somebody was quietly making their lunch completely unaware that a new national holiday was being fought for. After 17 June 1953, whenever I see a national conflagration,

I think of Katrin's quiet street. What does that quiet street want?

This particular street's youngest inhabitants wanted to know what I was. The children and the dog had given up their game and had silently gathered around me, leaning on their bicycles and joining me in looking at Katrin's apartment block while I tried to decide what to do next. I knew this was her apartment block, but I didn't know which was her apartment and it would have raised dangerous suspicion if I knocked on every door.

'What are you doing?' asked the boldest little girl.

'I'm looking for somebody.'

'Who?'

Should I ask them if they had seen Katrin? If the Japanese had managed to stay in Malaya for longer than just three years, then they may well have turned us children into their best little informants because they poured special attention into our education, filling us with wonder for their Greater East Asia Co-Prosperity Sphere. I didn't trust these children, because if the Japanese had managed to stay any longer, then I may have become a willing, if innocent, betrayer. This left me with a difficult choice because on this pleasant street lived many of the Communist aristocracy and it would be dangerous for me and, especially for Katrin, if I knocked on the wrong door and met a leading SED crony. But if I asked these children, then they might tell their parents about the strange brown man asking questions. I could just walk away, cross the border to catch my plane back to London, and return to my life. It struck me that one of my choices was slightly better than the others.

'I'm looking for Katrin Schule. Have you seen her?'

'She's gone. She went to Stalinallee.'

'Why did she go there?'

'She said she wanted to teach them a lesson.'

'But it's not safe for her there,' I blurted out anxiously.

'Her brother went to Leipzig this morning because the demonstrations have spread to there as well,' a tiny boy explained authoritatively while the dog looked on in agreement.

'These are very worrying developments,' another tiny boy said sagely. 'I knew something was wrong when Dahlem didn't appear at May Day.'

'My mother thinks this is the end of the SED,' said the tallest girl. 'But that is defeatist talk. Comrade Ulbricht has a plan, you can be sure of that.'

While the children were discussing the political situation, I was looking at their bicycles. I showed the tallest girl my FDJ badge.

'This is an FDJ emergency. I am requisitioning your bicycle.'

I thanked her on behalf of the People as I pedalled away furiously, chased by the dog. I had already ruined Katrin Schule's life, so there was nothing more I could do.

I needed to get back across the border and back to my life, whatever that might be.

Chapter 37

It was now the afternoon of 17 June, and the dog eventually gave up the chase as I pedalled back to the border on a ludicrously small bicycle.

Though a bit embarrassing, it was faster than walking, and the route was mostly downhill. I took the long way around to the Bernauer Straße checkpoint in order to avoid the unpleasantness of Stalinallee. I appeared to be part of a steady stream of young people heading in the same direction. This stream was distressingly interrupted by two men bleeding profusely from head wounds, running in the opposite direction. It is not in my nature to head towards trouble and the sightings of blood, the sound of desperate shouting, and the roar of engines made my pedalling slow to a crawl. I knew that I had to head into that uncertainty if I wanted to escape.

When I turned the corner onto Bernauer Straße, I witnessed a sickening sight, one worse than anything I had feared. Soviet tanks were on the streets, belching out black smoke as they jerked forward in menacing lurches while Berliners were ripping up cobblestones to throw at them in an act that was brave, if ultimately pathetic.

This was a battle and the most terrifying chaos I had ever seen, and I had seen executions at the end of the war after the Japanese had surrendered and before the British had returned. But back then, I had been a young bystander, confident that the British would soon be back and that the correct order would be reestablished. Now, I was trapped inside the chaos and although I knew I had nothing to do with any of this, I also knew that chaos finds its victims in the weak.

The Bernauer Straße checkpoint was just beyond the tanks. A short walk away on an ordinary day after a dreary lecture on Tolstoy. But this was no ordinary day. Today was my only chance for escape, but escape was on the other side of those roaring tanks. I couldn't just saunter towards the checkpoint and expect the tanks to appreciate that I was an innocent Malayan student. Nobody just walks past an angry tank. The final gap between me and safety was unbridgeable. Twenty yards ahead of me a tank was pawing at the ground, and then its unseen mahouts decided it had been baited enough. It reared up and charged straight into a group of rock throwing men, who only just managed to leap out of its path. And then a machine gun was fired into the air, the bullets ricocheting off Berlin walls, walls that had experienced bullets before. The ancient part of my brain that works on adrenaline, decided to take matters into its own hands by pushing my bicycle forwards and making me pedal with everything I had.

It is possible that some Berliners might remember seeing a young Asian man riding a girl's bicycle past Soviet tanks on 17 June 1953 but might have assumed that they were hallucinating. Although one part of my brain was consumed by absolute terror, the other, more civilized part was deeply concerned that I might, indeed, have looked ridiculous. My suspicion was confirmed when I saw a young Soviet soldier lower his machine gun to gawk at me as I made my dash for safety. The civilized part of my brain would have liked for everyone to have known that I had a lovely beige linen suit that would have been perfect for a summer's day such as this, but the ancient part was more concerned with weaving the bicycle past a tank while avoiding getting my wheel caught in a tram track. I had come this far and now I had no choice but to push myself past the final tank as fast as I could, even though its anonymous machine gun was tracking my every move. I could see the tank commander in his turret saying something into his intercom and watching me as I finally managed to surge past. Filled with relief, I raced towards my freedom.

But something was wrong. There was a thin line of Soviet soldiers in front of the border. This did not look right. I stopped my bicycle next to a young man who was shouting at West Berlin.

'What's happening?' I asked him.

'They've closed the border.' And then he returned to his shouting. 'Why are you doing this? Why don't you help us?'

'But I'm a Malayan student. I live in the West. I want to cross the border.'

'They're not letting anybody in or out.' And then he returned to his pointless shouting. 'Why? Why us?'

The border was signified by nothing more than a white line painted on the street, but now that it had been closed by Soviet soldiers, it might as well have been a wall. West Berliners stood on the other side, helplessly watching the chaos in the city that was no longer their city. It was now a separate city called East Berlin, and I was trapped inside it. I should have been one of them, in fact I should have been at the airport waiting for my plane back to London and my simple life. They may have been feeling scared, but from where I was standing, they were enviably safe because with the border closed, they were now cocooned in the prison of West Berlin, and the mayhem in the East would not dare cross that single white line. To do so would start a fire that would set the whole world ablaze.

The safe people watched me from the border, from their apartments, and from an observation deck, and on that deck, I saw the unmistakable figure of Tom Pelham. He lowered his binoculars when he saw me, and my lip reading was good enough to have discerned him saying, 'What the bloody hell . . .' My heart leapt with relief. Tom would save me. I waved to him and pointed at the border, as if to tell him he should get me across to the other side. But he just shrugged his shoulders, as if to say what I probably already knew. There was nothing he could do. Just like during the war, when I dreamed he would save us from the Japanese, I was not going to be rescued by Tom Pelham.

Another burst of machine gun fire reminded me and the shouting Berliner that we were horribly exposed in this open ground and we both exited for cover as fast as we could. There were other checkpoints and the border was porous. I could find another way out, perhaps through somebody's house and through a window. I cycled away. I had to find another way out.

Try as I might to hug the border and find an escape route, the presence of police and soldiers kept forcing me to go deeper into East Berlin. They may have been Germans and Russians, but to me they were all Japanese soldiers because I was feeling the same horrifying sense of isolation and abandonment I had felt throughout the war. And once again, I was blaming the British.

Why on earth had I put my trust in the British? Just because their women were attractive, and their tailoring was exquisite, it did not make up for the fact that Britain was a tiny, weak, and impoverished place that could barely protect itself, let alone me. I tried to promise myself that I would never make that mistake again if I ever got out of East Berlin. But the odds of escaping were lengthening at every corner I turned, where I saw yet more police and soldiers blocking my path. It was as if we were being funnelled into a single compacted area, and as I continued cycling, I began to realize that area was Stalinallee.

What could I do? I could bash on a door and beg for help but why would anybody risk harbouring me? Nobody could be trusted.

Behind me, police and soldiers were walking forwards to close the bag on the demonstrators.

I had no choice but to cycle into that bag.

Chapter 38

Being a new road, Stalinallee was not made with cobblestones. So, the demonstrators had to go to the older parts of town in order to arm themselves with stones to fight the tanks.

I cycled up to a group of young men ripping up a quiet side street and told them that the police were coming. But then there was a sudden burst of machine gun bullets that cracked above our heads. The sound was absolutely thunderous on the compact street. I couldn't fully understand what was happening even as I watched tracer bullets bounce along the walls. The Berliners, on the other hand, seemed to know exactly what was happening and so I copied their example as they ran, and we all threw ourselves into a doorway. But there wasn't enough space for us all to squeeze in and I had to scramble on top of them to get some cover. As I desperately clawed my way up the wall, I ripped off a poster of Walter Ulbricht and revealed, many layers below, an older poster of Adolf Hitler. Despite the present dangers, the huddled Berliners found the Fuhrer's reappearance to be amusing. Earlier in the day, the Soviet soldiers had fired high into the air but now their aim was getting lower. The oldest among us, and he wasn't very old, suddenly barked out orders like a platoon corporal—he had probably been one.

'Scatter. Zigzag. Stay close to the walls. Don't bunch. Out, out, out!'

We all burst out of our cover, some bravely and sensibly straight across the street, while I lunged for my bicycle. Soldiers kept on walking steadily up the street and let out a casual spray of bullets that smashed through the windows above. I pushed and pushed the bicycle, threw myself on and pedalled as best I could.

The chain suddenly slipped.

My feet spun pointlessly in empty air, and I crashed onto the ground from where I managed to catch sight of the young soldiers laughing at me. Somebody grabbed me by the hair, yanked me to my feet and pushed me on my way. It was the old corporal. I followed him as he expertly zigzagged his way out of trouble, and I briefly thought of Jim Plaistow. Perhaps, during the war, these two had faced-off against each other in the desert of North Africa, or perhaps this German had massacred the village of one of the Soviet soldiers walking towards us.

We all ran and ran until we reached Stalinallee, where we separated and hid inside the illusion of safety in numbers. My heart was racing. My legs were shaking. I had never been shot at before. If earlier that morning the workers had believed in the possibility of a victory over the SED, then by the afternoon, with the intervention of the Soviet Red Army that hope had been crushed—but not their spirit. In this chaotic battle zone, Berliners were still taunting and throwing rocks at the tanks that raced into the crowd in clumsy fury, and in the middle of the street was a dead body. He had been shot in the head. Some of his comrades were trying to reach him but weren't able to as they had to retreat from the tanks. I had not seen a dead body in a street since the war. It meant the complete collapse of order, safety, and society. But this was not my society, and this was not my war. I had neither friends nor enemies here, and yet it was becoming clear that I was going to die in Berlin.

Most of these demonstrators had probably not been beyond the battleground of Stalinallee all day long and so had not seen, as I had, that the bag was being closed and that the uprising would soon be snuffed-out in one final, bloody tumult. I circled the edges of the crowd, desperately looking for a possible escape route. I knew I would not make it out, but I continued looking, it was just the dying light of an old reflex for survival. I felt no hope any more. It was just a way to kill time before the final killing. It was all so unfair. Why me? There was so much more I wanted to do with my life but what could I do? We were all going to die that day. We were all already dead.

An angry group had gathered around somebody against whom they were directing their violence. *Faced with the indestructible tanks, the trapped crowd is now turning on itself*, I thought to myself. As an unknown Asian man, I would probably be next. But then I saw that in the middle of the mob, lay a man with a puffy and blood-soaked face and crouched over him was a woman trying to protect him, but being repeatedly punched for her efforts. It was Katrin Schule, and the mob were cursing and punching her for being a member of the now hated FDJ.

I had completely forgotten that my original reason for being in East Berlin that day had been to find Katrin. Now that I had found her it was clear that my mission was irrelevant because the mob was going to kill her before the tanks finally closed in. Unless, perhaps, I did something? But what could I do? If I stepped forward, then she and I would just end up being killed together. But I was going to die anyway. All my old instincts and calculations for avoiding trouble had been rendered useless in this warzone. Every possible calculation led to my death.

Some part of me made me step forward. Perhaps it was the part that doesn't like to see friends being beaten to death. I could do one final noble act. Actually, a first and final noble act. I pushed through the crowd and stood over Katrin, raising my arm to shield her from her assailants. I had not considered what I was going to say to them but in my quaking fear I suddenly erupted into a burst of rude words in Malay, and especially, Hokkien, which is always so graphically reliable. This seemed to stun the crowd, but I was rapidly running out of epithets about their mothers and goats, so I started shouting the words of old Mr Hargreaves that had always confused and frightened me at school.

'What are you boys up to? Am I talking to myself? Do you want me to speak to your Housemaster? Because if you carry on that is precisely what I'll be doing!'

The bizarre sight of an Asian man shouting at them in three unknown languages did stop the crowd, but I knew that this window of opportunity would close rapidly, because I did not, ultimately, have the authority to send them for detention.

'Katrin, go now. That boy! Have you been smoking?'
'But what about you?'
'Just go!'

The Berliners had surrounded us, and I could tell that the power of Mr Hargreaves' words was now as empty as when the Japanese soldiers took him away to Changi prison in '42.

'Now then, boys. I can see that you're upset but raising your fists to a Master is never the answer.'

I closed my eyes as I accepted the blows. These were not the expert boxer's jab that Sir Alfred Pelham had dealt to my nose, but fists to anywhere they could find on my head. Several people were also slapping me very hard on my ears, which was intensely painful, but between the flashing white lights of pain, I caught a glimpse of Katrin pulling her friend to his feet and dragging him away. I also caught a glimpse of a man walking towards me with a metal bar and raising it above his head.

So, this was how I was going to die?

Somebody grabbed me by the hair and pulled me up. I expected the metal bar to be smashed into my face. Words were being shouted, but after all the blows to my ears I could not hear very well. I could see the man with the metal bar considering his next action as he was being shouted at, and then I was yanked away by the hair, just as I had been by the old corporal. Somebody was talking to me, but I still could not hear, and then the words were being shouted in my ear.

'Why are you here?'

Despite being marched straight across Stalinallee by my hair, I managed to turn my head just enough. It was Saskia from Silesia.

'Why are you here?' I asked her back.

'I was shopping.'

'Me too.'

Chapter 39

A tank was roaring towards us. *Nobody simply walks in front of a tank*, I thought to myself, but Saskia, still grabbing my hair, kept marching me across the road.

The tank came to a sudden lurching halt in front of us, just before the dead body in the middle of the street.

We must have seemed a peculiar apparition to the young tank driver: A glamorous woman wearing a stylish summer hat marching an Asian man by the hair straight across a warzone. Nobody had been expecting this day, no plans had been made and no tactics rehearsed on either side. The crowd seeped back into the wide-open space and with a burst of gunfire they would run away again, carrying the wounded from the previous surge, and the entire time, Saskia was marching me through the chaos, with me trusting that her apparent certainty would make us bullet-proof.

I still could not hear very well after the bashing to my ears, but I could see the desperation on people's faces as they fought what they must now have realized was a lost cause for their future.

I just wanted to survive.

We stepped over a broken banner that said, 'We are not slaves!' and Saskia kept pushing me towards the outer edge of the warzone.

'There are police over there,' I warned Saskia.

'Keep walking,' she ordered me.

My hearing began to return to me as we were leaving Stalinallee, and things were beginning to get quieter. Away from the frontlines, the crowd had broken up to some wounded being bandaged and some scattered couples trying to work out what to do now that their world had been crushed by Soviet tanks and now that there was no escape. It was as if Berlin was again falling to the Red Army.

We turned a corner, and sure enough, there was a cordon of Soviet soldiers across the road. They raised their guns when they saw us.

'They are young and stupid,' Saskia told me. 'They don't know what they're doing, so we need to look like we do. Keep walking.'

Saskia was now grabbing me by the back of my collar, the first person to do so since Mr Hargreaves back at school, and she pushed me towards the soldiers, which did not seem like a sensible thing to do. An officer fired his pistol into the air. I instinctively flinched and pulled to run away but she kept pushing me forward. The officer fired again, and this time I could hear the cracking sound of the bullet as it flew past me. When we were close enough for her to be heard, Saskia shouted something in Russian. The officer lowered his weapon, ordering his men to do the same. We entered the group of soldiers and Saskia hissed something at the officer in Russian, I think she asked for his name. The man who moments before had been about to shoot us, now looked shaken as he said his indecipherable Russian name. Still grabbing me by the collar, Saskia led me away and only released me when we turned another corner.

'What the bloody hell are you doing here?' she demanded, with what I thought was a surprisingly English turn of phrase.

'There was something I needed to do.'

'I told you to leave Berlin.'

'I was about to. I'm supposed to be flying to London now, but I had to do something first.'

'What? What was so important?'

'I had to warn somebody about something.'

'Was it that FDJ girl?'

I didn't answer.

'Why did you do that?' Saskia asked. 'Why did you save her?'

'She's my friend.'

'But they were going to kill you.'

'I wasn't thinking. I just knew that she's my friend. I had to do something. I didn't want to, but I did.'

Despite the monstrous tumult around us she looked at me like I was the most curious thing she had seen all day. Then she spoke more to herself than to me, 'People don't think like that any more.'

'But you saved me.'

'That's different. I knew that man didn't want to kill you. All he needed was an excuse to stop. But will I regret my action? I told you that if anything happened, then you would get the blame. Now something has happened, and now you will be blamed. And so will I.'

'I just need to get across the border, and then everything will be fine.'

'If you go near the border, you will be arrested and then put on trial as a Western saboteur. You will never leave East Berlin. Unless I can think of something. Come with me. I can keep us safe for a few hours.'

Why was she helping me? I did not dare ask in case she started asking herself the same question.

Her apartment was nearby. It was the first home I had been invited into in Berlin, and as this one was in the Communist East, I was expecting a drab cubicle with a portrait of Stalin as the only embellishment. But Saskia's apartment was large and sumptuously decorated, and yet not in any style that I could recognize from my Malayan and English world. I could only imagine that it had been filled with all the luxury goods of an eastern European caravanserai. I did recognize a Russian samovar, from which Saskia drew me some welcome tea, but the colourful fabrics and glassware were all unknown to me, although there was an atlas opened on a map of Malaya. It was all a far cry from the chaos and violence of Stalinallee, and I slumped into a comfortable chair as Saskia went to the kitchen to make us some lunch.

I had forgotten that people ate lunch.

The adrenaline was draining from my body, leaving me with the awful awareness that I had almost been killed. I focused all my attention on a painting. It was a portrait of a 19th century German general who looked very severe with his grandiose moustache. I looked around and saw that the walls were covered with portraits of what must have been the same family through the centuries, all looking severe and very unlike the smugly whimsical portraits I had seen at the Pelhams' home. Saskia brought me a bowl of stew with dumplings.

'Are they your family?' I asked her.

'These people? No. They're Junkers. Prussian noblemen. The paintings were here when I took the apartment and I decided to keep them. They remind me that they are all finally gone, and I'm still alive. That little painting is a Rubens. Probably stolen from some Jews.'

'What do you do, Saskia?'

'I survive. Is it very hot in Malaya?'

'Yes.'

'Do you travel everywhere on an elephant?'

'No, of course not. I travel in a car. But I have been on an elephant. They're used to clear the jungle.'

After the awful events of the day, the memory of the heat of Malaya and the elephant mahouts jabbering in Thai was simply too unexpected. Saskia's apartment was so serenely safe, and I was safe, even if only for a few hours. My hands started shaking and I burst into tears. It just suddenly happened, I had no control over myself. Saskia watched me impassively.

'Don't worry,' she said. 'It's natural. You almost died today. Let it happen, and then you will be able to think clearly again.'

She ate her lunch disinterestedly until my sobbing eventually subsided.

'What are you doing in Berlin, Hamid from Malaya?'

I was looking at her face for the first time when she said my name for the first time. I wanted to tell her the truth.

'I'm studying Russian literature.'

But I didn't, even though I knew I could trust her because she had saved my life.

'But why?' she asked.

'I've always had a fascination for Russian literature.'

'In German?'

'German is a romantic language.'

'It is? Why have you been following me?'

'I wanted to sit and talk to you, like this.'

'You are attracted to me, is that what it is?'

'You are very attractive, but to me you looked, I don't know, normal.'

'I have never been called that before.'

'I mean you look normal in my world, or at least in the world I want to live in.'

She leaned back in her chair as she considered my words.

'In the cinema,' she said, 'you told me I was your only friend, but you know nothing about me.'

'I know what books you read. I know you find Schiller funny, but I don't know why. I know you are kind because you like giving your good food to the German girls, and I know you do not wear perfume.'

'I have never found my scent. You say you don't have any friends in Berlin, but what about that FDJ girl you saved? You said she is a friend.'

'She is more of a professional acquaintance.'

'I see, I think.'

'I need to ask you a question. The Colonel, he is your husband?'

'No. He has a family in Moscow. Don't worry about him.'

'I see.'

'That movie we were watching, how did it end? Did Stalin liberate Berlin?'

'Yes, he did. How did you know?'

Some tanks roared along the street outside to remind us that this was a terrible day, and we went to the window to look at them. I had only seen Saskia in the gloom of this room or from the corner of my eye in a café, but now, by the window in the early evening light, I could see that her skin was luminescent, especially when framed by her flowing dark hair, which I had barely glimpsed before because she was always wearing a hat.

'I hate seeing tanks on the streets. Those are T54s. I know too many tanks and I wish I didn't.'

'Saskia, how do you come to speak such excellent English?'

'I learned it during the war. I wanted to get to the Americans.'

We looked down at the tanks that were now waiting for orders.

'And yet, you are still among the Russians. Why don't you go to the West?'

'It is not so easy for me.'

'But I see hundreds of people crossing every day.'

'They are German, so they can. I am not German, I do not have any papers, and I would not be welcome if I did go. So, I stay here, surviving and waiting for a miracle to arrive.'

'I do not wish to appear selfish but how do I get across the border?'

'You will also need a miracle. And how do you speak English?'

'I'm Malayan,' I told her self-evidently, and yet the information did not appear to be self-evident enough for Saskia. 'Malaya is part of the British Empire.'

'So, you were safe during the war.'

'We were invaded and occupied by the Japanese. It wasn't easy.'

'You also lived in a hole in the ground?'

'But it also wasn't that hard.'

We traded war stories as the sun went down and we were sitting in darkness when she told me about Lidice.

'It is, or was, a village outside Prague,' she explained. 'We were living there in '42. It seemed safer than where we had come from. The stupid British sent two agents to Prague to kill the monster Heydrich, and when they succeeded, the Germans killed everybody in Lidice. What did they think the Germans would do? Surrender? I lost my whole family in Lidice. I wasn't there. I was in Prague, I had scarlet fever. My family thought they might lose me, and when I came out of my fever, I was told I was an orphan.'

'I am sorry.'

'We should not be sorry we have survived, and yet I am. My birthday with my family before I had the scarlet fever, when I was still a little girl, that was the last normal day I ever had. I want life to be boring and normal again, like it was in Czechoslovakia.'

'But you told me you are from Silesia,' I interjected.

'Did I? I stayed there for a short time during the war. I stayed in many places, always trying to get safer, but everywhere I went got worser and worser.'

Saskia laughed at her allusion to *Alice in Wonderland* but for me, her distinctly English English was becoming curiouser and curiouser. What suddenly struck me as being curiouser still was that during my entire time with Saskia, I had not once thought about marrying this woman. She was captivating, intoxicatingly beautiful, terrifyingly strong, and yet, immensely fragile, but I wasn't thinking about marrying her, probably because for the first time in my life, I could not see how I might have a future. I could only have a future if I could get to the safety of the other side of the border. Saskia held the only possible key to my having a future and we had not yet discussed it.

'This is not who I am.' Saskia continued. 'I am still that little girl looking for safety, but I think I might have found safety, thanks to you, Hamid.'

'Me?'

'Yes, perhaps.'

The silence in the room was broken by the sound of a key being put into the lock of the front door.

'I am sorry, Hamid, but I must survive.'

The front door swung open, and the light was switched on. I wanted to throw up. It was The Colonel. He was as surprised to see me as I him. Saskia went to him and kissed him as he said something in Russian. And then she spoke in English.

'This is my gift to you. A Western saboteur.'

The Colonel seemed delighted. 'Good girl. Is this the boy who has been following you?'

'Yes. I found him on Stalinallee, directing the hooligans.'

Chapter 40

'But I did no such thing,' I complained feebly. 'I'm just a student. Tell him the truth, Saskia.'

'Saskia?' asked The Colonel. 'Is that what she told you? Her name is Katya.' He turned to her. 'Clever girl,' he praised, 'but now I will take him back to headquarters for questioning.'

'No,' said my betrayer, this Katya. 'He's my gift. Question him here. Please.' He considered the request.

'I will have to change my methods but as you wish. The result will be the same.'

The Colonel must have been unbuttoning his jacket when he was walking up the stairs because now, he was doing them back up again as the woman poured some drinks. This horror was happening all so fast. The events of the day had been changing from one sickening direction to another at such speed that my head was spinning. Just a few minutes earlier, I had been safe with Saskia, but now, she was Katya, and I was about to be interrogated by a KGB colonel.

The Colonel sat in front of me. Under different circumstances, I might have been better able to appreciate that he was a very handsome man and that his uniform was very smart indeed.

'You are a Western saboteur,' he told me.

'No, I am not.'

'Yes, yes you are. The workers of East Germany have been confused and you have been sent to exploit them and lead them in the wrong direction.'

'That's not true. I'm just a student. I'm from Malaya.'

'This will be much easier for you if you just tell me what I want to know. We've been watching you for months. You've been marking chalk crosses all over Berlin. These are messages for your agents, yes?'

'No. It's a game we play in Malaya.'

The Colonel found this amusing.

'Ah yes, Malaya. This is where you write for the *Socialist Straits Times*, yes? But there is no *Socialist Straits Times*. You must never add unnecessary details. Didn't Tom Pelham tell you this? I know all about Tom Pelham from when I was stationed in London. This whiskey is from him. We trade sometimes. The English are clever, cleverer than the Americans, but the Russians are cleverer still. And I am Georgian. Would you like a whiskey?'

'Yes please.'

'This is very different from my usual technique, but I am enjoying it. Thank you, Katya.'

He thanked her for the gift of me and for the whiskey she had poured.

'You said the workers have been confused,' said Katya. 'How is that?'

'We made a mistake. Moscow and Ulbricht have been saying opposite things in public. I told Beria this was a mistake. Moscow wants a rapprochement with the West, even if that means the end of the DDR, but Ulbricht doesn't want to lose his kingdom. And they said it all in the newspapers, for everyone to see.

Ulbricht disobeyed us and kept pushing the workers, raising their quotas, lowering their pay. He made this happen. And when they started rioting, he told me, "It's over." He and his gang of weak fools were going to run. We had to send in our tanks. We cannot look weak. Today's uprising has changed everything.'

'So, what you're saying is,' I ventured, 'that I didn't have anything to do with any of this?'

'Yes, you did. You are a Western saboteur, and you engineered this attempted counter-revolution.'

'But you just said . . .'

'I was not talking to you, I was talking to Katya.'

I did not like that name, but then again, I did not like her either, so it suited her nicely. This Katya was pensively hovering over The Colonel's shoulder.

'Changes everything?' she asked, 'How is that?'

'I don't expect you to understand. Beria, and I, want to ease the people's burden and make peace with the West, but Ulbricht forced us to act against our wishes. And now, Khrushchev has his chance with the Central Committee. I doubt Beria even knows he's in trouble. But I do, and I have my chance, because I have captured the Western saboteur behind the uprising. I have Britain's best agent. Agent Hamid from Malaya. I will put him on trial and prove that the British did this, not us.'

'You're very clever,' said Katya. 'That's a brilliant plan. But do you have enough time?'

'What do you mean?'

Katya started speaking in German, and did I catch a glimpse of Saskia?

'Beria is your friend, yes?'

'Yes.'

'You are both Georgians, and you have been attached to him for twenty years.'

'Yes.'

'When he rose, you rose.'

'Yes.'

'And when he falls, you will fall.'

'Maybe not. I have my Western saboteur.'

'Do you have the time and power to conduct a show trial in Berlin? You are not Stalin.'

'Not yet.'

Katya got onto her knees before The Colonel.

'How many Berliners were crushed by Soviet tanks today? How many more have been arrested and will be executed? This was Beria's mistake and the excuse his enemies have been waiting for. If you were one of his enemies in the Central Committee, what would you do?'

'Arrest Beria immediately.'

'And then?'

'Put a bullet in the back of his head.'

'And who gave his orders in Berlin?'

'Me. But I have my Western saboteur.'

'It will never work. Look at him. Does he look like he could lead a quarter of a million Germans in a counter-revolution? If you put him on trial, the whole world will laugh at you.'

'But you gave him to me. You must think he's worth something.'

'As a toy for you to play with but not as something to save your life. Will Beria survive this?'

'No.'

'How long does he have?'

'A few days.'

'Do you really think you can survive this?'

The Colonel looked down and meekly shook his head.

'Only one person can save you,' said Katya.

'Who?'

Katya began speaking in English again. 'Him.'

'Me?' I asked, a trifle unhappy that I had been brought back into the conversation. 'What can I do?'

'Yes,' agreed The Colonel. 'What can he do?'

She took The Colonel's hands.

'If you are arrested and executed, then they will destroy your family in Moscow, and they will arrest and execute me as well. You only have one choice.'

She turned to me.

'Are you or are you not a British agent?'

It did not feel like a good idea to confess that I was a British agent to a KGB Colonel, but I didn't appear to have too many other options.

'Yes.'

Katya turned back to The Colonel.

'You must defect to the British and he will take us to, what is his name?'

'Tom Pelham,' I said.

'He will take us to Tom Pelham.'

'You are insane,' said The Colonel, casting aside Katya's hands. 'I have spent my life fighting the English. I destroyed their entire network. Tom Pelham is my last target and now you want me to join them? No.'

'But what about your family, what about me?'

'No.'

The phone suddenly rang, the noise excessively loud. The Colonel answered it and merely grunted a reply. Whatever he had been told left him looking deeply concerned.

'Who was that?' Katya asked.

'One of my agents. It's merely a detail. Khrushchev must be looking for allies. Marshal Zhukov has joined him. I must tell Beria.'

Katya grabbed the phone from his hand.

'No. You are insane. You cannot compete with the man who won the war. It's over. If you call Beria now, then you will go down with him. You must save yourself. This is your last chance. He is your last chance.'

They both looked at me.

'Perhaps we all need another drink,' I suggested.

Chapter 41

It was late in the night, or early in the morning, when The Colonel began to see some virtue in Katya's plan.

She had been supplying us with food and drinks while The Colonel sat in silence, considering his options and probably thinking about the great crime he might be about to commit. To save himself, he would need to betray the Soviet Union. I thought that Communism and the Soviet Union was an absolute travesty of nature, but this man had dedicated his life to it and must have believed in its mission, and although he was obviously a killer, and would happily have shot me, I did feel sorry for him.

But I was feeling sorrier for myself because if I was to have a future, then it depended upon his decision. He occasionally looked up to ask Katya for clarifications.

'What about my family in Moscow?'

'The British can get them out.'

'No, they cannot.'

'But you told me there's a British network inside the Soviet Union.'

'Then it must be true.' He squeezed Katya's hand as he looked at a photograph of his family. 'I will need to contact Tom Pelham.'

'He can do it,' Katya said, pointing at me.

'No. I can get him across the border, but then he'll just run away. I want to keep him here. He's my hostage.'

'Why do you need to contact Tom Pelham?' she asked. 'Get me the papers you've been promising, and we will all just walk across.'

'I want to know what Tom Pelham will give me first. I will be the biggest prize of his life, and I want something. But if I simply arrive, then I will be his hostage.'

'Then call him. You said you trade sometimes, so call him.'

'Don't be so naïve. Everyone will be listening if I call him now.'

'So, then you must contact him. I cannot go across. My papers are forged.'

During their conversation I had been silently considering my options for survival and had decided that the best one was to keep silent and hope that they forgot all about me. And yet, I found I was trying to stop myself from speaking. I realized that I might have a solution.

'I might have somebody,' I said.

They both looked at me with surprise.

'One of your agents?' The Colonel asked.

'Not exactly. She's my friend. Her name is Katrin Schule.'

'I know Katrin,' The Colonel said with a rare smile. 'She's a big girl. I sent her to seduce you. She was told to bring you back, but she didn't.'

'Can you trust her?' Katya asked.

'I don't know. But I think she owes me a favour.'

It was still before dawn when The Colonel drove us to Katrin's apartment. Because of the riots, there was a curfew and although the streets were empty, The Colonel still managed to hit several objects along the way. He was either a very bad driver or he was blinded by a distraction as dense as the London smog. Before we left their apartment, he and Katya had quickly penned a coded message to Tom Pelham, and now she was adding some finishing touches to it in the back of the car.

'The cipher is based on Goethe's *Faust*,' she informed me. 'Every German bookshelf will have a copy. All your girlfriend has to do is deliver the message to Tom Pelham and say "Mephistopheles".'

'She's not my girlfriend,' I stated.

'But how will he know we're using the first edition?' The Colonel asked, ignoring me.

'Because it will be obvious to him. Why would we have chosen the fifth or the tenth? And Hamid has seen him with a copy.'

'I saw him with a copy of it,' I pointed out. 'I don't know if it was a first edition.'

'It must be the first edition,' Katya stated.

'And how do you suddenly know so much about codes and ciphers?' The Colonel asked.

'How do you think we got messages past the Germans and the Soviets during the war? You concentrate on the road. And watch out for the dog.'

'What dog?'

There was the sound of a nasty little thud and The Colonel swore in Russian. I only saw it for a split second, but I could have sworn I recognized the dog lying on the road.

'She's not my girlfriend.' I said quietly to Katya. 'Katrin is just a friend.'

'You sleep with your friends?'

'I did not sleep with her.' I decided to change the subject. 'I've never read *Faust*.'

'You know *Alice's Adventures in Wonderland*?'

'Of course.'

'It's the same thing.'

'This is it,' said The Colonel as he stopped the car outside Katrin's apartment block. I slunk back into the seat when I saw a Soviet military patrol walking past.

'You two stay in the car. I will get rid of them,' he told us as he got out of the car.

With The Colonel temporarily gone, Katya turned to me.

'She must be your girlfriend because you never mentioned her.'

'That makes no sense. And I never mentioned her to you because you and I never spoke. But if we had spoken, would you have mentioned that you were living with The Colonel?'

'Anyway, now is not the time.'

'Really? Do you think so? Do you think we can discuss this tomorrow because today I'm probably going to die!'

'Quickly, listen to me. The Colonel will give your girlfriend her orders and she will not dare to refuse. But you will need to talk to her. Tell her you have been working for the Soviets and assure her it's safe. All she has to do is take this message to Tom Pelham. The Colonel will give her a pass for the border, and then she goes there and comes back. That's it. We cannot allow her to think this is strange because then she will go to the *polizei*, and then we are *kaput*.'

'Will she be safe?'

'Yes.'

'I mean afterwards. When The Colonel has defected. Will she be safe then?'

'She just did what The Colonel ordered her to do. She doesn't know anything else. Why would they do anything to her?'

'The Colonel thought I was a Western saboteur and I'm not. They don't need much of an excuse.'

'Either she takes this message to Tom Pelham, or you will die today. Now is not the time for having a conscience. It's your choice.'

The Colonel opened the door.

'They've gone. It's time to go.'

From what little I had seen of The Colonel over the previous months, he had always struck me as being a most terrifyingly self-assured man, but he did not look so confident this morning as he sat in his seat, resting his hands on the steering wheel. We sat in a peculiar silence waiting for the immobile Colonel to stir. It was the first silence I had experienced in over a day that felt like a year. I think, at that moment, The Colonel and I wanted to sleep, just to evade the terror of what we were both about to do.

'You should have shaved,' Katya told him.

'I have other things on my mind today.'

'No, you do not. That little girl must see the most powerful man in Berlin and his best agent. Stand up straight, and be a man. And if she won't do it, then you must shoot her immediately.' Her eyes flicked towards me ever so briefly. Was she suggesting that he must then shoot me as well? 'I'll wait in the car. Now go.'

It only took a matter of seconds for The Colonel to deftly pick the lock of the front door and as we climbed the stairs, I told him that Katrin lived with her brother.

'He is one of my informants. Who do you think tells me about Katrin's movements? But he's in Leipzig now so we won't be disturbed. I will talk to her, but you need to assure her it is safe. If she worries, then she will go to the polizei and then we are all dead.'

'I know. Katya told me already.'

'Did she? Clever girl. Remember, you are a top Soviet agent and no unnecessary extra details.'

He knocked on the door and we waited. He glanced nervously at the other front doors and then knocked again. I have never seen such a look of fear overwhelm a face as did Katrin's when she opened her door to find The Colonel.

'Good morning, Katrin. Do not be alarmed. You know this man, he is my top agent in the Western sector. I want you to do something. May we come in?'

I watched from the adjoining room as The Colonel gave Katrin her orders. I could see that he was beginning to look like his old self again, presumably drawing strength and comfort from the familiar role of instilling fear in another, and something about Katrin's round face seemed to invite the bully. I actually wanted to protect her, but I knew that my life depended on her being more afraid of The Colonel than of her own government. He stood up and gave her the piece of paper.

'Tom Pelham. Mephistopheles,' he told her.

'Mephistopheles,' she replied.

He walked towards me with a smile on his face.

'She's shitting herself. I think she'll be fine, but just in case . . .' He tapped his pistol. 'Tell her where to find Tom Pelham and no unnecessary extra details.'

Katrin was trying unsuccessfully not to cry as I approached her. A lifetime spent in Nazi and then Communist Germany should have taught her how to hide her thoughts and emotions, but the sudden arrival of The Colonel this morning must have been too great a shock.

'Why me? Why did you ever come into my life? What did I do? Why me?'

'Katrin, I'm sorry. But you must do as he says.'

'This doesn't sound right. Why didn't he have me picked up? Why did he come here?'

'Katrin, don't talk.'

'And who the hell are you? First, he told me you were a British agent and now he tells me you're a Soviet agent.'

'Yes, I am a Soviet agent. I love the Soviet Union and its communism of course. It's absolutely magnificent stuff.'

'You don't know anything about communism or the Soviet Union.'

'That's the brilliance of my disguise. I pretended I didn't know but, really, I do.'

'Where do you stay in Moscow?'

I only knew of two places in Moscow, and I was fairly sure that the Bolshoi was a ballet theatre.

'I stay at the Kremlin. It has a hotel for secret agents. It's very nice. There's a television in every room.'

Was this what The Colonel meant by unnecessary extra details?

'This doesn't sound right. I need to speak to somebody. I want to talk to my brother.'

'No, Katrin, don't do that. Just take the message to Tom Pelham and you will never hear from us again.'

'It doesn't work like that. First, he told me to sleep with you, now it is this, and then I will be running more messages, and then they will make me have sex with other men I do not love. I want a quiet life. I want to get married, have children, and work for the SED. That is all I want. Why did you ever come into my life? Why me?'

'Why is this taking so long?' The Colonel asked from the other room.

'Everything is good,' I said. 'I'm explaining the different addresses that Tom Pelham uses.'

'Do it faster,' he ordered, and I could hear the metallic click of his wedding ring tapping on his pistol.

'Katrin, I promise you. Do this and you will never hear from him again.'

'That makes even less sense. He is not going anywhere. Unless . . .'

At that moment, Katrin appeared to understand something, something that seemed to give her sudden defiance, and this frightened me.

'. . . Unless he is going somewhere. Somewhere far away.'

'Katrin, you will never have a quiet life if you do not take this message.' I had to think fast. 'Tom Pelham has film of you, of us together. He is the only one with proof that you were ever there.'

'So what if he does? You are a Soviet agent, and we just talked.'

That was a good point, but my life was on the line.

'Things change. Today Beria is on top, but it will be somebody else tomorrow. And they will ask why did you go to the Western sector to talk to me when I am Beria's man? Take the message to Tom Pelham, but only give it to him if he destroys the film in front of you. That film is dangerous to you, more dangerous than The Colonel because Tom Pelham will use it to make you become a British agent. If Tom Pelham destroys it, then I think you can have the bourgeois life you've always wanted. Take the message and destroy the film, and then you will never hear from anybody ever again.'

She was afraid and she was confused.

'Who are you? Who do you work for?' was all she could muster.

'It is time to go,' interrupted The Colonel. 'Here is your border pass. I have signed it. When you come back from the Western sector walk past the bakery on Hermannstraße and drop your handbag if you have successfully delivered the message. If not, then continue walking.

'And when you are there put on some lipstick for me,' I added. 'If you have succeeded.'

'I know she will be successful. Somebody will come here to retrieve Tom Pelham's reply.'

I told her the address of Tom's private apartment and then whispered in her ear.

'Your brother is informing on you. Goodbye, Katrin.'

'Goodbye,' she said.

'How is your girlfriend?' Katya asked insolently as we got back into the car. I didn't answer.

'I think she will be fine,' said The Colonel. 'She was terrified.'

'Hamid, what do you think?' Katya asked, but this time more softly, while putting her hand on my arm. I looked at The Colonel's pistol as he jolted the car into life.

'She will be good. All is good,' I said.

'I know she is not your girlfriend,' Katya told me.

'She is my friend.'

'Yes, I know that, and I am sorry.'

'I have to go back to work now,' said The Colonel. 'We have to clean up the mess of yesterday.'

'Will you be shooting anyone?' I asked bitterly as Katya squeezed my arm and shot me a look of concern.

'Perhaps,' he laughed. 'I will miss this. I read about a place called Las Vegas that sounds like fun. But I will miss this.'

Throughout the journey, I thought about my conversation with Katrin, about how I had somehow had the presence of mind to use Tom's film to blackmail her into doing what I wanted, or had I just freed us both? Katya was also lost in her thoughts, but her hand stayed on my arm. It felt consoling, like something a married couple might do, like something adults might do. It felt like something from a thousand years ago that I had dreamt Clare and I would do. But a short while earlier, Katya's eyes had suggested to The Colonel that he should shoot me. I didn't think Clare would have done that, but you never know what people will do when they're caught in a sticky situation.

Chapter 42

The Colonel's driver was waiting diligently when we returned to the apartment, so Katya hustled me in through a rear entrance.

Katya calculated that I could sleep for three hours before Katrin would return from her mission, a task I gratefully accepted. Katya gave The Colonel his final orders in Russian while he shaved quickly, and then he left for the office where he would presumably be interrogating, and perhaps executing, some of yesterday's rioters. A final fling before his defection to the West.

When I woke up, I felt confused. An old Prussian Junker was glowering down at me from a painting on the wall. Where on earth was I? In my dreams, I had been in the landscapes of Malaya with an English wintry chill.

Where was this place and why was I so scared? My eyes drifted down and rested on Katya, asleep on the sofa opposite me. Looking at her calmed me as I recollected my present dire predicament. Her hair was splayed out across the cushions, and she looked like she was drifting down a river. Now that her makeup had worn off, she looked much younger and more delicate than the woman who had saved my life just the day before. I had never imagined that I might ever need somebody to save my life or that that person would be so beautiful. She opened her eyes, and we just looked at each other for a while.

'What are you thinking about?' she asked.

'I don't understand how *Faust* and *Alice's Adventures in Wonderland* can be the same thing.'

She smiled. I had not seen her smile before.

'They knew what they were doing.'

'But he made a deal with the devil, and she had tea with the Mad Hatter. Two very different things.'

'She saw a rabbit with a watch. Is that normal? And yet she followed him and drank from a bottle that said "Drink Me" and ate a cake that said "Eat Me." She knew the risks she was taking but she did it anyway because she was bored, just like Dr Faust. Some of us do not have that luxury.'

'What luxury?'

'The luxury to be bored of life. How long were we asleep?'

'About two hours.'

'You watch for Katrin, and I will make us some coffee. And don't worry, it's Italian.'

It pleased me enormously that she knew my fondness for Italian coffee. It seems she had noticed something about me during our months of silent friendship.

'I still don't think Alice had a choice, or Faust for that matter,' I said as we sipped our coffees by the window, watching over the bakery below. 'I mean, perhaps at first they had a choice, but afterwards they were both caught in events beyond their control.'

'Perhaps. But beware the white rabbit and Mephistopheles, even if they come in the shape of a beautiful girl,' she said while blowing on her coffee. 'Is that your weakness? Beautiful girls?'

'Well, isn't that everybody's? But not really. Besides, is Katrin beautiful?'

In those days, people did not talk about their 'feelings' and you did not need to have grown up under Nazi or Communist rule to know that the utterance of one's personal thoughts could be dangerous, you just had to be born Malay, or Asian for that matter, where standing out from the crowd was a mortal sin. I did not dare to talk about what I truly wanted, and yet, I wanted to talk to this woman, just as I had once talked with Margaret de Vere.

'I think I just don't want to be alone,' I told her. 'I have had some trouble with women recently.'

'Is that why you are here? Did you follow them down the rabbit hole?'

While waiting for Katrin, we talked about the books we had read and the films we had watched together during our silent friendship.

'I did not enjoy *Oliver Twist*,' she told me. 'It was like a horror movie. It reminded me of . . . things.'

And she also told me some of her lighter wartime stories, if massacring a German patrol could ever be funny (the coda about the subsequent reprisal was most definitely not amusing). She made us breakfast and then lunch, and then my stomach began to churn with anxiety. Where was Katrin? Why was she taking so long?

'Did we miss her when we were asleep?' I worried.

'No, she couldn't have been that fast.'

'One of us should have stayed awake to watch,' I continued worrying but in a slightly more heightened manner.

'Calm down, Hamid.'

From our vantage point, we could see not only the bakery below, but also the border crossing at the end of the road that Katrin would probably use upon her return from the Western sector.

'I still have a problem,' Katya said. 'I will not be safe even if I can cross to the other side. You see, they will probably send me back.'

'But why?'

'I did some things during the war that they do not like.'

'What things?'

'Bad things.'

'That was a long time ago. Tom will take care of it. He'll keep you safe.'

'You have great faith in this Tom Pelham?'

'I don't know about that, but he's not a cruel man. He's a decent chap.'

'No. I will be an embarrassment to them. They will send me back and then I will be killed.'

'But you'll be with The Colonel. They want him.'

'But does he want me? He already has a family, and I am just his mistress. I am an embarrassment to him as well.'

'So, what do we do?'

'I don't know. Perhaps I will think of something. Look, there she is.'

In the distance, at the border crossing was the small figure of Katrin having her papers and bag inspected by the guards who towered over her. To my relief, she passed through the border checks. It would be a long walk from there to the bakery below us where she would either stop or continue walking. First, she had to cross the wasteland of the border zone and then walk up the wide street where Soviet tanks had been charging the day before. The curfew was still in operation, and she was the only person on the streets.

'We should have given her the driver as an escort.' Katya's voice betrayed her concern as we watched Katrin make her lonely way towards the bakery. 'She can be shot for breaking the curfew. Stupid.'

Witnessing a crack in Katya's usual imperious calm was distinctly unsettling for my traditionally hysterical nature, and I felt compelled to be the voice of reason, for some reason.

'But we can't get anyone else involved.'

'Yes, you're right. Yes.'

Katya took my hand and squeezed it as we watched Katrin walk the last few yards to the bakery. And then Katrin walked straight past it. A pulse of clammy sweat oozed from both our hands as we both came to the sickening realization that our worlds had just ended. Katrin had delivered to us Tom's reply. Our plea had been rejected. I had been abandoned.

'We run now,' Katya ordered me. 'There are gaps in the border. We'll never make it, but we must try.'

'But she only spoke to Tom. We can try the Americans, or even the French.'

'Don't be stupid. We cannot stay.'

'Wait. Look.'

Katrin had stopped walking. She was looking around. It looked like she was lost. And then she started walking back towards the bakery.

'This isn't her part of town,' I said with sudden hope. 'Maybe she didn't see the bakery because it's closed.'

Katrin stopped outside the bakery and started fumbling with the contents of her handbag. Was she torturing me for the terrors I had brought into her life?

'Just drop the bloody bag,' I demanded. 'Please, Katrin.'

And then she dropped her handbag. I instinctively gave thanks with Islamic phrases from my childhood while Katya babbled her gratitude in an unknown Eastern European language.

'What is she doing now?' Katya asked. 'She's putting on some lipstick.'

'Why the hell is she doing that?'

'It's a message to me. She's saying goodbye.'

'No unnecessary extra details!'

I agreed, but this one was worth it. Katrin didn't know where we were, or even if I was watching at all, but she looked so very pretty as she stood on that empty Berlin street, applying her lipstick. In fact, she was the most beautiful sight I had ever seen. Katya hugged me and we held each other tightly.

'We have a chance,' she said.

I watched Katrin Schule walk away.

Chapter 43

Katya called The Colonel's office and informed his driver that she would be cooking borscht that night, their prearranged message in the event that Katrin had been successful.

If Katrin had failed, then it was to have been some other equally awful cabbage-based dish. I was so exhausted that I simply collapsed in a chair and fell asleep. This time, I awoke with a sensation of deep anxiety instead of outright fear, which marked a pleasant change. It was getting dark outside, and the first thing I saw when I opened my eyes was not a painting of an angry Prussian Junker, but Katya.

She was looking at me, contemplating me. I had never seen a face like hers before. Yes, she had a rare beauty but what distinguished her face was its ability to change. Mostly, she looked like a ravishing but world-weary woman, and sometimes, one could catch a brief glimpse of an innocent young girl. What I saw now worried me in an anguished, yet familiar, way. She seemed so very much older than me. She looked concerned and disappointed. She looked like my father.

'What do you do, Hamid? I mean, when you're not being an awful spy.'

'I'm studying in London.'

'What are you studying?'

'Well, that's difficult to explain. Is that the time?'

'And what will you do when you have finished your studies?'

'I will return the Malaya and be a civil servant.'

'Does that pay well?'

'Not at first, but it comes with many perks: housing, healthcare, and prestige.'

'What do your parents do?'

'Why are you asking all these questions?'

'What do your parents do?'

'My father is a senior civil servant and my mother . . .' How do I explain that my mother seemed to enjoy permanently dwelling in a realm of romantic melancholia? 'My mother keeps herself busy. I say, why are you asking all these questions?'

'I want to know who you are. Tell me about your country.'

I was about to roll into my usual set of clichés about elephants and endless sandy beaches, but we were both saved from that nonsense by the sound of a key being put into the latch of the front door. The Colonel was looking very pleased with himself.

'I have Tom Pelham's reply,' he said.

'Can I see it?' Katya asked.

'I have already destroyed it, but it is a good deal. He says he will get my family out.'

'How? Does he have agents in Moscow?'

'Of course not. Probably a prisoner exchange.'

'What prisoner?'

'How should I know? He says he will have somebody they want.'

'A prisoner he will have, or he already has?'

'I don't know, it's a crude cipher, the tenses are very imprecise. It's a good deal. I accept. You should be happy.'

'Do you have my papers?' Katya asked with a hint of venom.

'Of course I do. I told you I would. You are now Marie Bierman, a Berlin Jew.'

'How did I survive the war?'

'I don't know, but you're a clever girl, you'll think of something.'

'These are very good forgeries,' Katya said as she read through her new identity.

'They're not forgeries, they're real. She once existed. She died in Cracow.'

'How long have you had these papers for me?'

'Does it matter? You have them now.'

'But why from Berlin? It's too dangerous for me. She might still have family or friends there.'

'She doesn't. You just need the papers to get you across, and then you can disappear.'

'It's so sad,' I said as I looked over Katya's shoulder at the papers.

'I saw these poor creatures in Cracow,' she told me. 'Maybe I saw her.'

We three, who had experienced the war in such different ways, looked at Marie Bierman's papers.

'She's dead now,' said The Colonel, 'but you're alive. We cross over at dawn tomorrow.'

'I want some insurance,' Katya stated to our confusion. 'Tom Pelham's deal is for you, it's not for me.'

'So, what if it isn't for you? Who are you?' The Colonel arrogantly pointed out.

'I am nobody. I'm just a woman with false papers and no past.'

And then she described herself with a word in German that I did not know but which I had heard Tom use.

'What does that mean?' I asked her.

'Disposable. I am disposable. I do not want to be sent back. I need insurance.'

'I am your insurance,' The Colonel told her.

They looked at each other for a moment and a silent understanding passed between them. His assurance was worthless.

'Then what do you suggest?' The Colonel asked.

'I want to get married.'

'But I am already married.'

'Not to you.' She turned away from The Colonel. 'To him.'

'Me?' I spluttered. 'Wait, what? Me?'

'Yes, you. I wish to get married to you.'

I had spent the last six months falling in love with and wishing to get married to every beautiful girl I had met, and yet, the thought of marrying Katya had never once crossed my mind. Our worlds just seemed too far apart and never destined to converge. And yet, both Katya and The Colonel were looking at me as if her scheme made some kind of sense.

'This is crazy,' I stated clearly.

'No, it's not,' she stated even more clearly. 'They cannot send me back if I am married to Tom Pelham's agent.'

'Tom Pelham can do anything he wants,' I said. 'He doesn't need much of an excuse. He can send you back even if you're his wife.'

'It will cause a diplomatic incident if he betrays you by sending back your wife.'

'What diplomatic incident? I don't even have a country. I'm a subject of the British Empire.'

'Then it will be an Imperial scandal,' Katya suggested, 'which is even worse for the British.'

'You're being crazy. Tom can just paint me as a Communist sympathizer and disown me. He can send me back as well.'

'Your father is important in your country?' she asked.

'A bit. He's known.'

'Not sending back you and your wife will be a small price to pay for keeping your country happy.'

I silently conceded that her argument made some bizarre sense. Then she turned to The Colonel, who had been unusually quiet.

'And this way, I won't be an embarrassment to you. I won't be your mistress, but his wife. You will have no need to dispose of me.'

'My Katya has grown up so fast and now she wants to get married. I like your idea, but I don't have enough time to forge the documents.'

'They don't need to be forgeries. Your neighbour is a judge. He can perform the ceremony now.'

The Colonel immediately started walking towards the door.

'I'll get him.'

'Stop!' I demanded. 'You have the bride's consent but you don't the groom's. Has anybody stopped to ask what I want?'

'What's the matter?' Katya asked. 'Don't you want to marry me?'

'It's not that, it's just that it's all happening so fast. I mean, I haven't told my parents anything, and there are a million and one other things to do for a wedding. Perhaps before rushing into getting married, we should take some time?'

'How about five seconds?' The Colonel suggested from the door.

Katya looked at me, took my hand and spoke quietly.

'I am asking a lot of you, and I apologize. But if you do this, it will save my life. So please, Hamid, will you marry me?'

I looked into the life of her dark eyes that had seen and survived so much, eyes that did not deserve to be killed in a Soviet basement by a bullet to the back of her head.

'All right then,' I mumbled. 'A thousand times all right then. Let's get married.'

What seems like a thousand years later my son, The Ayatollah, went through great trouble when trying to marry his third (or was it fourth?) wife, who was a non-Muslim. She adamantly refused to convert to Islam, which by then had become a legal necessity in my country. But back in the more flexibly understanding days of the 1950s, there were no such hurdles to jump over, and any country's recognized civil wedding was seen as a valid marriage. So I knew I was about to become truly very much actually married, as The Colonel pounded on the door of his neighbour, The Judge. When The Judge finally opened the door, dressed in his pyjamas and dressing gown, he had the exact same look of fear that poor Katrin had when she opened her door to the most dangerous man in Berlin. But The Judge was also confronted with the confusing sight of a beautiful woman and an unknown brown man. What, The Judge must have wondered, had he done wrong?

'You have done nothing wrong,' The Colonel blankly stated, which must have been as assuaging as a hangman telling the condemned that the drop won't hurt much. 'I want you to perform a marriage. Now.'

'Yes, of course,' said The Judge and I could see that he was trying to create logic in a statement that made no sense. 'I will get dressed and we can go to the courthouse.'

'It's nearly midnight. You will perform the marriage here.'

'Yes, of course. But,' The Judge was daring himself to say, 'I need the correct paperwork.'

'You know the wording. You can write it. I am sure that between us, we have the power to do this.'

'Yes, of course. We will need two witnesses,' he said nervously, as he realized that our number did not tally.

'Your wife will be a witness.'

'Must we involve her?'

'This is just a wedding, Your Honour. You will be doing nothing wrong. This is a private matter. Do you understand?'

'Yes, of course. Please come in.'

Despite being a judge in the new Socialist order, his apartment hid an old-world charm with paintings that could have been siblings or cousins to the ones hanging on The Colonel's walls.

'These paintings are not my own,' The Judge felt the need to say. 'They were in the apartment.'

'My apartment is the same.'

'Please excuse me while I wake my wife and dress in my robes.'

'Don't bother changing your clothes.'

The Judge appeared to have a surge of indignant defiance.

'They are not my clothes. They are the robes of my office. They show that none of us are above the law.'

As The Judge shuffled away, I saw that his words appeared to have some effect on The Colonel, but I couldn't understand why. Besides, I was concentrating on my own present situation, which was as difficult to comprehend as being suddenly confronted with a tank. I looked at Katya and tried unsuccessfully to comprehend that she was my bride. She did look lovely, but she was as unknown to me as a tank. *Was she, I wondered, in fact, a tank?* Was I going insane, and if so, when had this insanity begun? It must have been when I met Tom Pelham in the smog of London, or had it been a thousand years before, back when I used to sit with the Pelhams on the veranda of The Residence in my hometown?

When the bride-to-be suddenly ran out of the room, I was surprised, but it did make some sense. I had been abandoned on my wedding day, but it hadn't even been my idea to get married, and now, somebody needed to run away from this insanity. I turned to my unlikely best man (or was he representing the bride's family?) but The Colonel was lost in his own thoughts. And then she returned. She had changed into a white summer dress with the tiniest of blue polka dots that I had seen her wear before, I think it was when we had watched *Oliver Twist* together, and she had engineered a white veil from a scarf I had also seen her wear before.

'I want to wear white for my wedding,' she told me.

White is not a necessary colour for Malay weddings, it is actually worn for funerals, but naturally, I understood its significance and her effort helped to make this bizarre situation seem slightly less insane.

The Judge's wife emerged from their bedroom looking as terrified as her husband, and The Colonel made no effort to calm her nerves. But her presence did make it necessary for him to decide where he should stand. Should he be my best man or the father of the bride?

'She can be my mother,' said Katya, saving the situation and making the man who would happily shoot me my best man.

The Judge returned in his courtroom robes and in the DDR, a marriage ceremony was as rapid as one of The Colonel's executions. I am not even sure at which moment the marriage was legally bound, was it when I gave my consent or when she gave hers? Or was it when we signed our names on the marriage contract that The Judge had hastily written.

'Wait,' said The Colonel after I had signed my name. 'Do you sign it as Ekaterina or Marie?'

Without a thought, Katya signed it. The Judge stamped the document and handed it to me, but Katya took it.

'Is that it?' I asked.

'Yes,' said The Judge. 'You are married.'

'You must have some flowers on your wedding day,' said The Judge's wife as she pulled some flowers from a vase that was next to a black framed photograph of a girl. 'I am sorry but that is all I can offer you. Good luck, my dear.'

'This has been a private matter,' The Colonel pronounced. 'There is no need for you to speak of this to anyone.'

'Yes, of course,' confirmed The Judge.

We thanked The Judge and his wife and then The Colonel ushered us out. It seems I was married, but for how long?

I sat opposite The Colonel at the table while Katya heated borsht for our wedding dinner. I had no idea if this wedding was anything more than one of convenience, but my new wife's empty chair being right next to him suggested it was. When she brought us the food, she moved her chair so that it would be in the middle and we ate in silence, in an atmosphere that was more befitting of a funeral or wake than a wedding celebration.

When we finished, they left me, she to sleep with a man who was not her husband.

I was filled with nerves about our forthcoming attempt to cross to the Western sector, but I was more confused about my new marriage status. I wanted to talk to somebody, somebody I could trust.

I found a piece of paper and a pen, and I started to write 'Dear Clare'. But how could I be worthy of her trust when my news would simply compound the memory of my sins? I could only imagine her angry face when reading my letter. 'I am sorry,' I added, and then I took another piece of paper and wrote, 'Dear Margaret'. I think she had once briefly cared for me but had understood that I was nothing but a wastrel. 'Dear Hermione,' I wrote but all I could feel coming back was her scorn. I even started writing to my father in the Malay script of Jawi, but I was more afraid of him than

I was of a Soviet tank. The only person I truly wanted to talk to was one with whom I had barely spoken at all, but somebody I felt I could trust. I wanted to talk to Saskia, but she had been replaced by Katya, and Katya, I didn't know at all.

I realized just how alone I was in the world as I looked at all these opened and unfinished letters, seeing faces filled with disappointment looking back at me, because my new bride was already sleeping with another man. I sat there with my customary sense of self-loathing, when a door opened. It was Katya.

'I should sleep with my husband on my wedding night. I will sleep on the sofa, and you will sleep in the chair. What are you writing?'

'My confession.'

'You can finish that another time. Come, sleep opposite me. We have much to do in the morning.'

I folded the letters and put them in my pocket as she curled up on the sofa and I sat opposite. We looked at each other for a short while.

'You are the only normal person I know, Hamid.'

And then our eyes started closing, and soon, we were asleep.

Chapter 44

Tom Pelham had chosen the Glienicker Brücke checkpoint—the bridge—as the place where we should cross.

It made sense, Katya told me, because it was outside Berlin, and therefore, relatively secluded. But most importantly, it was under Soviet and not East German control, so The Colonel could hopefully dominate the guards.

The Colonel had not spoken a word since the wedding, and I found his silence to be unsettling as he drove us through the empty Berlin streets in the predawn darkness. Katya had packed a small valise and was wearing a lovely winter coat. She said she didn't want to leave it behind and it turned out to be a sensible choice because it was a chilly summer morning. As we approached the bridge, there was a mist hanging over the river, or was it a lake?

Katya appeared to be equally concerned by The Colonel's silence. She leaned forward and placed her hand reassuringly on his shoulder.

'All is good?' she asked him in German, but he merely grunted. She then started speaking to him in Russian, but he didn't answer. So, she spoke to me in English.

'It should be simple. We get out of the car and walk across the bridge, but he must talk to the guards first. He has to make sure that nobody makes any phone calls out until we are over the bridge. Everything depends on him.'

'Don't worry,' The Colonel finally spoke. 'I survived the siege of Leningrad. I can handle this.'

He stopped the car at the checkpoint and sat pensively for too long a moment. Daylight was beginning to emerge, and we looked at the cantilever bridge that could be our route to safety. The bridge seemed impossibly long. I did not know how long it was because its other end was still draped in the last lingering darkness and thick mist.

'You two stay here,' he said. 'I will talk to the guards.'

Katya and I watched as The Colonel sent soldiers scampering away in search of their senior officer. I felt reassured, because The Colonel had a commanding presence, and I, too, would have unquestioningly obeyed his orders.

'If your Katrin Schule talked to anybody,' said Katya, 'we're dead.'

Katya's very unreassuring words helped to elongate the seconds beyond their natural length, but when I saw the checkpoint's senior officer deliver an exemplary salute, I began to believe that Katrin had held her silence. The Colonel walked back to the car.

'It's time to go,' he said as he opened the door and took Katya's valise.

'What did you tell them is happening?' she asked.

'I told them it's none of their business.'

We walked towards the checkpoint, and despite my nerves, I realized that this was the first time in months that I had been outside a city, be it London or Berlin, since Christmas Day, when I had trudged away from the Pelhams.

I could hear the birds singing their dawn chorus and there was no other sound as the guards stood watching us in obedient silence. The Colonel barked an order that raised the checkpoint barrier and when we stepped beyond it, The Colonel handed me Katya's valise, which seemed to be a curious thing to do.

'I am not going with you,' he told us.

'What?' I demanded. 'Why the hell not?'

'Calm down, Hamid,' Katya ordered me. 'Act natural.'

'Nobody is above the law,' he said.

'What law?' I asked, at the brink of hyperventilating.

'Soviet law.'

'But that law is going to kill you,' I continued blathering.

'Maybe so, but it is the law I have lived by and worked for. I cannot betray it now, even if it demands me. And I have to think about my family.'

'Tom Pelham said he will get them out,' Katya told him.

'He doesn't have a prisoner that can equal me and my family. Apart from Tom Pelham himself, of course. You must go now, before they start getting suspicious.'

I glanced at the guards who were watching us intently, and I could indeed detect that their silent obedience was shifting to muttering concern.

'Go. I have made my decision. Walk now.'

'But Tom Pelham wants you,' Katya stated.

'Well, he'll have to be satisfied with you.'

'He won't be,' she said.

'Go.'

I looked down the length of the bridge, but I still could not see its end. We had a long way to walk and the checkpoint's senior officer was edging towards the telephone in the guardhouse. I took Katya by the arm, pulled her away and we started walking.

'He's dead,' she said. 'They'll shoot him today.'

'How long is this bloody bridge?'

'Don't run.'

'I'm going to.'

'Don't run. They'll shoot you if you run.'

'The Colonel will stop them.'

'His power is over.'

As if in agreement with Katya's grim judgment, the guardhouse telephone suddenly burst into a deafening ring. Even though each step took us further away from the telephone, its ringing just got louder and louder. I glanced over my shoulder and saw the senior officer moving to the telephone while The Colonel just stood there watching us.

'Hamid, calm down.'

If there is one thing that is guaranteed to make me not calm down it is being told to calm down, but then Katya put her hand in mine.

'Telephones ring all the time. It's probably nothing.'

'When are we safe?'

'The middle of the bridge is the border but if they shoot us after that, who is going to stop them? We can only be safe if we reach the other side.'

She squeezed my hand as we walked down the bridge together when there was suddenly the sound of shouting behind us.

'Don't look back, keep walking,' she told me. 'Tell me about your country. Is it hot there?'

Yes, yes my home was hot, and sunny and welcoming and safe. I couldn't help myself as I babbled to her about Ah Cheong's steamed pao in Kuala Kangsar, how we boys played Eton Fives at MCKK, how it hurt me to see my mother's sadness, how I loved my father and wanted only to earn his respect, and then the mist started thinning. I could see the other side. I could see American soldiers and the familiar, but not always reassuring, sight of Tom Pelham waiting impatiently. I looked back, and I could now barely see the Soviet side. Its sound was muted but I thought I saw The Colonel standing with his hands above his head before he disappeared into the mist.

'Are we halfway yet?' I asked.

'We're past that. We're nearly there. Listen, Hamid, when we get to the other side, whatever happens,' she stopped me.

'Why are we stopping? We must keep going.'

Suddenly, a powerful spotlight from the American sector was focused on us and a British army captain stepped to the edge of the barriers and shouted, 'Kill that bloody light!'

'We might not talk again, and I want to tell you something. I don't know your father, but you have earned my respect.'

Nobody had ever said anything even remotely like that to me before. The words were so alien to me that I could barely understand them.

'I have?'

'Yes. And I want you to remember, whatever happens, we all had to do what we could to survive.

But you are the only normal person I have known since before the war.

The British Captain started shouting to us, 'Come along!'

Katya ignored him, 'I liked us reading together in Berlin. It meant something to me. Something I thought was dead. Your mother is lonely, that's why she is sad. When I was with you, I didn't feel alone.'

'Me too.'

'And please don't hate me,' she said, while pulling me along.

'Why would I?'

Katya and I walked to The Captain, who led us through a chicane of sandbags, past American soldiers who were a silent mixture of sleepy, bored, and tense, and then under the raised barrier to deliver us to Tom Pelham. I had made it. I was safe. After the terrors of the last twenty-four hours, I was feeling overwhelmed by happiness and relief. I wanted to collapse, and I wanted to celebrate, but Tom did not look like he was in the mood for a celebration. It was the last time I ever saw him grace me with such a look, but he looked down at me with an Imperial disdain.

'Where is The Colonel?' Tom asked coldly.

Like generations of brown men before me, I was still subject to Tom's withering Imperial disapproval, and so I could not speak. Katya stepped forward instead.

'He didn't come.'

'I want The Colonel,' Tom demanded.

'Well, you have us,' she said glibly. 'Hello, Tom.'

'Hello, Hana.'

I didn't understand. Hana?

'But your name is Katya, isn't it?'

Somebody nearby started laughing sarcastically. It was The American I had met months earlier when I had first arrived in Berlin, and attached to him lurked the aristocratic German.

'Looks like your boy really messed up this time,' said The American. 'He's used up all your favours, Tom, and then he went and left The Colonel behind.'

'He wanted to stay,' said Katya, or was she Hana?

'And who the hell is she?' The American asked.

'She?' said Tom. 'I'd like you to meet Hana Neumann, but you know her as Disposable.'

'She's Disposable?' The American appeared to be overcome with both awe and incredulity.

'She most certainly is Disposable, aren't you, Hana?'

'But . . . you know each other?' I demanded to be told.

'Hana helped me during the war,' Tom said, disinterestedly.

'In Yugoslavia?'

'And other places.'

'And I've been paying for it ever since,' she added.

'So, your name isn't Katya?'

She shook her head.

'And what the hell is "disposable"?'

'It's my codename,' she told me. 'Tom gave it to me. I wonder why, Tom?'

'Are you kidding me?' gushed The American. 'Disposable is the best source on Soviet Intelligence we've ever had. That's if she really is Disposable?'

'Oh, she is,' said Tom. 'She's been The Colonel's mistress for the last two years. Pillow talk, I suppose. She's a very clever girl, and she always gets what she wants.'

'Miss,' said The American. 'I want to call you Sir, I don't know, Madam? I want to shake your hand. Great job, great job. I don't mind telling you that we've been blind inside the Soviet Bloc since all the Brits turned out to be Commie agents, but your work has been incredible, just incredible. Great job.'

'Well don't get too attached to her,' Tom interjected, 'because she's going straight back. And so is he.'

'What?' I blustered. 'What did I do wrong? I did everything you told me to do.'

'And you're going to do one last thing for me.'

'I put all my trust in you,' I said, unable to understand what was happening.

Tom leaned in.

'And we trusted you. You can't hurt my sister and expect to get away with it.'

'Wait a second,' said The American. 'You sent your boy into East Berlin for some personal vendetta? Is that all he was?'

'No,' said Tom. 'Of course not.'

'He was a distraction,' said Katya, or was she Hana? 'Tom sent Hamid as bait to draw attention away from me.'

'But I did things for you, Tom. I met Katrin, I sent messages, all those crosses I marked.'

'All meaningless,' she said. 'You were sent as a distraction, and it worked. The Colonel became obsessed with you. He talked about you all the time.'

I thought I knew Tom and I thought I knew this woman. I had trusted them, and they had both betrayed me?

'And The Colonel sent you to spy on me?' I asked her.

'No. I did that myself. I wanted to warn you, Hamid.'

'And I told you that was a stupid thing to do,' said Tom angrily. 'It ruined all my hard work. I don't know what you two have been up to, but you got that sly bitch Katrin Schule to destroy a perfectly good bit of blackmail, and you have failed to give me The Colonel. They'll probably shoot him tonight. What a waste!'

Tom made an effort to rein in his anger and he looked at me.

'But it doesn't matter now because I'm sending Hamid straight back. I want to give them something for The Colonel. They need to think they've won. And I'll be sending you back soon enough as well, Hana.'

'I'm not going back. I'm finished with you,' she told him.

'You can't very well stay here. I don't think you're welcome,' Tom said, giving a barely perceptible nod in the direction of The German.

'I'm not going back, and neither is he,' she said, standing her ground. 'We're married.'

She handed our marriage certificate to Tom.

'You can't send us back. See, I signed my real name. I've worked for you for ten years. I saved your life, and I got nothing. I'm not doing it any more, Tom. I'm not going back, and we're married, so he stays with me.'

'This doesn't mean anything,' said Tom. 'One of your witnesses is probably already dead. This makes no difference. You're both going back and that is that. You can say your goodbyes but make it fast. Hamid is going back tonight.'

'Whatever he did to you,' she said to Tom, 'he has paid for it a thousand times over. Please, Tom, let him stay.'

But Tom was unmoved.

'Captain, send this man back across the bridge.'

The Captain took out his pistol and waved it towards the bridge.

'Come along. Let's not have any trouble.'

'But my father will be angry,' I blurted out desperately to Tom.

'Your father? I'm sure he'll be ashamed to discover that his son was a Communist, but will he be surprised? And it will be fun,' Tom chuckled himself, 'to see him discover that he is not an important man.'

Tom stepped closer to me and whispered in my ear, 'I saw him, back in The Residence, with my mother.'

I was so frightened that I could not even remember The Residence. I had no past, only a present, and it was being taken away from me by the long ago actions of my father?

'This is all because of that?' I asked.

'You carry the burden of your father's sin.'

Katya, or Hana, and I, fell into a silence. We had fought our way out of East Berlin for nothing. I was about to be sent back but for once I wasn't thinking about my own predicament.

'He can't send you back if you don't want to go,' I told her.

'Yes, he can,' she said, spying The German. 'I'm sorry, Hamid. I tried everything. I thought that if we got married, then he wouldn't send you back.'

'You knew he would?'

'Yes.'

'Didn't you hear what I said?' The American cut-in. 'She has been the best source on Soviet Intelligence ever.'

'So?' said Tom.

'So, we're going to give her a ticker-tape parade. Well, a debriefing in a safehouse in Berlin, but we'll get a cake.'

The German whispered something to The American.

'I don't care what she did to you during the war,' exploded The American. 'Just as we clearly don't care what you did during the war either.'

'Now hang on,' said Tom. 'She's my agent.'

'And if I say she's ours now, what are you going to do?' The American's statement pushed Tom into a brief impotent silence but then Tom angrily pointed his finger at me.

'He is a subject of the British Empire, and I am sending him back.'

'Listen,' said The American in a mood of condescending exasperation, 'when will you people understand that all this European and Empire bullshit is finished. There's a new show in town, and until somebody else comes along, it is Uncle Sam. She is a hero, and if she wants him, then she can have him.'

'You can't do this,' Tom blustered defiantly.

'I think I just have.'

'No, you can't. I'll fight it, I'll take it all the way to the top, the Prime Minister himself if I have to.'

'I don't care if you send the King.'

'We have a Queen now.'

'Who gives a shit. And that, Tom, is that.'

By asserting his authority, The American had changed the situation and Katya, or should I say Hana, understood that before me because I was already walking towards the bridge as Tom had ordered me to do. She pulled me back.

'Hamid, you don't have to go back.'

'But Tom told me I have to.'

'You don't have to listen to him any more. We're free.'

Over the last twenty-four hours and ever since Christmas, I had caught far too many glimpses of safety being dashed to pieces for me to believe I might finally be safe. Like a schoolboy being sent yet again to detention by Mr Hargreaves, I felt at home following the certainties of Tom's orders. After all, I must have done something wrong.

Back in 1953, I was barely out of school and although I had experienced some moments of adulthood, I had accepted then that I would see no more. I had accepted that my future was a prison and then death, and yet, something in her words suggested that I might have instead crossed a bridge to a different future, to somewhere wholly new. I found it hard to comprehend what she was saying to me.

'We're free?' I asked. 'Are you sure?'

'Yes,' she said, trying to hide a smile.

She pulled me away from the bridge, towards a waiting car. We walked past a disconsolate Tom Pelham.

'Goodbye, Tom,' she said to him.

'Goodbye, Hana.'

'I'll never say anything about the past, so I hope we'll never meet again?'

'I hope so too. And good luck.'

'Thank you, Tom. And thanks for saving my life during the war. I'm sorry about the scar on your face.'

They shook hands and she walked on. But I wanted to say my goodbyes too. This Tom Pelham looked nothing like the fiery young Englishman I had listened to with reverent awe on the veranda of The

Residence as he railed against the very Empire that gave him his stature. This Tom Pelham looked smaller. The Colonel may have destroyed himself in the process, but by remaining in the East, he had stolen from Tom what would have been his greatest triumph. I felt sorry for Tom that he had been forced to face the humiliation of a new diminished status, but I was very happy to be able to walk away.

'Tom, please accept my apologies for what happened during Christmas. I didn't mean to hurt anybody. And please tell Clare that I am sorry.'

'Hamid,' Tom Pelham said with a sigh, 'just leave me alone.'

I walked away from Tom, now knowing that I did not want Clare and a purely English future, and towards the car where she was waiting for me. I already knew that her face had so many different variations, but now I was seeing a new expression. She was trying, unsuccessfully, to suppress a giddy excitement that she had perhaps not felt since her girlhood birthday before the war. Her face was happy, and I liked looking at it.

'Before we go,' I said to her, 'what is your name? Is it Katya, Hana, or Saskia, or something else?'

She thought about it for a moment.

'I've had many names and each one brings me pain to remember. I think I want a new name. You can call me The Wife.'

'I have a present for you.'

'Is it a wedding present?'

'Yes, I suppose it is.'

I fumbled around in my bag to open its secret compartment and pulled out a bottle of perfume.

'You bought this for me?' she asked with a hint of suspicion.

'Well, yes. Maybe it will be your scent.'

'Perhaps. I will try it tomorrow. But right now, I want you to tell me more about your country.'

As we were driven away, I told her about my country but this time I wasn't interested in rolling out my usual exotic clichés because, well, if truth be told, I don't really like beaches. Instead, I remembered breakfast in my hometown, *kaya* on toast in Ah Siew's coffeeshop, fragrant *nasi lemak* wrapped in coconut leaves, *thosai* and *dhall*, and all mixed with the usually awful, but now comforting, memory of stewing latex brought in from the rubber estates that morning. I told her these things because I knew I would see them again and because I wanted to share these moments with her.

I took one last look at Tom Pelham and the bridge. I could finally see the other side because the mist had lifted.

Epilogue

Home

'I'm sorry, what did you say?' I asked in a daze of confusion.

'I said The Haze has lifted,' she shouted from upstairs. 'I can finally see for miles around.'

The mist over Glienicker Brücke in 1953 had lifted, London's Great Smog of 1952 had lifted, and now, more than fifty years later, the winds had shifted away from Sumatra to lift The Haze over Kuala Lumpur. I was waking up by stages from a night of a fog of memory to happily discover that I was an old man again, in the comforting safety of my home. The morning sunlight was rapidly growing across our delightful little garden, and across the forested hill, beyond where the nighttime cacophony of unknown insect calls took place, the creature was settling down for the day.

My nocturnal jungle friend had gone to bed, probably down a deep hole. I wasn't quite sure what had happened but, clearly, I had not gone to bed last night and instead had spent the night downstairs where I now found myself surrounded by old photographs, old newspaper clippings, old unfinished letters, and several bottles of perfume. It was as if I was some sort of sophisticated and deliciously fragrant drunk who had been on what I think my grandson would call a 'bender'.

Stuck to my face was the briefest of notes that I had written to Irma, of my old hometown. You remember her, she imagined when still only a child that she and I were to be married. Well, she's never forgotten. Irma and I have tussled relentlessly over the years, just as I have with Malaysia itself. She married an army general. He wasn't a general when they met, but she dragged him up through the ranks and made for herself a fortune in developing property and arms trading. I had recently bought land in a forgotten valley, overlooking rice fields and misty mountains. It was the Malayan idyll I had once known, but then Irma bought the adjacent land and built an enormous hotel, topped with a blinking sign proclaiming: 'Irma D'Inn'. She knows I hate poor French grammar.

My note simply said, 'I'll see you in court!' She will win, she always does, and then she will send me a gift, usually cash that she knows I cannot afford to refuse. And then our cycle, our tussling would begin afresh. We would never have been happy together, although I would have been rich.

I picked up an old newspaper clipping from 1953. It was about The Colonel. He had not been shot on that night on Glienicker Brücke, but he was arrested on the charge of being a British spy. The newspaper report admitted to having only a hazy understanding of the Kremlin's inner workings, but it seems he was taken back to Moscow, where he was eventually executed alongside his old friend Lavrentiy Beria, when Nikita Khruschev staged a palace coup. The Colonel may well have been executed by his hero Marshal Zhukov himself, and I wondered if that would have been any consolation to him. In many ways, I owed my life to The Colonel. But he had been a vicious and dangerous man. I had clippings that I had cut out over the years from newspapers in Kuala Lumpur's Goethe Institut that charted the career of Katrin Schule as she rose from the leadership of the FDJ to eventually winning a seat on the Politburu of the German Democratic Republic. I looked at the photograph that showed an expression of utter bewilderment on her very chubby face as the Party spokesman unexpectedly announced the opening of their borders in 1989. Her world with all its power, privileges, and certainties must have collapsed as quickly as the Berlin Wall did. I felt sorry for her when I looked at an interview with her from decades later, showing that she had remained an angrily defiant Communist to the last, denouncing the colonization of her beloved country by West Germany. *Katrin really let herself go*, I thought to myself as I looked at her distinctly portly shape.

And then I removed a book that I had been sitting on: *I Spied for the Queen* by Tom Pelham, a title that must have been forced on him by his American publishers because he would never have chosen anything so crass, but presumably had to do as they said because the book was and remains banned in Britain since its publication in the mid-1980s. Tom had penned this book after his retirement as a tell-all exposé of Britain's Intelligence incompetence, its shameful subservience to the Americans, and as a warning of the dangers of an unchecked surveillance state.

When I heard about the book, I was terrified that he was going tell the world, and more importantly, everybody at The Club, about my Socialist past. Being exposed as a spy might have led to some good fun in The Bar, but having any awareness of dialectical materialism would have been an absolute disaster for my election as The Club Treasurer. And I really wanted that parking space because it was right next to the golf caddies. I immediately flew out to America to purchase the book on the day of its launch and tore through it in one feverish sitting. Mercifully, neither I nor Operation Disposable were ever mentioned. Perhaps he saw that that situation was not his finest hour. Satisfied that my secret remained safe, I gave the book a more leisurely second read and discovered a reminder of the Tom Pelham I had known in my childhood. The book's language had the same fiery and eloquent rage I had found so intoxicating on the veranda of The Residence, when Tom Pelham told the world where it was going wrong. But the crusading hope of youth had been replaced by the bitterness and regret of old age. He seemed to be arguing that his country's mission should be something more than just servicing America's wants, but he was never able to say what that something might be.

I put Tom's book back on the shelf, squeezed between a copy of *Alice's Adventures in Wonderland* and a first edition of Goethe's *Faust* that my grandson had managed to track down. Even though he had sadistically punished me in Berlin, had used me, and tried to send me to my death, I still admired Tom in many ways, and the first thing I did upon returning to London in '53, had been to make sure that his tailor became my tailor. Three Savile Row generations later, and I am expecting the imminent arrival of an exquisite velvet smoking jacket, which I know from experience I will be able to wear if I turn the air-conditioning to its coldest setting.

For the longest time, I did not know if Tom was alive or dead, until he published a little book about his extraordinary lineage and his lovely home called Tanamerah. It was nice to see that by returning to his deeper past, he had mellowed with age, and this book remains one of my favourites. I looked at its photographs of the garden, the stables, Sir Alfred's study that must have become his own, and of the library where one long ago Christmas, I had sat with Tom Pelham and three lovely, young women.

I started to put away some old unfinished letters.

'Dear Margaret' and 'Dear Hermione' were all they said.

I never met Hermione again, but attached to her unfinished letter were newspapers clippings from the society pages charting her subsequent journey through several marriages to stalwarts of the British Establishment. Each husband was ascendingly wealthier and well-connected and all of them met with untimely deaths. I especially remember the newspaper baron who met with a truly awful demise when he fell into the machinery of his own printing press, thereby mangling himself into that morning's edition. Poor Hermione must have suffered emotional anguish because she had witnessed the horrible event. In fact, she was the only witness. I enjoyed a furtive look at her photographs, that showed she had never lost her radiant beauty or her slim, yet athletic, physique. She truly was the embodiment of the English Rose, a beautiful flower with thorns that can cut the unwary, and she had aged gracefully, from being the princess that I once knew into something more like a queen. In the course of her marriages, Hermione has amassed a vast fortune and with the well-placed marriages of her children, she seems to have created a network of interests in European and American industries. She had also acquired some cash-strapped European royal houses. The most recent clipping showed that she was now married to an ex-Olympic horse rider, who was much less than half her age. Remembering, as I often do, my brief but savagely exciting night with Hermione, I considered him to be a very lucky fellow, but he might want to be extra careful when out riding.

As I was putting away the letter to 'Dear Margaret', I remembered with a smile that I did meet Margaret again on the streets of London, in the early 1970s. I had perhaps seen something in Kuala Lumpur that I perhaps should not have seen, and so with a little prompting, a certain Malaysian businessman paid for me to stay at The Savoy Hotel for a week, which was very nice of him. I was stepping out of Coutts Bank on the Strand, where the Malaysian businessman had deposited an extremely generous expense account for me, when I suddenly bumped into Margaret de Vere. She was a little rounder than when I knew her, but the extra weight suited her face, which was still incandescently beautiful, perhaps more so. There was something about her that looked different, and I quickly realized that it was because she was happy. She was with her son, who was a very handsome and charming dark-haired fellow about the same age as I was when I had met his mother. She told me that her marriage had not lasted long, but that she had happily embraced becoming a single mother while running her late and unlamented father's company. Being a divorced single mother in those long-ago times made Margaret the brave trailblazer that I knew she was, and as we were talking, our eyes did meet. There passed between us the silent understanding, that even across the decades, we still truly knew each other, and there was perhaps even a longing. We parted and have never met again. I actually do not know what she is doing now, and yet I am certain that she is alive and that she is happy. But remembering her in her RAF uniform, as I often do, makes it impossible for me to watch an old war movie without getting a trifle excited.

Beyond the introductions, I had not finished these four letters written on the East German paper of 1953, and yet, I now saw that two of them had been completed. I had no memory of it, but I must have written them in the night. There was a long letter to my father in Malay, written in the Arabic script of Jawi that I had not used since the 1960s. I didn't even know I could still write in Jawi, and yet, here it was, flowing across the pages.

Both my parents had passed away many years ago, when they were younger than I am now, but here, I had written a letter, telling my father how much I missed them both, about my regret that our relationship had been so formal, so Malay, and not as close as the one I now have with my grandson. And then there were several pages where I confided in my dead father and asked for his advice as I confessed my fears about my relationship with my own son. Why, I asked my father, were we so different? Why must he be such a lackey, happily abasing himself to people vastly inferior in the endless pursuit of money and prestige? And why must he keep marrying, where on earth did he get this fixation with women? I told my father that I love my son and that it is my ultimate wish for us to somehow reconcile. My letter to my father concluded with my saying that all I ever wanted was to earn his respect and that my most cherished memory was, when, in his dying days, he had said that he was indeed proud of me. Before folding it away, I signed the letter and I was fully aware that my father would never be able to give me the answer as to why my son was so eager for money as I dried my signature with a magnificent silver ink blotter from Asprey of New Bond Street and placed it next to its matching backgammon board, both courtesy of a certain Malaysian businessman. The reasons for my son's peculiar nature would have to remain a mystery to me.

And finally, there was a now finished letter to Clare Pelham. I knew she was dead. She had died many years ago, when she disappeared in the Amazon jungle searching for her beloved ants. I remembered the simple beginnings of her fascination for ants, when she had gleefully tortured the creatures on the veranda of The Residence a thousand years ago, and from that she had gone on to become the world's foremost authority on the insects. I knew that she had visited Malaysia on a field trip, but I had not dared to find her, partly because I was afraid of what might happen between us, but mainly because I simply do not have the wardrobe for a jungle expedition.

I had been absolutely devastated when I chanced upon the news of her death in a copy of *National Geographic*, but I have harboured the fantasy that she was saved in the jungle by an unmet tribe. I know that she would have happily forsaken the world and stayed with them forever, and that they would have quite rightly worshipped her as the Earth Mother goddess that she was. I have always felt deeply ashamed of how I betrayed sweet Clare, but in my defence, I was young, her friends were stunningly beautiful, and they liked me. I do not think I could have done things any differently, but as a consequence of my youthful passions, I did perhaps forfeit a life that could have been. If I had managed to keep my ardour to myself, then perhaps, I could have had an English life with Clare filled with English things in the soft English landscape.

The British Empire of Sir Alfred and my father had collapsed in the face of the Japanese invasion, and yet, I found it impossible to abandon the visions I had seen during my Imperial Malayan education in the humid classrooms of Malay College Kuala Kangsar, the Eton of the East. My family had served a Malay Sultanate for generations, my mother did not speak a word of English and had never even left our hometown, and so England should have been completely alien to me, and yet, its fables and romances had burrowed their way into me.

After the war, virtually all my old schoolmates vociferously rejected Britain, despite sending all their children to English public schools, but I like to think that I am more honest: An England that is ours and not theirs had burrowed its way into all of us, and it remains there. During the Christmas of 1952, I briefly touched that mythic England and briefly imagined that a corner of it could be forever mine. But I blew it, because I was gatal, and because the life of this brown man was meant to be lived in horizons far broader than little England.

I often think of Clare Pelham and the life that could have been, and yet, this newly finished letter to her was startlingly brief. I was looking at it when I heard the footsteps of my wife coming down the stairs. My instinct was to feel guilty and to immediately dispose of any incriminating evidence, but then I realized I had not actually done anything wrong. I was still unsteadily waking from my night of restless memories when she wafted into the room, and it was as if I had not seen her for a thousand years.

'Why are you looking at me like that?' she asked.

'Like what, *sayang*?'

'I don't know, but I don't trust it.'

I chuckled, because even after all these years, I find her lack of trust to be deeply endearing. She looked at the debris of mementos strewn around the room and started reading the clipping about The Colonel.

'He wasn't a bad man,' she said. 'Actually, he was. But thank you for forgiving me. You have forgiven me, haven't you?'

'Of course. There's nothing to forgive. You had to survive.'

'It would break my world if you did not forgive me.'

Last night, in my memories, she had once again been the mysterious and dangerous dark-haired beauty of Berlin. Now she was a grandmother, her hair entirely grey and her figure somewhat fuller, but she was unmistakably the same woman. The woman who had stared down tanks and soldiers, who could make and break coded messages, sniff any danger, and drag me to safety, who had finally found her home in the alien landscape of my homeland, who had more strength than I could imagine, and yet, she was still worried that I might not have forgiven her for something she had to do before we even met.

She wanted the world to be safe and calm because she had already lived through the horrors of a thousand lifetimes before we even met. After a bumpy start, we had become the other half of each other. She is The Wife. And I think she would kill me if I ever betrayed her.

"'Dear Clare,'" she said, reading the newly finished letter.

'You don't need to read that,' I said nervously.

"'Dear Clare, I am sorry. I am now married. When we got married, I thought I was saving her, but it turns out she was saving me.'"

'It's all true,' I said with a sense of relief.

"'Dear Margaret." I remember Margaret. We bumped into her in London in the seventies. She was with her son. He looked just like our son.'

'Really? I hadn't noticed.'

'Yes, he did. He's a bit older than our son but I swear they could have been twins.'

'I really don't think so. You're being most fanciful.'

'I know Margaret, but who is Hermione?'

'Hermione? I've never met anybody called that.'

'But you've started a letter to her.'

'Have I? Gosh, yes, now that you mention it, if I remember rightly, I think she was a Danish pen pal I had back in the 1950s. I never met her, but I was helping her to read and write. She was a great big girl, the size of a truck. And when she ate a sandwich, it was really quite horrible.'

'How did you see her eat a sandwich if you say you never met her?'

'Did I say that? I did, didn't I.'

'Hamid, how many times must I tell you, no unnecessary extra details. Now tell me again, who is Hermione?'

In my panic, I lunged for a bottle of perfume that I had bought the day before. It was a bottle that a genie might inhabit, and its scent had sent me into swooning into a haze of memory both terrifying and exhilarating. Perhaps it would also work its magic on The Wife?

'I bought you a present, sayang.'

'A perfume? You know I don't like perfume.'

'But this one is different,' I said while spritzing it onto her wrist. 'Now it's called Everlasting, but it used to be called . . .'

'I know it,' she said breathing in its dangerous aroma. 'It's Betrayal.'

It is her scent.